Diana, wakened by her absolute interior clock, touched Constance's face, and there were the dark worlds of her eyes, always the first territory of day. Not since they'd shared a war over forty years ago had they been alarmed out of sleep. Waking was silent, intimate, still even after all these years faintly arousing.

Diana was reluctant to leave their bed to confront her singular, upright self. This morning there were autumn messages in her bones. . . .

Constance, two years older than Diana, had all her own teeth, could hear birds sing, and only needed glasses for reading, which she had pretty well given up, and for intimate weeding of the garden which she could still do, hunkered down for minutes at a time and able to rise as swiftly and agilely as a young girl. Yet Constance often could not move from their bedroom without Diana's aid. Particularly in winter, she might forget that it was morning and be putting herself to bed again by the time Diana had finished in the bathroom.

This morning Constance had left their bed, taken off her pajamas and was standing irresolutely beside clothes put out for her the previous night.

"Have I had my shower?"

"No," Diana said, smiling.

MEMORY
BOARD

MEMORY
B O A R D

Jane Rule

The Naiad Press, Inc.
1987

Printed in the United States of America
First Edition

Edited by Katherine V. Forrest
Cover Design by The Women's Graphic Center
Typesetting by Sandi Stancil

Library of Congress Cataloging-in-Publication Data

Rule, Jane.
    Memory board.

    I. Title.
PR9119.3.R78M46 1987   813'.54   87-11112

ISBN 0-941483-02-9

WORKS BY JANE RULE

1964 *Desert of the Heart**
1970 *This Is Not for You**
1971 *Against the Season**
1975 *Lesbian Images*
1975 *Theme for Diverse Instruments*
1977 *The Young in One Another's Arms**
1980 *Contract with the World**
1981 *Outlander**
1985 *A Hot-Eyed Moderate**
1985 *Inland Passage and Other Stories**
1987 *Memory Board**

*Available from The Naiad Press.

For

Eileen and John

CHAPTER I

"Our father died in childbirth," wrote David Crown, bearer of bad news (retired), as he sat with his hearing aid turned off at his desk in what had been the ironing room in the basement of his own house. It was an old line, one Diana, his twin, had found melodramatic and inaccurate rather than funny. Their father had been killed in an automobile accident on his way to the hospital where their mother was already in labor. David used it again just the same, uncertain about whether he was writing it down for himself or Diana. Might she be able to hear it differently now, as a kind of cosmic joke on them both? But cosmic jokes had never been on them both. Throughout their childhood, years after they were a pair of bundled babies their mother didn't always dress in pink and blue, people asked if they were identical twins, a stupidity which

enraged David because for Diana it was a joke on him
without offense to herself.

It was David who had developed an obsession about
being a twin. He read that in nearly every culture twins
were bad omens. In some cultures certain foods were
prescribed for pregnant women to avoid multiple birth.
David used to know which kinds just as he knew the curses
twins had brought down and the tribes in which they were
routinely killed at birth, one or both of them.

"Well, they would have killed me," Diana said. "Why
worry about it?"

Because for the first twelve years their birthday was
also for their mother the anniversary of her young husband's
death, there was always something morbid about the fuss.
After that, when she married again and had two more sons,
it became a kind of apology to the twins, the unfortunates
she didn't know how to bring out of the shadow of her old
grief into the light of her new life. It was a day for
propitiating rituals and burnt offerings, against floods,
earthquakes and fires their neglected adolescence might
otherwise bring down on the new little family.

Appalled at being deposed by a stepfather, David clung
to that mythic sense of himself as twin. But what he
wanted of that sense was not identification but proof of
absolute difference, to have a negative, a shadow self, a
perfect inferior, available to him at all times when com-
parison was to his advantage, otherwise invisible. Later,
contrite, he offered that description of himself to his sister.

"Oh, D, you were never *that* bad. No five-year old is
that fully developed a male chauvinist pig."

But such desires didn't "develop," or didn't in David.
He could remember waking up with them, as one does with
the symptoms of disease, headache, sore throat, fever, and
it seemed to him they crippled him into his adolescence

much as polio might have. He could still sometimes feel the vestigial limp.

Until they went to school, David and Diana were two halves of an harmonious nature. Oh, they quarreled occasionally, but their griefs were far more often mutual and sympathetic, a wonderful defense against their instinctively gentle mother, whose discipline was guilty and sporadic and easily deflected by their indignant howling.

Acutely aware that they lacked a father, their mother was particularly careful to supply David with the masculine toys he might have chosen (or might not), soldiers, pop guns, cowboy hats, a doctor's kit. But he and Diana played with all their toys interchangeably. If David was the father and Diana the mother for her dolls, David bathed and changed and pretended to read to them in imitation of the only parent they had. They also spent hours designing battle fields for the soldiers, digging trenches, establishing look-out posts, arranging the troops in companies and scouting parties. At the end of the day, there was never a battle. They might occasionally pelt the soldiers with ripe plums from the overburdened tree in the garden, but it was more like breaking up building blocks for the next project than an act of destructive violence.

Out in the world, they held hands, David to protect Diana from cars, she to protect him from dogs. In bed at night, they sang through their crib slats to each other, giggled and were suddenly both deeply asleep when their mother came in to silence them.

It never occurred to either of them to tattle on the other. Their criminalities were shared. Even in the attention twins always attract, they didn't compete but closed ranks to be sure they weren't fussed over too intimately or deprived of treats adequate for them both.

"Thank you, and one for D," each learned to say. They had the same name for each other, which even their mother couldn't use since it didn't distinguish them from each other. For themselves they didn't need to distinguish. Differences didn't matter.

Yet in a single day David learned not only to drop Diana's hand but to call her all the new names of the kindergarten playground, chief of which was "girl," the generic insult from which all others stemmed. Diana was a *girl* among the other *girls,* the untouchables.

Some of the other boys were also cursed with sisters, but they were older or younger, not humiliatingly in the same class. Diana expected to sit next to David, to roll out her nap rug next to his, to share juice and cookies.

"You're a *girl,*" he said to her, frantic with this new information which didn't seem to mean anything new to her at all.

What took David only a few hours to learn didn't change her view of herself until months later and then only imperfectly. Some of her confusion might have come from David's own inconsistent behavior, for, when they were at home alone together, they often played as contentedly as they had before, though now only with David's toys, and he tried to make her feel it was a privilege.

"Girls don't usually play with soldiers," he said.

But he flatly refused to be bathed with her.

"Girls are dirty."

His mother gave in to him. He had only to say, "Boys don't do that." Except for such obviously masculine chores as emptying the garbage, he got away with it.

Diana was never as easily impressed as their mother, but she saw David daily in his less certain command among his peers whose recklessness and cruelty often terrified him. There were boys who withdrew, but they had to suffer such taunts and bullying from the others that they were made to feel even beneath the girls, a humiliation David couldn't have endured, for he would have to suffer it with Diana looking on. She was there, always there, watching.

"See Dick run . . ."

Little girls are not impressed with little boys. Only other little boys are. For them David tore his clothes and broke his bones. For them he caught the cat to be hanged from the school flag pole and stole light bulbs to be smashed in people's driveways. Their approval could not change his sister's growing disgust or their mother's dismay. They couldn't understand what David didn't either.

"I *have* to," David said.

Diana had no such compulsions.

"Why don't you have some of your own little friends over?" their mother asked Diana when David excluded her from the pitched battles that now went on in their once basically scenic back garden.

"They're silly," she said, a judgment she wouldn't apply to herself.

When David occasionally condescended to play on a boring Sunday afternoon, Diana more often than not wouldn't on the excuse that she didn't like the game or wanted to listen to some stupid radio program.

"You play with me if I say so," David demanded.

But he could never get her to do anything he wanted her to, but cry.

Nobody could, not their mother, not the teachers. How docilely David accepted the teacher's judgment that being left-handed was babyish. No such blaming touched Diana. If she couldn't use her left hand, she wouldn't draw or write.

"Baby D won't," David crowed to their mother.

"Why not?" their mother asked.

"This is my own hand," Diana answered, offering it.

How did she know that? Why hadn't David, who had been clumsily ambidextrous all his life?

The twins were separated in the third grade to give them emotional distance from the other. At the time, David was convinced that Diana had been sent to be among the slower and sillier children, and there may have been some truth in that, for Diana's stubbornness made her an uneven student. She not only refused to use her right hand but refused to read aloud any story she didn't like, and, since most stories reflected David's view of the world rather than her own, she was often silent.

David missed her with what he later recognized as that mixture of emotions which overcomes people trying not to fall in love. He dreaded seeing her in the halls or on the playground and looked for her everywhere. His pack of friends, somehow sensing that tension, would at the sight of her begin to chant, "There's your stupid sister. There's your stupid sister." If she looked at David, he made a face. If she didn't, something as sour and heavy as tears lodged in his throat.

At home he couldn't leave her alone. He stole her pencil box, hid her shoes, tied up the dolls she now neglected, put dog turds on her pillow, worms in her milk. Sometimes she ignored him. Sometimes, if what he had done was really terrible, she'd hide or break a favorite toy of his, but more often she simply cried.

Their mother never spanked either of them. Their punishment was to be sent to their now separate rooms where David read his big-little books or listened to the radio, trying to pretend he liked being alone. Diana often exiled herself, preferring her own company, but David would choose anyone, even his sister, to avoid being by himself.

From the moment David realized he was supposed to be superior, he was terrified he wasn't. It was a cruel trick being played on him, rather than on Diana. If you were a girl, you didn't have to be somebody; you could be yourself. Nobody cared, or cared as much. Yet he wouldn't have dreamed of trading places with her.

It took their mother as long as two years to decide to marry again because David got along so badly with Hugh Bacon, the man she wanted to marry. Hugh wasn't in those early days unkind to David, or at least not often and then under such provocation that even David had to acknowledge it. He didn't like to have fun when Hugh Bacon was around.

"How about a game of catch?" Hugh would suggest.

"That's okay." David would shrug to let Hugh know that he didn't have to put himself out on David's account. David was willing just to hang around the house keeping an eye on Hugh.

"Why don't we go out for ice cream?"

"There's already some in the fridge."

But David learned to sense when he'd pushed Hugh's good humor to its limit, and David was afraid of him. Hugh was a large, strong, grown man. David was an underweight, bespectacled ten-year-old.

Diana wasn't as blatant in her dislike of Hugh Bacon. Her practice of staying out of David's way was useful to her in staying out of Hugh's. Neither did she share David's fantasy that they had power enough to prevent Hugh from taking a permanent place in their lives. Also, when Hugh was around, David was too busy laying traps for him to pay much negative attention to his sister. In that way, Hugh seemed something of a relief to her.

Their mother never paid as much attention to Diana as she did to David, though David didn't feel certainly her favorite. Diana didn't demand attention simply for its own sake. Though David could squirm under his mother's pleading little lectures about trying to be kinder to his sister, kinder to Hugh Bacon (whose first name David pronounced as if it were a bad smell, whose last name inspired David to grunt and squeal), any attention was better than none.

What small tenderness David allowed in his ten-year-old heart was reserved for his mother. She seemed to understand that, though gestures of affection were taboo in front of other people, David could be petted like a cat before he went to sleep at night. He hated the thought that anyone but he could bring that look of bright pleasure to her face when he surrendered a treasured stone or wildflower to her. David had no notion that he could protect and care for her because he didn't see her need—a grown woman, his mother, whose role in life was to protect and care for him . . . and his sister. Even when she married Hugh, David understood it as a quite unreasonable punishment for his own worst misdeeds.

What shocked David even more than Hugh's presence in his mother's bed was her sharing of Hugh's name, that awful name, when she had before been so nobly called, like her children, Crown, a gift from their mythically careless father. Hugh, the pig man, was turning her into a pig woman, disenfranchising her royal children. David's two-year-long rebellion turned into stunned mourning, a mood Hugh could misinterpret for a while as something more positive and civilized than defeat. His mother knew, but David turned away from the apology in her eyes.

Hugh would, David supposed, have adopted both children if they had been at all receptive to the idea. They weren't. Having had two years to hope the marriage wouldn't take place, they were, at twelve, too old, too used to be being fatherless, to risk the experience. If Diana wasn't as shocked and threatened by the marriage as David, neither was she enthusiastic. It might, other things being equal, have drawn the two of them together again in the nearly forgotten mutuality which had worked so for their benefit when they were little children.

But suddenly other things weren't equal. Did David notice, even at the wedding, that Diana was visibly taller than he? Within a year, she was six inches taller than David, two inches taller than their mother! Not only did David have this awful man towering over him but his own sister as well, and she was developing *breasts*. David's mainly scornful attachment to her changed to pure hatred. He teased her brutally, as if both her height and body were grotesque. "Giant boobs! Giant boobs!" he taunted in his piping, as yet not even cracking child's voice.

Diana was slow to realize her physical advantage, perhaps because David had succeeded in making her feel as mortified by it as he was. But finally one evening just before Hugh Bacon came through the front door, Diana gave David a mighty shove which toppled him over a chair. Then she fell on her brother, her hands at his throat, and he struggled helplessly under her intimate, astonishing weight.

Hugh pulled her off, saving David's life, but then he thrashed David to within an inch of it while David howled, "It's D's fault. She pushed *me*." Hugh didn't care if she had started it, he said, and then he gave David a brief lecture on what his behavior with his sister would be henceforth, all protective gallantry, which was the only decent manifestation of his natural superiority over her.

"But she's bigger than I am," David whined.

"Not for long," Hugh said, "and that's beside the point. She's a girl."

At dinner Hugh decided they had too informal a household. From now on, he would hold their mother's chair, and David would hold Diana's. When she looked around mistrustfully, Hugh reprimanded her, telling her that a lady commands trust. This rotten new rule meant that David couldn't pull the chair out from under her unless she was looking.

Later that evening, a remarkable thing happened. Hugh went to David's room to apologize.

"Your mother has pointed out to me that I set you a poor example by using physical force, and I agree with her. I also trust that in future I won't have any reason to use it."

After his own two sons were born, he thrashed them without reserve, but he never touched David again. Perhaps Hugh had been newly enough in love with David's mother to listen to her. Perhaps the memory of David's dead father also helped to stay his hand, but David gave his mother full credit for that small victory. If it cost Hugh anything, it cost David a great deal more.

To be a gentleman, he not only could not hit girls but had to somehow prevent them from attacking him. And he had to be trusted.

"Oh, David darling," his mother pleaded, "do try to be a better boy."

That's all he was, after all. If he had to have a new role model, why could it not be someone his own age and size instead of that great big bully? And if he had to be kind and polite to a girl, why couldn't she be his own size as well instead of someone capable of killing him if he didn't fall in line?

Hugh would have taken David to hockey games and taught him how to fish and hunt if David had let him. But David's policy was to be indifferent to anything that interested Hugh. He was no great reader. David took up books with a passion. Hugh thought music was simply a form of noise. David listened to it while he was reading to block out all domestic sound. He loved the walking base of boogie, the slow drag of the blues. He confessed to his mother that he'd like to try piano lessons.

Hugh might have been more generous about David's interests if he hadn't perceived them for what they were, mainly ways of annoying Hugh. If he had bought instead of renting a piano, David might have quit in the first six months. By the time Hugh grudgingly gave in and bought it, David was too hooked for such revenge. There was so much more power in filling the house with his own sound than in simply turning up the volume of the radio, which could be unplugged and removed. And his mother actually liked it.

But his mother was pregnant. David had a fantasy that the pig man blew into her a bit more every night until she was so huge she was in danger of exploding. Now her size, too, was repellant. All bodies began to disgust David.

His only relief, aside from playing the piano, was being disgusting with his pack, whose excremental sexuality suited his own. They stank up rooms with their farts and foul language, giggling more hysterically than girls over how dirty it all was, how revolting. They retched and rolled with laughter.

"You'll like having a baby sister or brother," their mother said.

"Oh, I guess a brother would be okay," David answered, a momentary vision of someone who would be smaller than he, who would have to mind him, for a change.

David could not have imagined a creature so really tiny, helpless and commanding as Carl when he arrived. His fragility terrified David. It would be far too easy to kill such an enemy who nevertheless had the power to silence David as even Hugh couldn't.

"Not while the baby's sleeping," his mother cautioned as David sat down at the piano. The little creep slept most of the time.

It was his crying which irritated Diana. "It doesn't sound human," she said once, almost under her breath.

"Girls are supposed to like babies," David said, not with rancor so much as surprise that she could dislike Carl as much as David did.

"Girls are supposed to be a lot of things they aren't."

She was looking David directly in the eye. They were the same height.

"Do you want to get out of here and go to a movie?" David asked.

They couldn't hold hands any longer, but David could walk on the outside. They were fourteen that winter of their peacemaking, and nothing was ever quite so hard for David again. His sister was the first real friend he ever made.

David looked down at the only line he had written and shrugged.

Even with his hearing aid turned off, David could hear the thumping of footsteps and the slamming of doors above his head, the hostile rumbling of his son-in-law, the outraged high notes of his younger daughter, Mary. If any violence occurred, it would be one-sided, Mary hurling yet another piece of family china at her husband's head.

From the time Mary was a baby, it was like living with a faulty smoke detector. You could usually locate the cause of her tantrums, but her outrage was out of all proportion to it. Her parents' bewilderment and increasing lack of sympathy inadvertently encouraged Mary to develop a generalizing self-righteousness to bolster her fury. If her older sister, Laura, was on the phone when she wanted to use it, Laura was *always* on the phone, *always* borrowing Mary's favorite blouse without asking, was *forever* trying to boss Mary around. Laura, mild and self-possessed from the cradle, avoided Mary's temper when she could and otherwise ignored it.

Mary's husband, Ted, showed some forebearance, but Mary, as an adult, had improved her aim and was sometimes able to hit a source of guilt the victim generalized for himself. For Ted it was usually money. Although he made a decent amount of it, he was apt to hand it out indiscriminately like a latter day apostle.

"Your wife and your children don't happen to be lilies of the field!" David had heard Mary shout, and he shook his head in sorrowing admiration, thinking she might be better off not married to a basically good man.

But Mary was also affectionate, funny, and lovely to look at. Her storms of temper blew like sudden winds over the city leaving the landscape clarified and shining, sometimes for days at a time.

Though the rooms David occupied were in the raised basement of the house, he could still look east out over the steeply sloping lawn and across the low roof tops of Kitsilano to the high-rise cluster of downtown Vancouver, and to the north on clear days he had a glimpse of the mountains, in mist now on this damp fall evening. The children had gone out, and so should he to a film perhaps since neither his futile memory nor his television could block out the row upstairs.

David slipped his wallet and keys into his pockets, took his raincoat and hat out of the closet, and let himself out his own back entrance quietly. He could have walked round the house and down onto the street, but to be less conspicuous he went up the back steps to the alley to walk the several blocks to the bus.

David rarely missed having a car. He had been a nervous, inattentive driver, and he'd always preferred to take the bus to the center of town to work. In the last years before Patricia died, she not only kept the car during the day but did what night driving there was. She enjoyed being in control; he did not. The only positive pleasure he had ever had from the car was giving it to his oldest grandson, Ben, right after Patricia died.

"But what will you do, Dad?" Laura had asked him.

"I only ever drove it to the hospital," he answered.

Laura worried about him. Though she admitted he'd arranged the downstairs very comfortably, she wasn't sure it was dignified for him to live in a space originally designed for a student. But there was a really decent little kitchen and bath along with a bedroom and the ironing room he'd made into a study. He had everything he needed.

Laura probably disapproved of his generosity to Mary as well, for it dispossessed Laura of what had, after all, been her home, too, but she and Jack would never have wanted to move back in. They had been planning to sell their own large house in order to help educate their two bright sons. David had suggested they postpone the move until the boys were settled for themselves. He would take over the burden of their education.

"But can you afford it, Daddie?" Laura had asked.

"What better way to spend the money?"

Patricia would never have done it, of course. Left alone, she would have stayed the head of the household, at the wheel of the car, managing her good life as she'd planned to manage theirs together which by now would have included winter holidays on the desert, cruises to South America.

"I sometimes think you could be satisfied with a subscription to *The National Geographic*," Patricia had said to him, but fondly.

The world he had never seen had tainted David's taste for travel, worn away what wonder he might have felt, for every landscape had come to him as a background for death and disaster, which he had broadcast night after night, year after year, on the evening news. There wasn't a place on the globe to which he couldn't assign flood, earthquake, explosion, assassination. Other people thought that record of "Beyond the Fringe" was funny. "This is Alva Ladell, bringing you news of fresh disasters." David Crown came to hate most those stupid human interest stories at the end of the broadcast, hypocritical sops to the nightmares he had been helping to create. It was a very odd way to have spent his life—in a soundproof box. Nearly everyone else he knew of in his own generation had taken part, placed the world catastrophe inside their personal experience and learned over the years to contain it. His disqualifying eyesight had spared and deprived him. None of his memories were his own, words rather, falling on him as impersonally as acid rain.

A bus on its way to town in West Point Grey at 8:00 p.m. is nearly empty, a student or two who have stayed late at the university library, a couple of old men like himself, incompetent to drive. The bus driver still wanted to see his Pharmicare card for the reduced fare. Everyone said David didn't look his age.

If David had been an actor, as he'd wanted to be, he could have made the move to television in the fifties. As a newsman, he simply didn't do. He sounded sincere enough on radio, but he looked like an actor. The men chosen were avuncular, square-jawed, dependable-looking fellows.

"You're too seductive, darling," Patricia had said, and, though she would have liked the money, she claimed she was glad she had to share only his voice so that they could still be private people in the public world.

One of his fellow stay-behinds in radio had said to him, "The guy who never has doesn't have to be a has-been."

David had never regretted it. He wasn't sure his nerves could have stood the film clips to illustrate the horrors of his nightly announcements, and he was glad not to have to pass the test night after night of being made up to look like himself. Could his hand have been steady at the mirror if his job had been to shave a public face? He would have been ashamed to have to become interested in ties. It was frivolous enough, what he had done, without having to endure the world looking at him while he did it.

Acting would have been different. What little he had done of it as a boy and a very young man gave him a sense of how he could rise out of himself into a creature of intent and direction, articulate even at the heights of emotion, which weren't emotion at all but an energy-charged will, focusing.

David Crown had not believed he was gifted enough nor was he foolhardy enough to go against all the practical and outraged advice of mother and stepfather. He had a very ordinary and clear-cut part to play in the real world and one advantage: he could begin his career just before nearly everyone else his age came back from the war half-educated and ill-adapted for civilian life, confused about what was owed them. David married Patricia, too, before a real man came back to claim her as the flower of his victory.

His mother hadn't approved of Patricia who even as a girl was sure of herself. "Opinionated" was his mother's word for it. "But please yourself," she had said.

Only extraordinary people pleased themselves, surely. It wasn't really a matter of privilege. Other people didn't know how, even if they were free to, except in the small details: the bus driver there with his Zero bar on the dashboard who otherwise wheeled his life under the trolley lines at the mercy of the traffic.

Night had come on, ablaze and aglitter compared to the dullness of misty evening, and the city rose up on the other side of Grandville Bridge, a chicanery of lights. David never got used to this new skyline, its cancerous swiftness obliterating what he wanted to remember, the town of his growing up, modest at the foot of mountains, at the edge of the infiltrating sea, a place for modest lives in the shadow of wilderness and remote snow. But there before him was an inflated city where you had to be at least twenty floors up for a view of the mountains and the water and pay dearly for it by the square inch.

David's younger colleagues, those who weren't being laid off as redundant without severence pay or pensions, had been moved down instead into the underground studios in the new CBC building, where newscasters joked about weather reports in a sky they could not see.

It was a fault of age, David knew, to be glad to be old, but he was. He wouldn't be either of his sons-in-law, Ted or Jack, so much more trapped than he had been between what they had been raised to expect and what they now confronted—a middle class being peeled like an onion, stinging the eyes of wives and children for all they wanted and increasingly could not afford. Ted was afraid as David had never had to be. Ted gave away what he did, not out of benign condescension but out of a real awareness that there, but for luck, went he, and there might he still go any day.

As David walked along Granville Street, a street kid

called out to him, "Hey, Gramps, how about a five? What do you say?"

He had nothing to say, past failure, past being frightened into generosity.

Stripped across every movie ad were warnings of obscene language, nudity, excessive violence, calculated to induce anyone but an old fogie like himself to join the lineup at the box office. He walked on through the theatre district into the sky-roofed tunnel of department stores, manikins keeping their own company in bright boxes. One display had been stripped down, leaving nothing but flesh-colored torsos with bald heads. "Minimal nudity," David labeled it for the censors, as he passed on down toward the working water. He stopped in the parking lot of the train station where he could look out at the docked freighters, at the dark water, at the misted lights of the north shore.

He was cold. His right shoulder had begun to ache from the damp that was settling into his coat. He was too old to walk the city streets like a brooding teenager, yet that was what being retired and being a widower had turned him back into, a person who simply went out, having nothing but a marginal role to play in the strife and striving of family life, his destination this parking lot at the edge of the world, from which he had never had any desire to run away to sea.

Laura had said to him, "You should marry again," a suggestion that had shocked him, for, though he missed his wife and lacked her defining presence, he had no desire to hand himself over to yet another responsible keeper. He needed his freedom even when he did not know what to do with it, even when its only purpose was to humiliate him as it did now. He had spent his adult life not doing what he shouldn't, being told to do what he should and doing it, occasionally with grace. Any way forward now had nothing to do with beginning again but somehow with returning to these blank destinations where as a boy he had broken himself to his life and lived it.

If David had nothing more to learn than that long-ago lesson of giving in, he needed now only the patience to experience the process of giving out. He did not much regret the fading sight and sound of a city so changed from his boyhood that he no longer felt at home in it, but, as he turned to retrace his steps, the pain in his shoulder which should have encouraged the mortal direction of his thoughts felt more like a lively protest.

He could no longer report it to Patricia, who would administer to or dismiss in her judgment. Not even his body, never mind his life, had been in his own hands for years. He looked at those hands, steady and articulate even now but with that old reluctance which could built to fear if he had to direct anything.

Another body brushed against his: "Watch where you're going, you old beggar."

David, startled, looked down at his old raincoat which Patricia might have by now told him to throw out, and he knew his hat wasn't in much better shape. But "old beggar?" Surely he didn't look as disreputable as that. He supposed without much effort he could.

His tongue touched the roof of his mouth and nudged the upper plate out of place. With it in his pocket, he had a partially toothless grin, and consonants would only softly form and slur at their escape. He next removed his glasses, to which his hearing aid was attached. The sound of traffic disappeared. He heard no footfalls of approaching pedestrians, and the traffic lights blurred into their larger auras. Finally he let his stance accommodate the pain in his shoulder, hunched up against his ear.

Now all he needed was to pick the right victim, one of

the Teds of this world, and with just the balance of cringing aggression ask for, well, a five, trusting that the street kid had sized up the current market.

"I need a five, son," he said to a man young enough to have been his son, well but casually dressed, who paused, reached into his pocket and handed David a two-dollar bill. "Much obliged."

Halfway down the block, David stepped into the shadow of a doorway to replace his teeth and glasses and to file his begged bill in his wallet, trying not to laugh aloud. But, restored to himself, he felt suddenly self-conscious. Mary should have told him not to go out looking like a skid row bum. But he was really no business of Mary's. He intended not to be. and he couldn't tell her, as he could never have told Patricia, about what he had just done. Unable to understand his comic sense of triumph, they would think him demented.

"Don't play the fool," his mother used to say to him.

Once he had, in *King Lear*, and knew it was a better part than the king's, in the play and in life. Patricia would probably see him as an old Lear now, giving up his authority to his daughters. The difference was that he'd never had any authority over them and didn't want it.

"Where's your gumption, David Crown?" his wife would demand when he didn't stand up for himself at work, in a restaurant, in a ticket line.

David rarely regretted the loss of it, then never in public. On one or two things he should have had the gumption to stand up to his wife before she was too ill, dying, and it was too late. He had been too close to her, had watched at too close range her natural young confidence transformed by the death of their first child into protective self-righteousness. She took that inexplicable crib death as punishment for whatever random sins she could assign herself, imagined neglects, self-absorptions, and lived increasingly as if the slightest moral lapse would wreak such vengence. And should. That was the overstep she made from which he should have drawn her back. In his silence, he had been her accomplice. He had gradually learned to forgive her for it, but not himself.

Sitting on the brightly lit and empty bus going back to West Point Grey, David wished his memory could be as aimless as his wandering had been, but it never was. It snagged again and again on that pair of deaths, his father's and his son's.

David made an image of them. They looked exactly alike. They shared his name, and they were both the same age, twenty-three—the age his father had been when he died and David was born. It was also the age David had been when his son died. If his son had lived, he'd be forty-two and David's father would be eighty-eight, both far too old for his romantic mourning of them. Why sentence either of them to a long life they didn't have?

Yet it eased David to imagine his son as a grown man. He lacked the emotional courage to grieve for him, as Patricia had, a baby who hadn't taken his first step or spoken his first word.

And those deaths had made David the cautious man he was, obliged to stay alive as the first duty to everyone he had loved, mother, sister, wife, daughters. But now lonely, reaching into the past for the companionship of his sister or his wife, he came up against another pairing of failures, his inability to reconcile those two women, a failure which had cleaved his life in two for all these years. What perverse loyalty to Patricia was it that still kept David from doing what he desperately wanted to do, to go to his sister and ask her forgiveness?

Oh, he had seen Diana. For forty years he had had the

furtive courage to go to her on their birthday, a day, like the home free in their childhood games, where none of the rules applied. At those meetings he was too nervous to observe much more than her appearance and manner, "photo opportunities" such occasions were called in the trade, where little real information was exchanged. He had watched her change from a handsome, self-possessed young woman, Dr. Diana Crown, obstetrician and gynecologist, into an increasingly heavy and slow-moving middle-aged woman until now she seemed old, much older than he, having given up at her retirement the habit of expensive clothes and her hair dresser. Now she wore loose smocks with large pockets full of things, trousers and flat, loose shoes to accommodate her arthritic feet. It did give him a brief relief to see her, but it did not excuse how he lived his life on every other day of the year. Or let his children live, accepting the cruel pieties they had been taught. They did not even know they had an aunt who lived in the same city.

David let himself into a blessedly quiet house, folded his coat, put it and his hat into a paper bag in the laundry room, went to his study and picked up the phone.

CHAPTER II

Diana, wakened by her absolute interior clock, touched Constance's face, and there were the dark worlds of her eyes, always the first territory of day. Not since they'd shared a war over forty years ago had they been alarmed out of sleep. Waking was silent, intimate, even after all these years faintly arousing. Diana was reluctant to leave their bed to confront her singular, upright self. This morning there were autumn messages in her bones. She didn't achieve a steady gait until she was halfway across the bedroom. It would be a day for her cane, as well as all the other hardware she now required, upper and lower bridges, hearing aid, glasses, and finally the row of pills neatly set by her place at breakfast.

Constance, two years older than Diana, had all her own teeth, could hear birds sing, and only needed glasses for reading, which she had pretty well given up, and for intimate weeding of the garden which she could still do, hunkered down for minutes at a time and able to rise as swiftly and agilely as a young girl. Yet Constance often could not move from their bedroom without Diana's aid. Particularly in winter, she might forget that it was morning and be putting herself to bed again by the time Diana had finished in the bathroom.

This morning Constance had left their bed, taken off her pajamas and was standing irresolutely beside clothes put out for her the previous night.

"Have I had my shower?"

"No," Diana said, smiling.

While Constance showered, Diana took up a small slate, lifted the cellophane to clear it of the crossed off items of yesterday, and began to write the list for today, the first item intended to amuse Constance:

> Put on your clothes
> Breakfast
> The morning show
> Lift bulbs in the bed by the garage
> Lunch
> Rest
> Errands on the avenue
> Walk on the beach
> Dinner with David

The last three items had been scribbled impatiently and had to be erased and redone. Even taking care, Diana formed letters only Constance and druggists could read. Reinforcing any cliché about her profession irritated Diana, but even now she couldn't slow down her mind to make her hand its adequate servant.

She propped the slate against Constance's gardening

clothes and went downstairs to plug in the electric kettle and put the eggs on to boil, taking pleasure in these homely chores which for so many years had been done for her. She wondered how many retired husbands became smug about their talent for boiling eggs.

Constance arrived at the breakfast table, dressed, with the slate in her hand, the first item crossed off.

"David who?" she asked.

"My brother."

Constance stared away from Diana at the blank slate of her memory.

"My twin brother."

"Is it your birthday?" Constance asked in sudden agitation.

"No, no, of course not."

"Then why is he coming?"

"I'm not really sure. He invited himself."

"With . . ." Constance paused.

"His wife died last year," Diana reminded her.

There were times when Diana envied Constance's memory loss. Even a year dead, David's wife Patricia was lodged in Diana's memory like a tumor.

"Are you glad he's coming?"

"I don't know. I'm not sure I have room for him after all these years, if that's what he wants."

"You do finally have to forgive men for marrying."

"Even badly?"

"Of course."

"Am I a grudge holder?" Diana asked.

"I'm the one who would be if I could be," Constance said. "I can't even remember what's the matter with me most of the time."

"There's nothing the matter with you, except that."

"Isn't there?"

"No," Diana said in the certain tone she had learned to use in her office, coagulant for the random fears of pregnant women, menopausal women. She hadn't had much to do with old women like herself and Constance.

"Were you a doctor in real life?" Constance asked.

"Yes."

"You sound like one," she said dismissively.

Diana laughed.

"Oh, I know you," Constance said. "I've always known you, Dr. Crown."

She crossed breakfast off her slate and then looked in a puzzled way at the litter on the table.

"What happens to this?"

"I'll do it. You go watch your show."

"Don't you go to the office?"

"No," Diana said, also in a learned tone, bleached of regret.

If it hadn't been for Constance's sudden deterioration of memory, Diana knew she might have been one of those people unable to recognize the time for her to retire. Sixty had been quite old enough to be done with playing doctor/mother to all those women in such intimate, limited, impersonal ways and to accept the limitless intimacy of Constance's need.

After Diana had put the dishes into the dishwasher, she consulted her own list, left by the kitchen phone. In the last five years she had gradually taken over the cooking from Constance, never able to develop her flair, but methodical enough—"scientific" Constance called it for all the consulting of cook books—to offer adequate meals for the two of them. They did not entertain. They never had.

David would not know the precedent he proposed to break in inviting himself to a meal. Even Constance might not remember how rarely anyone else had sat with them at their table. Diana mostly lived alone in their past except when sudden rushes of it overcame Constance, not as memory but as an invasion of the present when Constance briefly became who she had been and suffered again what she had suffered, out of reach of Diana's comfort.

Diana did not even know what her brother liked to eat, what allergies he might have developed. He had been a frail, near-sighted boy, for a year or so a head shorter than she, before he suddenly grew to eye level, and then she was looking up to him, and they were friends again as they had been as small children.

On his brief, yearly birthday calls, he liked to hark back to that adolescence as a bond between them which couldn't be broken, before they exchanged his potted plant and her book and he went back to a life from which she and Constance were entirely excluded. Diana had never laid eyes on his two daughters. She did not even know their married names or how many grandchildren he had.

Her only real connection with David had been impersonal. She used to listen to him read the news on the CBC as she drove home from her office. He had retired only a week after she did. But she had become so familiar with his voice that she could still recognize it on the phone.

A roast chicken. Would he feel obliged to carve it? Would she feel obliged to ask him? How did a sixty-five-year-old brother and sister who hadn't had a meal together for forty years behave?

David followed his sister into the living room, nodded to Constance, chose Diana's chair, sat down, covered his face with his hands and wept.

Diana couldn't move. It was Constance who went to

him, put her hand on the back of his neck and gently rubbed it. Two or three long minutes passed, through which Diana stared unmoving, before David recovered himself enough to apologize in an almost offhand way, as one might for a cough.

"Would you like a drink?" Diana asked.

He nodded.

"I don't know what you drink. Whiskey? Gin?"

"Gin, just with a bit of ice," he managed to say.

When Diana came back into the room with his drink, whiskey and sodas for herself and Constance, Constance still stood beside him, her hand on his shoulder now, and he was speaking to her with a kind of helpless urgency, as if there were no evening before them, as if he expected to have to leave momentarily. He looked up at Diana, and stood suddenly, dislodging Constance's hand.

"I know I don't have any right to be here."

"Take your drink," Diana said quietly.

He did and looked around him as if to discover where he actually was.

"I must be sitting in your chair."

"Do calm down," Diana said. "Sit down, have your drink."

Constance had taken her own drink and moved away a little, but her eyes stayed on David, concerned. He was seated again, looking into his glass.

"I've thought about coming for months," he said.

It startled Diana. David was a very occasional visitor to her thoughts, consigned to the past. Had she been callous not to reach out to him when Patricia died? But how could she have when there was no question of her going to the funeral, no question of her even calling at the house where other family members might be?

"What kind of a man must you think I am?"

"I don't really know," Diana said. "I'd have no way of knowing."

"Patricia never knew that I came on our birthday. When she died—it's ridiculous isn't it?—I somehow felt I couldn't."

Out of loyalty to her memory? Diana was tempted to ask sardonically, but Constance was probably right. Finally she would have to learn to forgive him for marrying so badly. Patricia was, after all, dead.

"The dead take their own time letting go," Constance suddenly contributed with detached sympathy.

Diana wasn't sure Constance even knew who this man was, so recently in tears in their living room.

"David, I don't really see what else you could have done, short of leaving her, and that's not the sort of man I'd expect or even want you to be. It's all long past. I certainly don't want to deal with it again, and I don't see why you should either."

"You did deal with it, you see. I never did. I never confronted Patricia and told her she was wrong."

"Would it have done any good?" Diana asked.

"It wouldn't have changed her mind," he said, "but my children should have known you, should have been made to understand what a wonderful person you are, what wonderful people you both are."

"Do you know us?" Constance asked.

"Not as I wish I did," David replied.

Diana excused herself to attend to dinner, carrying that old, uncovered fury out of the room with her. What right had he now, after all these years, to drag this corpse of remorse into her house, stinking of adulation? No wonder he behaved as if he were to be thrown out at any moment! She would put dinner on the table, and then she would tell him either to stop his groveling, maudlin act or get out.

The chicken had a rough trip from the oven to the platter. He would just have to stand up like a man and carve the damned thing because in her present state she didn't trust herself with the implements.

Diana and Constance had always sat across the table from each other, leaving the two heads of the table deserted; so it was natural enough for Diana to have set David's place in that vacant authority. He assumed it with protesting diffidence, again fearful that he was taking his sister's place.

"I want you to carve the bird," Diana said.

He did so painstakingly while she opened and poured the wine.

"Do you remember," David asked, "how Hugh always butchered the job and then blamed Mother, saying she'd cooked it too long or not long enough?"

Diana had put her stepfather, along with most of her growing up, in the furthest attic of her mind. What she remembered now was David's resentment of him rather than her own.

"It's some time since I've done that," he said with some satisfaction, finishing his carving.

"Do you live alone now?" Diana asked.

"Yes and no. A few months ago I moved into the student suite so that Mary and Ted and their kids could have the house."

"What's their last name?"

"Searle," David answered, and then he shook his head.

"Is it in the basement?" Constance asked.

"High basement. Nothing sordid. I even have a view of the city."

"I wouldn't like to live in the basement of my own house," Constance said.

"Yes, it's probably too accurate a place to be," David said.

Diana smiled, aware for the first time of what she liked about her brother, when his self-effacement was ironic, as it had been with Hugh. But David had been young then, biding his time.

"What do you do with yourself?"

"I garden some and read a litle. I go out too much. It reminds me a bit of the war years when everyone else my age was gone. Some of the widows are even the same women. I wish I'd never learned to play bridge."

"Why do you go?" Constance asked.

"Habit, I suppose. Patricia enjoyed that kind of thing. What I'd really like to do is get closer to my grandchildren. I've got three of them right there in the house, but I've been so busy keeping out of everyone's way that I haven't made much progress at it, except when I look after them occasionally in the evening."

"Who are they?" Diana asked.

"Christine, who's fifteen, Patsy, and that would make her thirteen, and young Tyler. He's eight. Those are Mary's kids. Laura has two boys, Ben and Mike."

Diana didn't ask for Laura's last name. She was curious and at the same time reluctant, not sure what it meant to her to have all these kin named. She should think of them as she thought of the hundreds of babies she'd delivered as no continuing concern of hers.

"Do you miss your work?" David asked, but he addressed his question to Constance rather than Diana.

"Did I ever work?" Constance asked.

"That's answer enough," David said, smiling.

How often Constance's real questions were taken instead as comments as, in a way, they were. Was it possible to miss what you'd entirely forgotten?

"And you, D.?"

Their childhood name for each other caught at Diana, a snagging affection.

"No. It's not work for an old woman."

David didn't seem to her old in the same way, though he probably had fewer of his own teeth than she did, but he had always seemed to her younger than he was. Now he looked like someone made up for his part, the grey brushed-through still vigorous hair, the lines penciled onto his face, the slight stoop assumed. As a boy, he had wanted to be an actor.

"I was so grateful to quit," David said. "I don't even read the newspaper now, and I don't listen to anything but music."

"I miss listening to you," Diana admitted. "And I still feel I have to check in on the world at least once a day to see if it's still there."

"But you've always lived in it," David said. "I've spent my life in a sound-proof studio."

"Bomb shelter," Constance said.

Diana glanced at her, but she showed no sign of distress.

"Either there isn't any real world, or it's all of a piece," Diana said. "Your life seems to me nearly cluttered with reality, compared to ours, for instance."

"Am I real to you?" David asked.

"I don't know who you are," Constance said.

"He's my brother, my twin brother, David."

David looked from one to the other of them, and Diana knew that neither answer was of any help to him, but they were not meant to be.

Constance slept peacefully, the evening erased from her mind. Diana, lying next to her, rehearsed the names of her great-nieces and nephews: Christine, Patsy (for her grandmother, of course), Tyler; Ben and Mike, and those two would be older since Laura was older than Mary. David's first child had been a boy and a crib death when he was only a few months old.

I'm afraid of him, she thought, *afraid of what he makes me remember, even of what he wants me to remember.*

Though David had managed to be guided away from his early emotional outburst, the last thing he said before he left was, "May I come again?"

Constance had answered, "I expect you will."

"Am I real to you?" How could such a question be answered after all these years? At the level he probably meant it, the answer was, no, he was not, a disembodied voice which once a year materialized with a token offering to indicate that, though his wife had ordered Diana and Constance out of the house while he stood silently by, he still maintained this ritual connection.

Diana could be no more real to him, an idea he had, a project for his old age, the last expression of his passive tolerance for the disasters, sins, and peculiarities of this world. David had always been able to cry.

Diana got up quietly to take her mounting anger away before it disturbed Constance's sleep. What she needed was some hot milk. As she sat at the kitchen table, she wondered if David did the same in his set of rooms in the basement of his house, all those related lives asleep over his head.

How often they had sat together late at night, quiet to keep from rousing their sleeping parents and the two little boys. In those days there was never enough time for David to tell her all that was on his mind. She had been his best and really his only intimate friend. He never seemed to notice that she did little more than listen.

That wasn't exactly true. Diana's habit of being dismissively critical of David had been more self-protective than accurate, for there was a time when she trusted him, counted on him for the protection she needed, and she had enjoyed his company. The first betrayal of that relationship hadn't been his.

"If I hadn't left him, we'd still be together, a couple of fussy old maids."

Diana had never wanted to think about how hard it must have been on David that not only she but Hugh had gone off to war, leaving David to look after his mother and the little boys. Diana had taken her life into her own hands because she had to be able to be herself beyond the range of David's protection. She had fallen in love for the second time with a young woman her brother was interested in, and this time Diana could feel an answering attraction, to which she did not dare to respond, appalled by it for the sake of her brother. Instead, she warned him off.

"Don't ever marry someone like that," she said to him.

"But I like her because she somehow reminds me of you. You should be flattered. And she thinks the world of you."

"Be more original than to act out our incest taboo," Diana said.

He had taken her advice all too well. Patricia was as heterosexual as Eve. She put an end to Diana's occasional speculation that David himself might have been happier with another man, for more than one of her own young men had been flirtatious with David, but David never seemed to notice.

What a sexual confusion they had both been to their friends! Virginal, devoted to each other, setting up crosscurrents of desire they hardly understood themselves, though for Diana it became increasingly clear that she was as fixed in her sexual direction as she was left-handed. David's choices had always been wider than her own.

The milk was gone, and Diana was now relaxed enough to know how tired she was. Her hips and knees complained all the way up the stairs. How much better it would be to move into something smaller on one floor, but it was out of the question while Constance could still work in her garden, while the place still seemed familiar enough to her to keep her oriented. There might come a time when Constance didn't know where she was, when her mind slipped back into her past and stayed there. Now she occasionally mistook Diana for her own sister or mother. Both women had been killed by a bomb that had also buried Constance for forty-eight hours. Constance was saved suffering, it seemed, from no more than exposure and a broken collar bone. Her present confusion was understandable, for Diana had tried to be mother and sister to Constance as well as lover all their lives together.

When Diana finally got back into bed, Constance turned and welcomed her into a sleeping embrace, the body's memory flawless.

Dear D.,

I so badly regret the way I behaved tonight. I don't know why I couldn't have imagined it more clearly and realized that, however good the motive, I could not possibly walk back into your life, apologize, and go on from there. I have a bad habit of thinking about us when we were young and good friends and blanking out everything that came later. It's been thirty years since I've actually tried to meet your level gaze and say something that mattered.

I can certainly see why you don't want to go back over
what happened so long and maybe irretrievably ago. I don't
really have any more excuses than you have already offered
for me, and, now that Patricia is dead, there's not much
point in making excuses for her.

There was no point in my visit at all, except inadvertent
cruelty, if I really am no more to you now than a painful
memory. And I also see now that there is no point either if
my only intention was to clear my guilty conscience.

This is the fifth draft of what has been, at one stage, a
ten-page long letter assuming a concern for me I have no
right to expect, but it has had the virtue of making clear to
me how much it matters to me to see you again, to know
you as you are now, to be a brother to you in whatever
ways I can.

Your brother, D.

"No point. No point. No point," Diana said aloud as
she read the note which David must have delivered by hand
some time in the early hours of the morning.

Constance, sitting across the breakfast table from her,
looked up inquiringly.

"It's a note from my brother, David, who was here last
night for dinner."

Constance gave the resigned nod for information she
had to accept on faith.

"You were very kind to him. I was very impatient."

"What did he want?"

"To make friends again. We haven't seen him except on
our birthday for nearly forty years."

"Do you want to?"

"It doesn't feel to me as if I have any choice. I don't
like that."

"You don't like to be forced to be as kind as you can be."

"No," Diana said and smiled.

"Is he dependable?"

"I suppose so, within his limits."

"I'd like you to have a brother, or someone of that sort."

"Why?"

"For when I can't any longer keep you in mind," Constance said.

"No one else would do for that," Diana said.

But after breakfast she went to her desk to draft an answer to her brother.

Dear David:

I didn't behave very well either last night. We see so few people that I'm out of the habit. You may not have been aware of the extent to which Constance has lost her memory. She only intermittently knew who you were. Since it is her recent memory which is most affected, you would have to expect to introduce yourself not only each time you came but several times during an evening. You would also have to learn to find your way in conversations which have no discernible direction, to be content with non sequiturs, and to accept sharp changes in mood which have no apparent relation to the moment.

We rarely go out because the confusion of unfamiliar places can frighten Constance, and I don't go out without her, unless it's absolutely necessary.

I suppose it sounds a terribly confining life, but it is one we've learned to live with with a good deal of contentment. It's as much for my own sake as for hers that I don't want it disturbed. I have had to cut off friends who have wanted to "rescue" me from it.

I'm not sure what there is I have to offer you under

the circumstances. I don't entertain with any pleasure the idea of evenings caught between someone who rarely remembers the past as we've lived it and someone who wants to remember what I'd as soon forget. I'm not capable of nostalgia.

But perhaps there are things we can do and be for each other in the present. Let's try again.

Diana

Diana reread the letter, thinking it sounded more grudging than it should. But, just as she would not resort to their childhood initial, she would not fiddle with drafts for hours as David claimed to have done. Nor would she rush off with it like a lovesick girl and stuff it through his mail slot. What had waited this long to be done needn't now occur with the suddenness and speed of a flash flood. Diana licked a stamp and placed it on the envelope which bore the address of a house she had never been in.

As she walked to the corner to mail it, Diana wondered whether she was now also opening the door to a lot of unknown young relatives. On her own terms, that would have to be, terms she would have to discover.

To change the direction of her thoughts, Diana stopped, leaned on her cane and deliberately looked about her at the human attempts to transplant an eastern autumn to this temperate evergreen and alder shore. In every yard at least one bush or tree was in the process of scarlet dying, giving the lie to human expectations. The alder might be good for nothing but firewood, yet its long, dull, shabby shedding which went on from October until the end of the year was in keeping with much more of human experience. The flameout of accident or trauma was for old grumps like Houseman to romaticize.

She found Constance in the back garden, stymied, her

memory board in her hand. Some days she could occupy herself for hours. On other days she was like a child's toy, needing to be wound up every few minutes, set in a direction which couldn't be changed, stopped only by whatever was in its path.

Her relief, when she saw Diana, lit her dark eyes, opened her smile to her white and perfect teeth, opened her arms wide and welcoming.

"Ah, you're a lovely woman," Diana said.

"I feel more like a dog," Constance said. "If only I had nothing to do but be interested in my bodily functions, distracted into barking by anything that moved, into wagging my tail at any sight of you, I'd be fine. But by the look on your face, I can see that more is expected of me."

"Would you like to come in the car while I go shopping?"

"That's a good, doggy thing to do. Leave me a crack of air and I'll growl at strangers."

Self-disparaging jokes were part of the hard days, and Diana had learned not to protest against them because they were one of Constance's weapons against falling into stupefied depression or further still into a past she couldn't find her way out of.

Diana kept Constance with her through the day, glad that her own life could be suspended in this way any time Constance needed her. They were practiced now in good diversions. Music was better than reading aloud, for Constance couldn't hold a story line or argument in her head for long, but themes in music repeated themselves, and, even when they couldn't serve to remind her of what had gone before, they had immediate as well as consequential meaning. Card games gave Diana too great an advantage, but they could work at jigsaw puzzles contentedly for hours. There were certain walks they had taken often enough, along the beach, out in the university grant lands, which didn't confuse Constance, but Diana's increasing lameness made those shorter and shorter pleasures.

Often in the evening Diana would begin, "I'd like to remember something for you."

That invitation sometimes triggered simple questions from Constance.

"How old am I?"

"Sixty-seven."

"That old? You're not that old."

"I'm sixty-five."

"We're old women. What color did my hair used to be?"

"Black, like your eyes, but it turned early, before you were forty."

"I've always lived with you."

"Since you were twenty-five and I was twenty-two."

"Always just the two of us," Constance said.

"No, once there were three of us."

"Three?"

"Jill Carlysle. You can remember Jill."

"Jill," Constance repeated, and then she smiled.

Diana would not take her farther in that memory than she asked to go. As a younger woman, Constance had been sexually restless. Lovely to look at, intense and tender, she was hardly aware of how it happened that so many people were drawn to her. It prejudiced her against friendships with men. She criticized in them the very random appetite she shared with them. She didn't recognize that kinship because she had such various rationalizations for her affairs. This one was like a child to her, that one like a mother. All this one needed was to experience her sexuality to get out of a bad marriage. All that one needed was a little comfort and reassurance.

They had quarreled fiercely over Constance's women in their early years together until the emotions involved became so negatively patterned that Diana determined to break out of her own jealousy. Constance had, after all, never chosen any of them over Diana, and perhaps it was time Diana believed her when she said she never would.

At first Constance mistrusted Diana's change of heart. It was either feigned or a sign of indifference. Constance began occasionally to suggest that sometimes she and the woman who currently interested her might do something together with Diana, go out to dinner, go to a film. Diana reluctantly agreed and found to her surprise that getting to know Constance's lovers made it easier to accept them as a necessary part of Constance's life, even of their life together. Diana didn't realize for some time that her new sense of security was based on a dangerous smugness, for none of these women had ever been in any position to offer Constance that blend of security and freedom Diana could once she had established her practice. They were mainly, as Constance said they were, women in transition, with as yet very little control over their own lives, and they all suffered in varying degrees their inability to compete with Diana, a jealousy which overtook erotic pleasure and broke it into emotional scenes. They irritated and finally bored Constance.

"Is it worth it?" Diana asked her one night when she came home particularly exasperated.

"It's inevitable, I suppose," Constance replied. "You're the only person I know who doesn't want eventually to own me."

"Only because I can't," Diana replied. "It's no virtue."

"But it is. I don't own you either. What would it be like if I were jealous of all your patients?"

Diana was tempted to remind Constance that she had no cause. Yet, though Diana had always been scrupulously professional in her work, she would not have chosen it if she hadn't liked the intimate confidence she had to inspire in women entirely vulnerable to her.

Wives of her colleagues certainly complained of the extraordinary hours they kept. Not only did babies seem to prefer the small hours of the morning for their arrival, they came in batches which could sometimes be traced back to a city-wide power failure or, more curiously, natural disasters, volcanic eruptions and earthquakes.

"You lead a beautifully sublimated life," Constance said.

Diana agreed with her. There was more than enough high drama in her work for her to have any taste for it in her private life.

Constance had tried to go back to school with Diana when the war was over, but a Canadian university was foreign to her idea of what a university should be, full of practical choices when she had expected to be required to study Greek, to cultivate her mind with no other motive than that. She took a course in Canadian literature to become more familiar with her new country and decided it was like studying English literature from a Boots lending library. And she felt stifled by the hard-working earnestness of all those returning veterans, whose scant social lives were carried on amid drying diapers and collicky babies.

"I've been to the employment office," she announced one day. "What Vancouver needs is gardeners. All the Japanese were sent away from the coast and still haven't been allowed back. I love to garden."

Diana didn't object. All solutions in those days seemed to her temporary, everything else postponed until she had finished her own training. Since the bombing, Constance had suffered from claustrophobia. A few years of healthy outdoor work might be exactly what she needed. And the money would be wonderfully welcome.

Constance was happy in her work and gradually successful. She bought a truck, the side panels of which announced, C CROWLEY, GARDENING SERVICE, and she hired students, always girls, to mow lawns and edge, while she planned and worked in the beds through the long growing season. But for four months every year she had very little to do. Diana had expected that Constance would use her free time to discover what she really wanted to do with her life.

"Don't be such a snob!" Constance finally shouted at her. "I'm doing what I want to do, and my customers think I'm just as marvelous as your patients think you are."

It was not snobbery, Diana realized, it was a judgment even more suspect. She had hoped that Constance might discover work so demanding that she had no time left for amorous adventures. Actually, Constance managed her winter affairs far more skillfully to suit Diana's erratic schedule than she could have managed a year-round job.

"Why don't we ever see Jill?" Constance asked from a silence they often fell into.

"We do occasionally," Diana answered. "She's afraid her visits upset you."

"Do they?"

"I think they upset her."

"Because of the way I am?"

"You're very good with her really. You can sometimes fake remembering and even fool me."

"I sometimes really do remember," Constance said, protesting.

"Of course. I don't think it's that. Jill is lonely."

"She lives alone now?"

"No, she had protégés, but you were the great love of her life."

"I shouldn't have been," Constance said.

"I don't think she regrets it."

"What did happen?"

"At the time," Diana said, "we thought it must have been the emotional strain. Both Jill and I were so busy with our own heroic stoicism, we hadn't really thought how difficult it must have been for you, even though it was what you thought you wanted—to live with us both, not to have to choose between us. But now I doubt that. I think it was a delayed reaction to everything that happened during the war."

Diana watched Constance's face carefully even though she knew actually talking about the past didn't trigger Constance's disappearances into it.

"But what did happen?"

"Jill found you one night out in the garden. You didn't know where you were or who she was."

"And I've been that way ever since?"

"Oh, no, darling. You spent five months in hospital. You had a series of shock treatments, and you were much, much better. You had the ordinary memory loss associated with the treatment, but we thought in those days it would be temporary. In a sense it was. It's only been really bad in the last five years, and this may be something entirely different."

"Time is so hard for me," Constance said.

It was for Diana, too. The arthritic ache in her hands could make her think it was only yesterday that she had dug painfully with them through the rubble to deliver this beloved woman who had delivered Diana from the prison of her desire. "Constance, Constance, Constance," she kept calling. "I will get you out." But first there had been the mother, then the sister, stillbirths both, and only hours later, Constance, alive. Diana had chosen a field of medicine where the odds were better than that, and her practice had given her the faith that she could always reach Constance again, wherever she had gone, however badly she was trapped in the rubble of the past. But those aching hands reminded her, too, that she was old, failing in body much more quickly than Constance, and sometimes she was afraid.

CHAPTER III

David handed his damp new raincoat and hat to his son-in-law, Jack Geller.

"I do wish you'd let one of us pick you up," Jack said.

"I hoped you'd admire my new rain gear," David said. "When somebody handed me a couple of dollars on the street a few weeks ago, I decided I'd better do something about myself."

"They didn't, Daddie!" Laura said, scandalized.

He kissed her for answer and followed her into the living room where his two grandsons, Ben and Mike, sat hunched over a game of chess. They rose to greet him.

"Don't let me interrupt the game," he protested.

"And miss the grand inquisition?" Ben asked.

"Oh, you are awful!" Laura said.

"Grand inquisition?" David asked.

"Don't worry about it, Granddad," Mike said. "We've

got her well outnumbered."

In this household Laura would always be outnumbered if the boys' male solidarity were joined by their father. But Jack almost always stood against them with his wife. Today he stayed at the edge of whatever game this was.

"There are dark rumors about you, Granddad," Ben said, "and Mother's determined to get to the bottom of them."

"Why don't you let your grandfather sit down and have a drink before you start all this nonsense," Jack suggested mildly. "Gin on the rocks?"

"Thank you," David said, sitting down gratefully.

"Isn't that a new jacket, too, Dad?" Laura asked.

"As a matter of fact, it is. Do you like it?"

Mike gave a low whistle through his teeth to express his approval. Ben took a lapel between his fingers and rubbed.

"It's very nice," Laura said.

"One more clue, eh, Mom?" Mike asked.

"That really is enough, Michael," Laura said, coloring.

David looked at his older daughter and thought how young this affectionate male teasing kept her.

Jack came back into the room with a tray of drinks, gin for his father-in-law, glasses of wine for himself, his wife and sons.

"First taste of last year's plum," Jack said. "You'll have to try it at dinner, David."

Ben and Mike make elaborate show of the tasting.

"A bit puckery, would you say, old man?" Ben addressed his younger brother.

"A bit green still," Mike answered through pursed lips.

"It's delicious," Laura decided. "I knew it would be. Those plums were dead ripe."

"It will get better still," Jack said, always the moderator of opinions.

David liked the number of projects this family shared, the vegetable garden, the wine making, and they were all ardent sailors. He could not remember a time when the boys weren't friends. Perhaps it helped to have them so close in age, not a year apart, but each with his own birthday. How Patricia had doted on them, as if they did, in some measure, compensate for her own loss.

Laura slid back the door of the cabinet behind her chair and produced a large dish of salted nuts.

"So that's where they were!" Mike said.

"If I'd put them out earlier, there wouldn't be any left."

David still ate nuts and then slipped away to rinse his bridge rather than call attention to his problem. After he had helped himself modestly, each boy took one nut from the dish, mocking their mother's rebuke until she was distracted and they helped themselves to large handfuls. David noticed that it was Mike who led in the prank. Probably some of this foolishness was really beneath Ben's new college dignity, but he would keep that from his brother, in no way wanting to exaggerate this sudden gap between them. He would hang back at home until Mike caught up with him next year.

"Now what about these rumors?" David asked.

"Aunt Mary thinks you're courting," Ben said. "And she also thinks it's undignified for a man of your age to ride the bus for such important purposes. Would you like your car back, Granddad? It would be a fine test for me to discover whether all these women are throwing themselves at my feet or the tires of your Volvo."

"No, I don't want the car back," David said. "Whatever put such an idea in Mary's head?"

"She only said," Laura protested, "that you'd been

going out lately to see someone in particular. That's all she said."

"And that you were buying new clothes," Ben insisted.

"And, if it didn't involve a woman, why would you be so secretive," Mike added.

"Well, you know Mary," Laura said.

"Put two and two together and make twenty-two," Mike helpfully added.

"My contribution to this conversation," Jack said, "was to suggest that David was free to do whatever he pleased without family prying, but, as you can see, it fell on entirely deaf ears."

"I've been going to see my sister," David said.

"Your sister?" Laura repeated, amazed.

"I have a sister," David said.

"Why didn't we ever know?" Laura asked.

"She and your mother had a very bad falling out. It was after little David died, and your mother really wasn't herself for a long time after that."

"They didn't make it up in even all those years?" Laura asked.

"No," David admitted.

"It was so bad you couldn't even tell us we have an aunt? Does she have children?"

"No, she never married," David said. "She was a nurse during the war in England and went to Holland with the Canadian forces when it was liberated. When she came home, she went to medical school. She's an obstetrician and gynecologist—or was. She's retired now."

"Right here in Vancouver?" Ben asked.

"Right here in Vancouver," David confirmed. "She lives with a woman named Constance Crowley."

"Why is that name familiar?" Jack asked.

"Crowley?" Laura repeated. "C. Crowley Gardening Service. That extraordinary woman? You remember, don't you, boys?"

"That little white-haired woman who used to come with her team of girls to do the spring and fall cleanup?" Ben asked.

"She was just wonderful, as good at squatting as a Jap."

David flinched inwardly as he always did at his wife's vocabulary on his children's lips, but he would have had to correct her to be free to correct them.

"Is she the one?" Ben asked.

"Yes," David said.

"She's English, isn't she?" Laura asked.

"Yes. They met during the war. I don't know just how," David began uncertainly and then rushed into the story of Constance's being buried alive, her mother and sister dead, as if that extraordinary experience had anything to do with the relationship between his sister and Constance.

"How awful!" Laura said. "Was she badly hurt?"

"It didn't seem so at the time, but either the shock or some damage to her head, no one's really sure, cropped up years later. She's got nearly no present memory at all."

"She could never remember the names of the flowers," Laura said. "She made a joke of it, but she kept a flower book in her truck so that she could point them out. No, it wasn't a flower book. It was a large board of seed packets."

Diana would have thought to make her that. David was a little thrown off balance by this focus of interest on Constance, about whom he hadn't thought he would speak much just at first. He was not even sure he was ready to talk about his sister.

"What was it like to see your sister after all these years?" Jack asked.

"Oh, it isn't that I haven't seen her. I always went to see Diana on our birthday. We're twins."

"Twins!" Laura exclaimed. "I can't get over this."

"Is there something you're cremating for dinner, Mother?" Mike asked.

"Oh dear," Laura said, hurrying out into the kitchen where the peas had just cooked dry.

"Next time your good nose smells the alert, follow it yourself," Jack said to his son.

"Yes sir," Mike said, flushing, and he followed his mother to the kitchen.

"Are we going to meet . . . Aunt Diana?" Ben asked.

"I'd like that," David said, smiling. "I'd like that very much."

In a way it might help, this coincidence of their knowing Constance already. It might reassure Diana that at least this part of the family took a real interest in her. Constance would, of course, not remember them, but that didn't so much matter.

"Do you remember, Daddie, when I was first pregnant with Ben?" Laura asked once they were seated at the table, "and I saw there was an obstetrician named Crown? Mother got really angry with me and said you didn't choose a doctor out of a phone book at a silly coincidence like that, and I'd go where my g.p. referred me."

"Yes, I remember," David said.

"Whatever happened between them? Was Mother jealous, or what?"

"It's a long time ago," David said. "It was very personal . . . and convoluted, and, since neither of them would . . . There was nothing I could do about it."

"You haven't told Mary yet?"

"It's a peculiar thing to have to explain," David said.

"Should we ask her to dinner?"

"Give us all a bit more time to get used to the idea," David said.

"What's she like?" Mike asked.

David's instinct was to describe Diana as a girl, but that would make no sense when they must be prepared to meet the old woman who was now his sister.

"She's quite lame and heavy and a bit deaf," he began. "She can be fairly abrupt, but she likes to laugh. I'm quite sure she'd take to the two of you."

David looked at his two grandsons, so clearly brothers, Ben the better looking of the two, more substantial and pulled together than his younger brother Mike, who clowned away a basic shyness, a sensitivity he had yet to find any use for. For a moment it all seemed quite simple.

As David took his leave that evening, accepting a ride frankly forced on him by Ben, he said to Laura, "I hope I haven't upset you."

"Not at all," Laura reassured him, "but you've made me very curious."

"Will it upset Mary, do you think?"

Laura looked thoughtful. "Perhaps it would be better to tell her by herself." Ben drove cautiously along the narrow residential street around the obstacles of parked cars and large piles of raked leaves in a neighborhood planned before anyone had projected three-car families or rental accommodation in the basements and attics of what used to be one-family dwellings.

"Settling in at the university all right, are you?" David asked.

"I guess so," Ben said. "Dad told me before I went out there that I was expecting too much of the place."

"And you were?"

"In a way. It isn't nearly as hard as I expected it to be. The only real difference from high school is that nobody gives a damn whether you work or not."

"Enjoy that," David said. "They will care again once they're paying you to do it."

"By the time I get out, I hope there's someone around who can pay me. Do you think it's true what they say, that the party's over for the west?"

"For British Columbia?"

"No, the western world."

"Ah, Ben, I've never pretended to understand economics. So many of the theories have always sounded to me like excuses for unwise or unjust spending, all round the world. The wonder to me is that the whole thing hasn't come down like a pack of cards long ago."

"I guess we're closer to it than we ever were," Ben said.

The big questions and general prophesies depressed David, but he hadn't the resilience of spirit of a young Ben who contemplated with more curiosity than terror what lay ahead. These worldly worries were his new mantle of manhood rather than mortal burdens.

"It must have been interesting to be right at the centre of everything the way you were," Ben said.

"The centre!" David exclaimed.

"You could have started a coup or a war or an evacuation."

David's laugh was incredulous.

"Well, you could, if you'd wanted to," Ben said a little less certainly.

"The only thing I ever wanted to do," David said, hearing how little his grandson wanted to sound foolish, "was just not to read about a plane crash or assassination. You know that old argument about whether or not the falling tree makes a sound if there's no one around to hear it? The real point is that the tree falls in any case."

"But look what the rock stars have been able to do for Africa, all because of the media," Ben said.

Even David, living in a news blackout as much as he could, had heard "Tears Are Not Enough" and "We Are the World." His granddaughters sang such songs around the house, and they did rise up above the vicious lyrics and nerve pounding of hard rock to reassure the children that their superstars had power and purpose beyond their faddish millions.

"And the first thing any revolutionary does to overthrow the government is to get control of the media," Ben went on.

David didn't try to explain that his job was never to write the news but simply to read it, his only responsibility the correct pronunciation of foreign names. He knew Ben wanted to think well of his grandfather to reassure himself of a significant role to play in the affairs of the world.

Giving Ben an affectionate shoulder hug, David got out of the car and made his way from the alley down the back steps where he'd left a light on for himself. Once in his bedroom, he sat down on the bed and turned his bedside clock to face him.

Raincoat collar turned up, hat pulled down, he said into it, "This is David Crown bringing you the CBC news at six. You have twenty minutes to get out of town."

He paused. Taking on the power to save or destroy the country was too ambitioius a role when his only recent success had been begging two dollars from a likely stranger. David didn't even feel competent to talk with his younger daughter; yet he must now soon before she heard it from some other member of the family.

David often joined Mary in the garden, a pleasure they had shared in her childhood and renewed now that she had returned to that childhood place, but David encouraged Mary in making new decisions so that the garden would become her own. More than once she had said, "I don't think Mother would like that," and David was careful not to confront that sentimentality directly, counting on time to loosen the hold Patricia's memory had on her daughter.

They were in the process of dividing the large iris bed, the prize corms which had been ordered yearly from Oregon carefully marked so that they would be divided rather than thinned.

"I haven't really meant to make a mystery of my social life," David began as they squatted together at their work.

He felt Mary look over to him, but he kept his own eyes on his busy hands.

"I've been going to see my sister."

"Your *sister*!"

He repeated the details and explanations he had offered the night before with one exception: he did not mention Constance Crowley.

"But what could have been that awful, Daddie, that we couldn't even know she existed?"

"Only their inability to apologize and accept their differences. Perhaps Diana could have if your mother had made the first gesture, but she couldn't."

"Do you blame Mother?"

"I don't suppose it's a matter of blame," David said.

"You don't expect us to see her, do you?"

The question did not surprise David, but it discouraged him.

"I don't expect anything," he said.

"It's just that it would be so embarrassing," Mary said, alerted by the tone in her father's voice.

"Initially," David agreed.

"And somehow, I don't know, offensive. You don't want me to tell the children, do you?"

"Their cousins know."

"What will they think? After all these years?"

"The boys seemed no more than curious. I don't think old troubles mean very much to them."

"Well, they're certainly upsetting to me," Mary said. "It's as if you'd done something awful to Mother, now that she's dead."

Her tears came as easily as his own, and he was irritated with them for that reason, but he stood up and went to her, putting a gentle hand on her bowed head. This was the scene which he should have played out with her mother long ago. It seemed to him now uselessly painful.

No explanation or argument would alter Mary's gut reaction. She couldn't see the revelation of Diana's existence as anything but a requirement to shift sides, a betrayal of a mother she loved for a complete stranger, and David was not sure that Mary, even in good will, could ever warm to Diana. He felt as sorry for Mary as he had for his wife, trapped in such narrow loyalties.

Suddenly Mary shook herself free of him and ran into the house. David stood, watching her go, hoping this, like all of her angers, would play itself out rather than harden, as Patricia's had, into unrelenting judgment. Sighing, he crouched down again to go on with the sorting of the iris corms. Alone, he took the liberty of slipping a few of the prize ones into his pocket as a gift to Constance.

"Hello!" David called to Constance where she stood with a garden fork in her hand.

It was the first time he had tried dropping in without a

specific appointment, and the mistrust in Constance's eyes made him regret it.

"I've only brought you some iris corms from my garden," David said, holding them out to her.

She backed away from him as if he might be an intruding stranger, and only then David realized that for her he was.

"Constance," he said gently, "I'm David, Diana's twin brother."

He stood as still as he would for a nervous dog while Constance looked him over.

"I've never seen you before in my life," she decided and turned firmly away from him to go on with her digging.

"I was here just three nights ago for dinner," he tried to remind her. "We talked about these iris, and I told you I'd bring some over."

Constance lifted her fork out of the soil and held it in front of her, a ridiculously small creature for such fierceness. "Get off this property!"

"Constance!" It was Diana calling from the back door. "It's David, my brother."

Constance lowered her weapon.

"I have no way of knowing," she said to David, "unless I'm told."

He wanted to say, "But I did tell you." How could he teach her to trust him if she was never able to know who he was except with Diana's confirmation?

After they had found a place for the iris and set them out, David left Constance to complete her garden assignments and went to speak to his sister.

"It isn't a good idea," Diana said, "to drop in like that without warning."

"Do you think she'll ever recognize me?"

"Probably not," Diana said, dismissively.

"Isn't there anything I can do?"

"Oh, David, just accept it."

"But I'd like her to be able to trust me," he persisted.

"If she really did remember who you are, that might be more difficult."

"As it is for you," David said.

"I need time to get used to you," Diana said. "I can't be bullied into it."

"Am I making a nuisance of myself?"

"Not yet," Diana said and gave him a reluctantly friendly smile.

"You'll have to set the limits. I don't have any."

"Of course you do," Diana said. "You just don't know what they are until you've stumbled into them."

She was referring, of course, to his loyalty to Patricia, which could, presumably, be transferred to any other member of his family, like his unreasonable and beloved Mary.

"I won't ever hurt you again, D.," David said earnestly.

"You may not be able to help that," she said. "I hurt you simply by being who I am."

"That isn't true."

"Isn't it?"

"No," David insisted, but at that moment he resented her as fiercely as he had as a boy when she wouldn't accept his view, the world's view, but persisted in her own.

"Oh David," she said wearily, "there's so much I don't want to think about any more . . . or deal with. It isn't you but all you call up."

"I know that," David said.

"And I really don't want Constance to run you through with a pitchfork just because I didn't know you were coming. There may come a time when she knows you, but we'd never be able to count on it."

"You don't really think she'd have . . ."

"No," Diana said, "I don't. But don't you see how difficult this is? You can't even know when I'm joking, and I'm so used to Constance I don't know what to explain."

"I'll learn Constance," David said. "I'll phone next time . . . or you might phone me."

"Do you have your own phone?" Diana asked.

"My own extension," he said. "I'll phone you."

Diana would make no move into his life, not even so slight a thing as a phone call, and, though it pained David, he knew she was right. If there was to be a reconciliation, he had to do the work of it and offer it to her as an accomplished fact to accept or refuse.

Meanwhile, he would get a phone of his own to be accessible to her. Even that simple resolution, however, daunted him. He could hear Mary's protests, exaggerating this small privacy until she would make it into a betrayal of her trust. Though the family byword had always been, "Don't give in to her; ignore her," everyone in the family was guilty of evasions with Mary. If David had been sure he could smuggle a new phone into the house without her knowing, he wouldn't have hesitated to do so.

David signaled his stop almost too late for the driver to pull up. The sharp breaking caught David off balance, and he would have fallen if a young college student hadn't reached out a hand to steady him.

"Thank you," David said.

His legs felt a little shaky as he got himself to the ground.

"Dad?"

David looked toward the call and saw Laura leaning out

the driver's window of her car, parked just beyond the bus stop.,

"Are you lying in wait for me?" he asked, a jauntiness in his tone to cover his sense of frailty.

"As a matter of fact, I am," she said. "I wish you'd get your own phone."

"That's odd," he said. "I was just thinking the same thing myself."

She had opened the passenger door for him, and he sat down gratefully beside her.

"Will you come home with me?" she asked.

"Trouble?"

"I just think you'd be more comfortable out of that house for this evening. You know Mary is sometimes simply a maniac."

"Oh dear," David said.

"Both the boys are out tonight. We could have a lovely evening, just the three of us, and by tomorrow she'll have worn herself out."

"Is Ted there?"

"Yes, he got home just a few minutes ago. As long as she'd not mad at him, he's very good with her."

David nodded. He was suddenly completely exhausted. Even the short walk to his own house could have defeated him.

"What you need is a gin, a meal, and a bit of peace and quiet."

"That sounds about right," David said and made an effort not to put his head back against the seat while Laura drove.

Left alone for a moment in Laura's living room, David dozed into an unpleasant quarrel with someone, his wife? Diana? Mary? and was relieved to be roused from it by Jack, who was offering him his gin.

"So," Jack said, "another eruption from Mount St. Mary."

"Let's not talk about it yet," Laura said. "Let's enjoy our drinks and dinner."

Why couldn't everyone have as sweet and sane a disposition as Laura? David was very glad he had two daughters. If there had been only Mary, he would have felt more to blame for what he had finally accepted as her inevitable chemistry. His first sip of gin warmed him, and by the time they had finished eating, he felt quite himself again.

"There's a great deal to be said for creature comforts," David said, though he refused Jack's offer of brandy.

"Dad," Laura began in a tone that meant this emotional recess was over, "I think maybe one problem for Mary is not knowing exactly what happened between Mother and your sister. With her imagination she can invent scenarios anybody else would laugh at. I understand why you'd rather not go into details, but maybe they are necessary . . . for Mary anyway."

David sighed.

"You sure about that brandy?" Jack asked.

"Yes," David said. "I've kept thinking that gradually I'd see a way to do all this, but I suppose, knowing myself, I would have put it off indefinitely rather than think it through. I promised Diana just this afternoon that I wouldn't hurt her again. She said I might not be able to help it. She's always been more realistic than I."

"But something that far back," Laura said, "can it still be hurtful?"

"Your mother ordered Diana and Constance out of the house because she disapproved of their relationship. She'd heard gossip, confronted them with it, and Diana told her their private life was their own business."

"They're . . . lesbians?" Laura asked.

"I would have said Constance Crowley was too good looking to be a lesbian," Jack said with nervous lightness.

"Do you know that, Daddie, for a fact?"

"Of course not," David answered impatiently. "Their private life is their own business."

"But then why wouldn't they deny it?" Laura asked.

"If someone accused you of loving Jack as if it were something despicable . . ." David began.

"That's not the same thing at all," Laura said.

"I think it is," David said more firmly. "The truth is that Diana and Constance love each other and have lived together for over forty years."

"But not as . . . perverts," Laura said.

"That's a pretty heavy word in this day and age," Jack said.

"For the sort of people whose sex lives are not just killing themselves off but spreading it to the general population?"

"Laura," David said sharply, "we're talking about Diana and Constance, not a group of randy young men."

"But if you don't *know,* why would you even suppose? Why would you have to suspect? Why would you ever mention it?"

"You thought knowing why your mother disapproved might make it easier . . . for Mary."

"Oh God," Laura said. "Even she couldn't come up with something like this."

"I don't intend to tell her," David said. "At least not yet."

"But either Mother was some sort of monster, or they're actually . . . what she thought they were," Laura said. "Was Mother wrong?"

"She was wrong to behave as she did," David said. "I

was wrong not to confront her with that. But she was very upset at the time. She thought the baby's death was a punishment, a judgment. If she had to be punished, other people should be punished, too."

"So she went around accusing other people of all sorts of crazy things?" Laura asked.

"She was harsh in her judgments," David said.

"But she got over it," Laura said. "She wasn't really . . ."

"Your mother did like to be right, Laura," Jack said gently.

"Maybe I'm beginning to sound a bit like Mary, but I wish Mother were around to defend herself."

"I'm not accusing your mother of anything," David protested. "I'm trying to *explain* what happened. If anyone's to blame, I am, for letting it drag on all these years. And I'm to blame now because what I'm really doing is wishing I'd been a different sort of brother, a different sort of husband and father, when it's far too late."

"Oh, Daddie, I'm sorry," Laura said, putting her arms around David. "It's awful for you. I can see that. I didn't mean to make it worse."

It was more reassurance than David by now expected. His several encounters on this day had held more potential for disaster than reconciliation. Why had he ever thought that his daughters might be more enlightened than their mother when he had allowed her prejudices to dominate their lives? David Crown, the bearer of bad news, hadn't after all retired; he'd simply transferred his talents to the private sphere.

"I'll take you home," Jack offered.

In the car, Jack said, "These daughters of yours are too sheltered by half."

"Yes," David agreed glumly.

"It's not all your fault, you know. I go on doing it. So does Ted. We like being married to 'good' women."

"But do 'good' women have to be fixed in stone?" David asked.

"No, and Laura isn't. It was a shock to her, that's all. And shocks come to her in black and white, not like Mary's off the wall technicolor, thank God."

"I wish I'd never gotten into this," David said. "It's not even like me."

"She's your sister after all," Jack said.

"A point far more important to me than it is to her, understandably. If I said to her tomorrow, 'Look, this is a bad idea,' she'd give me credit as a slow learner."

"Pretty tough old bird, is she?" Jack asked.

David looked over at Jack's amused profile and suddenly laughed.

"She was a tough young one, too."

"What I'm going to tell Laura—well, maybe not to-night—is that anyone who caught and kept Constance Crowley's fancy for forty years is someone I want to meet because I very much doubt it's what they do or don't do in bed."

"Thank you, Jack," David said. "For the ride, too."

"Bomb shelter," David recalled Constance remarking on that first evening he was with them, as he turned the key in his basement door. His own shelter felt frail protection from the war that had been declared upstairs though, for the moment, it was quiet. He would have been a wiser man to stay in it, live out his guilts and regrets without involving all these other people who couldn't help, who didn't want to be helped. They were sheltered, good women, his daughters, and he really had no right at this late date to be confronting them with the hypocrisy and ignorance from which their shelter had been constructed.

Did he expect them to make something useful out of the wreckage? At best, Laura might, for his sake, be persuaded to meet this monstrous myth, his sister, but Laura couldn't get beyond fearful curiosity without help from Diana, who would not trust her not to be her mother's daughter . . . and shouldn't.

Why did both his daughers so often call him "Daddie" as if they enjoyed infantilizing their relationship with him? They were grown women of a generation supposed to be far better informed and therefore more tolerant. They should be encouraging him out of his conservative shell rather than frantically stuffing him back into it.

David recognized the ironic look in his sister's eye. A part of him was maddened by it, but just behind that look there was also a question. He was someone she could need, and he had somehow to prove it to her, for his sake as well as her own.

"A lady commands trust," David said aloud in the pompous tone of his step-father.

David had taught that lesson to his own daughters: if you don't look around you, the chair will always be there. Now in his perversity he was pulling it out from under them.

Guilt and self-righteousness, those common incompatibles, were the rewards of this ridiculous day. David's anger bounced around like a pinball, lighting up now this figure, now that, until all the women in his life blazed at him, the smallest and brightest of them Constance with her pitchfork, saying, "Get off this property!"

CHAPTER IV

Diana was out in the kitchen, getting out cheese, sausage, and crackers, not because Jill Carlysle or Constance would be hungry so much as because she always liked to give them a little time alone together. She shook her head to remember how often Jill or she herself had invented not only purposeless little tasks like this one but whole evenings of pointless excursions to give the other time alone with Constance. If it had been Constance's problem, she would have solved it with imagination and pleasure. Both Jill, who was a lawyer, and Diana were far too straightforward, too directed toward clear goals to handle emotional detours with any grace. They both had gone alone to movies which bored them, arranged to have dinner with friends whose conversation was never enough distraction. Diana wondered if Jill had ever also been as badly reduced as Diana to join the periodical readers at the public library who would otherwise, like herself, be out in the cold.

Jill and Diana were both women strongly self-disciplined and naturally forebearing where they loved. But no matter how much they denied they were competitors—and they played their game by such subtle and strict rules that even people close to them might have denied it—they could not become friends until Constance's breakdown united them in the mutual fear of losing her. Even that bonding might not have occurred if Jill hadn't conceded defeat. She had moved out of this house which the three of them had chosen together for its uncommon arrangement of private spaces, long before Constance came home from hospital.

Jill blamed herself, but, if she'd found someone else then—twenty years ago by now—or if Constance hadn't suddenly, after nearly fifteen years of vibrant if sometimes fragile health, deteriorated, that guilt might have flickered out. Diana was sometimes impatient with Jill, for Diana saw Constance's life in a longer view—the accidents, the strains, the times of erotic chaos—as a complexly interrelating pattern. Jill's guilt could seem to Diana only a self-centered claim for how important a place Jill held in Constance's life, Constance's grand if doomed passion. When Jill had really suffered, Diana could comfort her by saying that any number of other things could have been equally or more responsible for Constance's condition. Now, if Diana offered the same observations, she deprived Jill of a tragic view of herself, without which her emotional life would be considerably diminished, for Jill had turned to her work with an intensity that didn't any longer leave room for intimacy. Her lovers were much younger women with a political attitude toward lust which made them critical and casual in their affairs.

"It's all very convenient for me," Jill confided to Diana. "I'd otherwise be labeled a male-identified pig with notches in the butt of my rifle, but that sometimes seems to me what I am."

Only once, in a moment of unusually vulnerable self-revelation, Jill had said, "I can wonder if I would have gone within a mile of Constance if you hadn't been there already to make it all impossible."

"A lot of things can look like choices years after the fact," Diana had said to her.

Diana certainly had not chosen to live with Jill or then to become her close and finally now her old friend. Diana did know that what initially made it very difficult now made it very easy. She admired Jill's competence, her youthful and now abiding loyalty to human rights, the hard, often discouraging work she did for minorities and for women.

"I'd rather be right than rich," Jill said. "In the long run, it's so much more fun."

Diana had admired that, too, the genuine pleasure Jill took in her work which she expressed in wonderful anecdotes and long outlining of strategies. Her energy came at such a steady flow, never depending on the adrenalin of crisis, in fact not good at crisis, her forte a long distance intelligence, dependent on being in control.

What Diana admired, Constance often had no patience for. If Jill was preoccupied with her work, let her be preoccupied and not involve Constance in the long listening required to share that preoccupation. Diana realized that she rarely brought her own work home except in explanations of changed schedules. But the triumph of childbirth was something that couldn't easily be shared with anyone but those immediately involved. And losing a life was not like losing a case.

'Well, I don't talk about my work either," Constance said, "whether it's earthworms or slugs."

She wanted evenings erotic or at least witty and certainly musical, which either Diana or Jill might have provided alone with her, but three together, Diana and Jill could only be talking heads, Constance impatient audience, wishing she had more than one channel to choose from. They increasingly arranged their life together as a carefully orchestrated series of scenes offstage until the stage itself was nearly always empty. "Two Without One" Diana came to think of it, but, while she focused on the problems of being without, she did not see the strain on Constance of never being alone.

"May I help?" Jill asked, standing in the kitchen door.

That old tact remained, the invitation to come back in before too much time had elapsed, like a childhood game in which the one left out had to go back into the room to guess what had gone on.

"I don't suppose anyone's hungry," Diana said.

"But how else would we figure out your Christmas present?"

There still had to be, after all these years, the excuse.

Constance's color was high, as if her blood held pleasure longer than her mind could. Diana smiled at her, long since feeling anything but gratitude for whatever, whoever could bring that vitality into her face.

"Food?" Constance asked. "Haven't we just eaten?"

"Four hours ago, before Jill arrived," Diana said. "But don't eat if you're not hungry."

"What I wanted to talk about with you," Constance said, smiling at Jill, "is what I'll get Diana for Christmas."

"You just have, darling," Diana said quickly, "but Jill didn't give away the surprise, and now you won't either."

"We have?" Constance asked.

Jill nodded.

"Well then," Constance said, "I could say, one less

thing to worry about, but I won't remember that either."

Jill took a ritual mouthful of cheese, standing by the fire which was burning itself out. What a romantic figure she still cut, trim in the trousers she had had made for herself, in a silk shirt nearly the color of her hair which was brown with not a trace of grey and made the strong lines of her face seem more marks of character than of the passage of time. Jill was a decade younger than Diana and Diana envied those ten years, though she would have little use for them except to be surer she would outlast Constance.

"Are you going home for Christmas?" Diana asked.

"No," Jill said. "Holidays are too much for Mother by now. My sister's taken over, and under her roof we've never even pretended to get along. I'm going to Mexico."

"All by yourself?" Constance asked.

"No," Jill answered.

"Good," Constance said.

Diana was relieved, for Jill was the only person they had ever felt required to include in what was otherwise a sweetly private day. One reassurance in including David in their lives was his absorption in his own family. Diana could trust that he would disappear into it on every ritual occasion.

"I must go," Jill said, moving to Constance, whom she kissed on the mouth.

At the door, Diana helped her on with her coat.

"You would call . . ." Jill asked.

"Of course, you know that," Diana said.

"*Anything*," Jill said.

Diana doubted that without doubting Jill's sincerity. She needed Jill only for the long haul, which was her talent.

"Who was that at the door?" Constance called.

"Jill," Diana answered, "just leaving."

Constance looked down at her memory board and crossed off Jill's name, the last entry of the day.

"It must be time for bed."

Constance went upstairs while Diana put the hardly touched food away, knowing that Constance would welcome her tonight, innocent of the source of her desire, as perhaps she always had been, even in their early years when Diana accused her of bringing her whole day's accumulation of lust into their bed. "What better place for it?" Constance had asked. Diana had had to grow old and lame, not even able to hurry up the stairs, to accept desire as the gift that it was, no matter who happened to bring it into the house.

"You didn't like babies when you were a girl," David said to Diana as they sat by the fire with Constance.

"I certainly didn't like *those* babies," Diana said. "What I really didn't like was seeing what a prison sentence they were for Mother . . . and realizing that we must have been, too. I couldn't have borne her life."

"Do you think she was unhappy?" David asked.

"No, not once she married again. Oh, I'm not sure she wanted those children all that much. They were to make up for Hugh's having to put up with us. But there wasn't really anything else she wanted to do."

"I never thought she was happy with Hugh," David said. "She hardly seemed to miss him during the war."

"She had you."

"Cock of the walk again for four years," David said.

"I never imagined it was fun for you," Diana said.

"It should have been, but at that silly age I wasted time being jealous of all the fun you and Hugh were having. The way you both wrote about it, all theatres and concerts and museums for you, Italian seaside resorts and lovely old hill towns for Hugh. You know, I don't think I ever believed Hugh saw action until they delivered him home."

"He might have lived on for years," Diana said. "There are still a few in the veterans' hospital."

"I didn't even feel sorry for him then. All I could think of was what a horrible burden he was going to be for Mother. I wanted to shake that poor, broken bastard and shout at him, 'Why did you have to be so damned careless?' "

Constance laughed and David looked over at her in earnest surprise.

"It's the way everybody felt," Constance explained, "furious with the dead. There they are right there, lying in the road or in the rubble and won't get up and walk away. We *were* careless, all of us."

"I've always thought of it as a masculine trait," David said, "one of the worst."

"You don't seem much of a man to me," Constance said.

"That's supposed to be a compliment," Diana said, smiling.

"Not really," Constance said, "an observation."

"I used to be sorry I didn't have much opportunity," David said. "The war defined all our generation, even those of us who were left out."

"Not defined, surely. Damaged," Diana said.

"Did you feel damaged?" David asked.

"Of course I did, and it disgusts me now, all this war nostalgia forty years after the fact. What can it teach your grandsons but that they've missed the great adventure, that ordinary life isn't enough?"

"She has a great affection for 'ordinary life,' " Constance confided in David.

"Well, ordinary death, if you prefer it," Diana said. "Why isn't it challenge enough to be one of the eight out of ten to live beyond seventy?"

Diana was impatient with the conversation, as she often was, out of the habit of the reminiscing and free association that stalled into platitudes which made her argumentative. But her impatience was more particular than that. David seemed always to invite criticism of himself, not to start an argument but to be confirmed in all his inadequacies. That was unfair to him, she knew that. The source of her impatience was inside herself, but she didn't know what her real quarrel with him was, an interior itch out of reach of scratching.

David was now speaking about the value of being ordinary, which wasn't what Diana meant at all.

"Surely you can't think of yourself as ordinary!" she burst out. "You have nearly nothing to forgive yourself for, which is extraordinary in itself."

"I see. Even when I claim to be ordinary, I'm self-dramatizing," David said, amused.

"Diana, don't be so hard on him. It's extraordinary to think of oneself as ordinary," Constance said. "It's quite saintly."

"How can you say I have nothing to forgive myself for?" David was in earnest again.

"I could have forgiven Patricia," Diana said. "It was my profession to forgive people like Patricia. But first I had to forgive you for marrying her, and I didn't even get round to that until after she was dead. You want it on your conscience. I don't."

"She was in a good many ways a wonderful woman."

"I hope she was," Diana said.

"What a lot of qualifiers!" Constance said. "Did I know this woman?"

"Briefly," Diana said.

"She was my wife," David said.

"A hard thing to be, a wife. I never could have managed it."

"I think on the whole she liked it," David said, lightly mocking.

"And you?" Constance asked in the same tone.

"On the whole," David said again.

"Do you still play the piano?" Diana asked.

"Occasionally, when Mary and Ted are out for the evening."

"We have a new Liszt," Diana said, "with Jorge Bolet."

"Did you hear him last fall?" David asked.

"No," Diana replied, as she got up to put on the record. "We don't go to concerts any longer."

"He's got so thin I wondered if he was ill, but I never heard him play better. He must be nearly eighty."

Diana had bought the record, as she had bought the roast they'd had for dinner, to please her brother, but she managed to present it as a rebuke. He knew he might just as well have said, "Do shut up. I can't stand another minute of this," but instead he stayed on the pleasant surface, turning his attention where she directed him.

It was Constance who had introduced Diana to classical music. No wonder David had imagined her life during the war as filled with concerts and plays. She wrote about what she heard and saw in passionate detail as a way to share her experience of Constance, who was inextricably involved in every pleasure Diana had. In love she was newly open to receive any gift, any wonder, for London was Constance's world, that great, fragile city, exploding and burning before them even as it offered up its treasures. Diana had never loved Vancouver, so puny a human clutter set against the reaching waters, the rising mountains. In London, loving

Constance, Diana had learned to love human accomplishment and to hate how nearly casually it was falling into ruins all around them, how casually Constance's life had almost been taken. At the end, there had been no question of staying there, for the city was nothing more to Constance than a grave.

Then Diana had to write about Constance herself, her closest friend, without family of her own now who would, Diana hoped, become a part of theirs. David answered that letter with the news that he was married. Diana's first reaction was that David was far too young to marry. Only then was she aware that she had left him behind where he had been at war's beginning, a boy.

"It will make it much easier, won't it?" Constance had asked.

It could have.

Diana looked over at her brother, attending to Liszt. She'd asked him once if he wanted to be a pianist. No, he'd said, it was just his way of building up his muscles so that no one would kick sand in his face. He had been prodigal with so many gifts. The only one he had consistently developed was an awareness of himself and his motives.

Diana was not unscrupulous, but she had lived out her desires mostly on blind will. She did what she had to without counting the cost. If she would simply put David back on the list of her imperatives, she could stop resisting him as an intrusion, as a threat, and accept whatever came to her because of him. Why, after all, did she want to see him as a matter of choice? He was her brother.

"Lovely, lovely," David said at the end of the record. "It's a marvelous instrument."

And he stood up, reading this offering as the end of the evening, as it had been intended. But Diana was now reluctant to have him acknowledge the sharp limit of his welcome.

"Shall we make a habit of Wednesdays," she suggested, "or don't you like habit?"

"I'd be delighted," David said, "if you'll let me do some of the providing. Do you like fish? I'm quite good with fish."

"You cook?" Diana asked, surprised.

"I cook," he answered, smiling.

"Are you reliable?" Constance asked.

"Within limits," David replied.

"Do I cook?" Constance asked.

"You're a wonderful cook," Diana said, "except for timing."

"Next Wednesday then," David said, "and I'll do the dinner."

Diana turned from seeing him out to find Constance in tears.

"What is it, love?" she asked.

Constance shook her head.

"Is it something about David?"

"It's nothing," Constance said softly.

Diana put a comforting arm around her and let her cry. Whatever sorrow this was, its name was locked out of reach somewhere in the storehouse of Constance's memory, out of which only emotions could sometimes escape, whether from years ago or from the music she had so recently listened to.

Diana had to reach far back into her childhood to know what it was like to cry without being able to explain, even to herself, the source of her grief. She could remember enraging David with her tears, his shouting at her, "I haven't done anything!" And often he hadn't. Perhaps she cried only because he no longer cried with her. By the time he had relearned those tears, she had given them up.

Constance grew quiet, and Diana took her up to bed. Then, singing to her in a voice no longer confident of the tune, Diana undressed her as if she were a small child, took her into the bathroom to wash her swollen eyes, and put her to bed.

"You are so patient with me," Constance said.

"I love you," Diana answered, a statement that had never become routine, for, even after all these years, she did not take the returning love for granted.

It was not only that Constance was a woman but such a desirable woman that had made her choice of Diana so unlikely. It was Constance who had chosen. Diana wouldn't have had the audacity without clear encouragement, but she had had the courage to love Constance and go on loving Constance in a growing sureness of heart, which had never been suitor.

Diana's early loves, aside from her brother, had been secret. The little girl with dark curls who lived in the next block was popular with all the children. She led about a gang of little girls always vying to be her best friend, and the boys were always tormenting her. Diana made no effort to join the gang or the torturers, but she watched for that head of dark curls on the school playground and in the halls. Very occasionally they met, but Diana never answered that ready smile because she didn't want to make friends, nothing as silly as that. She wanted to make a pact for shared, high, solemn heroics in a wonderful myth that left childhood far behind, never mind that the myth was made up of the stuff of her brother's junky comic books.

In high school Diana was in love with her chemistry teacher, a young woman of indifferent looks and sharp intelligence who was obviously proud of her distinction as the only female chemistry teacher in the school system. Far from wanting to be a role model for girls of similar ambition, she was determined to keep that place for herself. She encouraged the boys, mocked the inept girls and only tolerated the few like Diana, bright and dedicated not only to the subject but to her. Yet Diana never volunteered to answer a question. She was called on only when she might not know the answer. She always did. She never stayed after class to ask questions. But she did not join the mockery and complaints the taskmasters always inspired in their students.

"I was quite surprised, Diana," the teacher said at the end of the year, "to find you at the top of the class."

It was not this admission Diana's fantasies had wrested from her teacher, but it would have to do.

Diana had never turned to her mother for attention when she was old enough to be aware of it, after she and David had started school. She felt her mother's other child, not necessarily less loved but somehow one too many for her mother's attention since David demanded more and more of it, often if only to make their mother cross or disappointed in him. Diana trusted her mother to take care of them both, but it never occurred to Diana to trust her mother to understand either of them. By the time Diana was six and her heart had retreated from her brother sufficiently to clear her eyes, she understood him—that is, she saw through him—as their mother never would. He had figured out that boys were monsters, so he had to turn himself into a monster, at least when anyone was watching.

David at his worst was never quite able to kill Diana's love. He drove it off far enough so that it, too, had to be nourished in her fantasies, which were nothing like those she invented for black curls and taskmasters. In them Diana and David were brother and sister as they had been, inseparable and unselfconscious, playing together in a world—this was the only unreality—where there were no other children whose cruel games she had always hated.

The day Diana had actually wanted to kill her brother, had her hands around his throat, what she wanted to kill was the idiot monster who possessed David in order to set him free, to give him back to her. She had been differently afraid of him after that, not for what he could do to her, but of what he could change her into, a person capable of killing. She was certain Hugh had saved David's life, not only on that occasion but in the discipline he had imposed.

Diana hadn't actually disliked her stepfather as much as felt a distance from his large male body, the natural menace of it even in repose. There was a different smell in the house after Hugh came, not the acid sweetness of her brother or the fug of his room. Hugh was like one of those room deodorizers that obliterate all the smells one expects (for Diana her mother's smells: bath powder, baking, flowers) and leave something foreign and unnatural in their wake.

Their mother had been so timid, so self-effacing, that the presence of anyone else robbed her of herself. Diana and David had accomplished that long before Hugh and then the little boys arrived. But Diana didn't notice how much her mother was a house from which the occupant had fled until she was pregnant with Carl. She wore thick stockings to cover and ease developing varicose veins. In the last heavy months she walked with her left hand perpetually pressed against the small of her back. Diana didn't think so much about the baby to come as the relief and release the birth would be for her mother, but, once Carl arrived, he owned their mother as no one else did. His cries could suck her out of the kitchen as mightily as his mouth could suck nourishment from her breasts. No one else could interfere with that, not even Hugh.

Diana developed no natural sympathy for Carl until he

was two and had to turn over his reign to yet another
baby. Unlike the others in the house, resigned to the
process, he expressed his outrage freely against his mother,
against the baby, and, if neither was available, he punched
Diana or David. Carl threw the baby's empty juice bottle at
his father only once. Hugh took his diaper off to spank
him, and even those betrayed cries didn't bring his mother
back to him. It was Diana who went to find him, hidden
among the coats in the hall closet, who coaxed him out
with a cookie and cleaned up his grief-smeared face.

But she never really thought of those two as her
brothers. They were her mother's children, conceived and
born as offerings to Hugh, who responded to them with a
delayed need for ownership which made Diana pity rather
than love the children. It was pity in David, too, which
taught him to be milder with them than he might have
been expected to be. When they got into his old toys, he
offered them up without complaint, and he let those little
boys climb about him with no respect for his anatomy, a
neutral territory into which their father rarely reached to
demand new civilities and accomplishments. When Diana
speculated about how Hugh might have been with a
daughter, she didn't think of her own experience as a
measure.

Hugh dealt with Diana from the beginning as a potential
sexual fact to be denied. He did not encourage displays of
affection but practiced a strict courtesy with her for the
purpose of establishing mutual respect. Superficially, she
gave it to him, for he never tried to reach into her life for
control as he did into David's. Every aspect of David's
behavior was under scrutiny. The only moral authority
Hugh wanted over Diana was sexual, and the easiest way
for him to have that was to delegate it to David.

They could have the car, and their curfews were

generous as long as they went out together. Since Diana had no interest in boys with sexual ambitions and David's newly learned civility was focused on the elaborate taboos of brotherliness, they were both comfortable with the arrangement. A daunted boy might taunt, "You can't have one, you can't have one without the other." A girl used to more amorous pursuit might get bored. Diana and David didn't care. They nurtured the impression that they were inseparable not only for their own protection but because it inspired an envy and admiration among their peers. At a time when boys and girls were in unhappy adversarial relationship, dependent on each other for mutually exclusive needs, David and Diana displayed a friendship, chaste, serene and genuine.

It was a long time before Diana really trusted it. They had passed through two years of armed truce before they actually joined forces to retreat from a house that had become nearly unbearable, and both of them were at first embarrassed not only by their own behavior but the encouragement it received from both Hugh and their mother. David would sometimes regress into surliness and Diana would retire to her room when they were at home. So his gallantry in public and her amiable response to it seemed an act they were putting on, a milder and less threatening form of the clumsy courtships that were beginning all around them and falling apart after the first date or the fifth, anatomical gossip always raising the stakes for both success and failure. David and Diana were the only boy and girl playing by the same rules in either the front or the back seat.

David initiated each new interest they took up. Tennis, because it was the one sport Hugh mistrusted for vague social reasons, became David's passion. When he couldn't play the piano, he drove balls against the garage door, a sound rhythmic enough not to disturb a sleeping child which could, nevertheless, get on adult nerves. Diana learned for David's sake, and they played against each other to practice. Otherwise they were a doubles team who outplayed others not with superior skill so much as instinct, a complementary, intuitive balance.

Hugh was a poker player. David and Diana took up bridge. But their friends objected to their being partners because they were perceived to read each other's minds. What other teenagers lacked—a trusting familiarity with habit of mind and address—they saw in David and Diana as a mysterious power.

David discovered chess, for which they didn't need other people. They could sit for hours in the same room with Hugh and their mother, ignoring them, and David fancied it was also a silent rebuke to Hugh's lack of subtlety of mind.

Acting was David's one interest which seemed to have no ulterior motive, and he didn't encourage Diana to share it with him. Hugh disapproved of that, too, but even if he'd been a theatre buff, it wouldn't have discouraged David. Diana more freely admired David on the real stage than she did in the social parts he played, which were so often conspiracies rather than simple pastimes. Diana had no talent for being anyone but herself.

"Why don't you ever try out for the lead?" Diana asked him.

"Lazy, I guess," David said. "But the minor parts are more interesting, too. You have to get further into them to stay in them when there's nothing else to do."

Diana didn't know how to do anything without working hard at it. David, with more natural facility, got second class marks in subjects which bored him. For Diana the only choices were first class or fail.

"Skim it," David would say, so agile on the surface of things, so quick at picking up clues.

What she had despised him for, his need to be what was expected of him, she grew to admire as an ability she could develop only in conjunction with him, but, as they practiced dance steps together or played long volleys of tennis, she knew that what was best for her, the pleasure of being with him, was a rehearsal for David for the spring dance, for the tournament. Alone with him, she felt innocent. In public, she came to realize that it was not David but herself who was the fraud. Gradually he was constructing a social self he intended to take on, to play for life, while she only hid herself in it until she could discover the means for escape. Being David's sister would become as much a confinement as a protection.

The monster David had acted out of his system lay in wait for Diana, so ill-equipped at disguises because she recognized them for what they were. Sometimes she suspected there was no stubborn, unchangeable nature at the center of David, or perhaps anyone else, that she alone was cursed with desires as unmalleable as they were unacceptable. If a Patricia had pointed a finger at her then, Diana would have felt exposed, as the innocent and inexperienced do to the world's judgment, rather than outraged as she was when it actually happened.

And relieved, she could now admit, because David had been her only requirement in that world which she'd left so far behind her. Oh, it had been awkward with their mother, who had to know of the rift.

"You were always so close," she protested, of that time Diana came to think of as a brief interlude.

With Hugh's death, her mother's fiction of family collapsed for a second time, and she was left again with two growing children, in their turn despising each other.

Until she died, there was always an awkwardness around holidays, but gradually David's children provided a comfortable reason for choice, which had nothing to do with taking sides.

As nothing but a skeleton in David's closet, Diana could focus her full attention on the way she wanted to live her own life with Constance, to whom she could now never say, "But what will people think?" as a substitute for doubts and fears which were her own.

"We're not *married*," Constance insisted. "We're two very separate fleshes."

All the more so now as Diana sat in the dark, long into the night, with only Constance's even breathing to accompany her musing. Diana didn't imagine that a rehash of all those sexual conversations would interest Constance even if she had a mind for them. She had never engaged in them by choice but of necessity, to dismantle the conventions of Diana's wisdom.

"It seems to me peculiar to have to explain to *you* in your line that what we're doing has nothing to do with making babies. We have no excuse. And it's a terrible waste of pleasure to spend energy trying to invent any."

Long before the rhetoric of women's liberation, Constance took the view that linking sexuality with procreation was as misused a piece of information as the splitting of the atom. In the midst of a population explosion, peaceful uses of sexuality should surely finally be considered.

Had Diana not been insulted and outraged by the moral piety of her sister-in-law and had she not lived with a lovely iconoclast who refused a pious prison of their own, she knew she would not have been as good a doctor as she had been. Patricia and Constance, each in her own way, had taught Diana that passing judgment on her patients was something she had neither the right nor the desire to do.

But she had often wished for more time to teach them to protect themselves from so much harm. Sometimes what she saw in her office made the war between the sexes all too literal. She had also seen more women, and not just young women, turn from bad marriages to better relationships with other women. But that would never be the solution for the majority of women as some utopians now liked to suggest.

There was the other half of the human race, whom Diana had seen little of for years, except in hospital waiting rooms and at medical conventions. On the whole, she preferred young fathers to male doctors, even in the delivery room, into which they increasingly came to learn the lessons of birth, most of them with the proper humility.

It was so much impersonal intimacy which had spoiled Diana for social life, made her impatient with the inconsequence of it. But she was lonely now, she admitted it, and David had seen that and reached out to her with the only thing he had to offer, his own loneliness. If she was going to be good company, he would have to teach her to be as he had so diligently taught her when they were young. Could he also teach her to be an aunt, a great-aunt? She had long since lost count of the children who had been named for her, a gesture which had little more meaning for her than the children who would now go on being named Diana for the Princess. She'd had even less to do with children than with men, once she had brought them into the world.

Diana wondered how David would flesh out that old skeleton and bring it back to life. Would he, when he faced the real difficulties, even try? Diana was not at all sure she wanted him to.

CHAPTER V

The apartment David had set up so comfortably began to get on his nerves in the darkening days of November. His study turned into a cave, and he found he couldn't read for more than half an hour at a time before he had trouble finding his focus, distracted by the floaters which had begun to develop years before. Generally David was absent-minded about his health. It was Patricia who made appointments for his routine checkups, who told him it wasn't young people's mumbling but his own increasing deafness that was the problem. But, once his eyes had been declared so defective as to render him useless to his country, he had been neurotic about them. He would have gone to his opthamologist every six months if Patricia had let him, and he would have changed doctors every other year, unreassured by the bland diagnosis that he was in no danger of losing his sight, that floaters were a very common condition without significance, that everyone aging had increasing difficulty with changing focus.

Patricia insisted, once he became Dr. Thomlin's patient, that he should be satisfied. Dr. Thomlin was the best eye man in town. She looked into those things. Sometimes David teased her for using a cocktail or dinner party like a research project or a polling opportunity.

"People are my resource," she said.

If she'd had the opportunity to advise him now, Patricia would not begin with the problem of his eyes. She would castigate him first for giving up his bright study upstairs next to the living room. Though he did, indeed, miss it when the November fogs swirled in off the water low and muffled the base of the house while the upper floors were still in a watery sunlight, he didn't regret his decision. He would have to put to her his suspicion that, though Dr. Thomlin had been the best eye man in town, he was David's age, and there must be younger men with more up-to-date training. And she would answer, as she had before, that the good younger men had six months' waiting lists because they thought too well of themselves to set aside more than a couple of hours a week for refractions.

So it was that David found himself back in Thomlin's office, nervously critical of the five-year-old magazines and the cracked vinyl on the chairs. Thomlin had lost his wife, too, some time back, and perhaps she had been the one who looked after such things. There was no receptionist on duty. Thomlin himself showed the previous patient out. David noticed how slowly the doctor moved with an old man's shuffle.

"Well, David," he said without enthusiasm. "Come in."

David tried with a nearly poetic accuracy of description to make his complaints vivid enough, fresh enough to catch Thomlin's interest.

"Same old eyes, eh?" Thomlin said.

"Worse," David replied.

"We'll have a look."

"I can't read directions on medicine bottles without taking my glasses off. My granddaughter asked me why I had to *smell* the label. Even newsprint defeats me—not that I want to read a paper, but I ought to be able to."

Thomlin put him through the tests he had taken so many times before, finally handing him a paragraph in small print which David read out with the fake interest of the news reporter he had been.

"There's really nothing the matter, David," Thomlin said.

"How can that be when I can't read?"

"The scientific answer is that you can read. You just have," Thomlin said. "A lot of people your age couldn't read that without a magnifying glass, which, by the way, might help for medicine bottles."

David left the office, humiliated and enraged. A magnifying glass! It was like being told to get an ear trumpet, for god's sake! And there was no one to bluster home to who wouldn't think him as silly an old fool as he thought Thomlin was.

When Mary called to him from the kitchen to ask what the doctor had said, David refrained from any reply but, "He says they're much the same."

"Maybe you need a better reading light," she suggested.

Mary had been so solicitous of him in the few weeks since her temper tantrum that David had indulged her as well as himself in sharing a few complaints. But he didn't want it to become a habit between them, when what he really needed to do was declare greater independence from that household.

"Mary, I've decided to put in my own phone," he said as casually as he could.

"Whatever for, Dad?" she asked in surprise.

"The girls are getting to that age . . ." David began.

"I'll speak to them," Mary said decisively.

"No, no I don't want you to do that. They're very good about getting off the line when I want to use it."

"And I couldn't take messages for you . . ." Mary went on.

"I'd rather you didn't have to. Even when I'm home, you have to answer the phone and buzz me."

"Daddie, you're so little nuisance now, I mostly don't know you're there."

"Good," David replied. "Oh, and by the way, I'll be out Wednesday evenings, when you're making your own plans."

"Have you joined something?"

"No," David said. "I'll be spending those evenings with my sister."

"Daddie," Mary said stiffly, "when I want to know anything more about your sister, I'll ask."

David looked sharply at his daughter and said, "Wherever did you get a line like that?"

"Out of *Chatelaine*," Mary confessed, "in an article on how to control your temper better."

"I would say it's not guaranteed to stop other people from losing theirs."

"It does sound ruder than I thought it would," Mary admitted.

"I'm not going to talk with you about Diana for a while," David said gently. "But I may not be able to wait until you think you're ready."

"I understand about the phone."

"Thank you," David said. "I'll just go put in a call about that now."

The number in the phone book was in large, dark type. When it was *their* business, the phone company knew their regular listings were as safe from old eyes as if they were in code. He ought to join the Grey Panthers or whatever the organization was here in Canada, probably less aggressively named.

But he was really feeling as ridiculously proud as he had earlier felt ridiculously humiliated because he was ordering his very own phone and because he had reestablished a more normal equilibrium with his daughter—not large achievements some might think, but for David they were giant steps of liberation.

David's first call, when the phone had been installed, was to Laura.

"How did you manage it?" Laura asked. "Mary hasn't even mentioned it to me."

"I simply told her I was getting my own phone," David said. "Mary isn't tyrannical. She's simply candid. I'm learning to be a bit more candid myself."

"Did you get anything fancy?" Laura asked.

"You mean Mickey Mouse or white and gold? No, but it does have a volume adjuster."

"Where is it?"

"By my bed. I'm calling to ask a favor, too. I was wondering if you had a free morning any time soon. I haven't done any Christmas shopping for years, except for your mother."

"I can do it for you," Laura offered promptly.

"No," David said, "but I'd like you to help me this first time round. And then maybe we could have lunch."

"Tomorrow?"

David was particularly grateful for his new coat and hat

when he got into the car with his elegantly dressed daughter. Patricia had instructed the girls very well in the mysteries of color and fabric and line as well as the appropriate time of day, the appropriate season for each fashion, a knowledge David doubted his own mother possessed. Sometimes Patricia had seemed to him unnecessarily rigid. It could be the hottest day of the year, but, if it was after September first, she would not put on light colors or white shoes. If the girls ever protested that everyone else they knew would be wearing jeans, she told them there was nothing to recommend the herd instinct. She would have been horrified to see how lax both Laura and Mary had recently become with their children, letting them go on neighborhood errands in anything they happened to have on, and Ben and Mike no longer wore ties when it was just David coming for dinner. But Patricia's code was too deeply ingrained in Mary and Laura for them to change.

"Where are we headed?" Laura asked.

"The Bay, I think," David said. "I've been trying to establish some framework for this or theme or what have you. It may sound too arbitrary, but if I don't have some guidelines, I'm lost."

"Quite right," Laura agreed.

"So what do you think of this: for each one something to wear, something to read, something to listen to, something to work with . . . and, let me see, something to eat."

"A great idea, Daddie, but too many presents."

"We could cut out something to eat," David said, "or make that one a household matter."

"Mother never gave the kids more than a couple of presents each."

"She had less to spend than I do," David said.

As they compared the virtues of watering cans, trowels, and work gloves, as they browsed through books, as they looked at shirts and sweaters, David wondered why he'd never shopped with Patricia and shared the pleasure of speculating on the taste of each of their children and grandchildren. He found he knew a lot more about tools, books, and records than he did about clothes. Laura even knew what colors her nieces liked, what kinds of collars they wouldn't wear. She knew that Christine wanted both to be with-it and at the same time would feel self-conscious in anything too modish while Patsy was a no-nonsense sort about clothes.

When they finally stopped for lunch, David was exhausted not only by the shopping itself but by all he had to learn if he was ever to be able to do this by himself.

"I need a drink," he said. "How about you?"

"I'd rather have coffee," Laura said. "Otherwise I'd fall asleep at the wheel. But you go ahead. You've earned it."

A gin restored David to the festive mood in which he'd set out.

"We've done rather well so far, don't you think?"

"We certainly have," Laura said. "You know, you amaze me."

"That I can survive a morning in a department store? I rather amaze myself."

"Not only that," Laura said. "I always thought of Mother as the one who held the world together."

"As she certainly did."

"But you know, if she'd been left alone, I don't think she would have managed half as well as you do."

"Don't fool yourself," David said. "Right now she'd be on a South American cruise looking over the rich widowers."

Laura laughed at what was obviously for her a preposterous image of her proper mother.

"I'm serious," David said.

"Well, you're wrong. I know she wanted to go, but

she'd never have gone without you. She wouldn't have gone out after dark without you."

David picked up the menu and was looking at it. "Your mother always said she had to choose what we ate all the time; so it was my job when we went out. How do you feel about it?"

"Not the same way at all," Laura answered. "At home I eat what Jack and the boys like. I want that extravagant crab salad."

"Good for you," David said.

He ordered a hot meal for himself so that he wouldn't have to be bothered with anything more than a snack in the evening.

"You know," Laura began, "after we talked about Aunt Diana that night, I was shocked, but when I talked it over with Jack, I realized I was partly shocked because you weren't. And he told me I might be shocked by a lot of things you think because there was so much in our family that was never talked about. Do you think that's true?"

"Jack thinks you girls were very sheltered, and I suppose, insofar as we could, we did shelter you."

"But even from what you privately think is right and wrong?"

"Not so much that as not admitting I didn't put as many things in those categories as your mother did. If it had been my job to teach you to brush your teeth, I probably would have talked more about cavities and less about moral obligations."

"You used to say, sometimes even to Mother, 'Don't be so quick to judge.'"

"Well, your mother thought she could spot an embezzler by the color of his tie and a lecher by the shine of his shoes. I'd hate to admit to you how often she was right."

"How do you really feel about Aunt Diana, Daddie?"

"Much as you feel about your sister, I suppose," David answered, "loyal, critical, protective, puzzled. But, if you mean how do I feel about her relationship with Constance, it awes me a little. It always has."

"You don't feel there's anything wrong with it?"

"No," David said, "but I've known quite a number of gay people. You do in my line of work. It's my experience that the only people shocked by homosexuals are the people who don't realize they know any."

"That would certainly include me," Laura said.

"Yet you have," David said. "Do you remember Peter Harkness, for instance?"

"Peter who used to work with you when we were kids?"

"That's right."

"But Mother loved Peter. We all did."

"He transferred to Toronto. He thought it might be easier in a bigger city," David said. "One thing I've always regretted is that those of us who cared about Peter didn't make it easier for him here. He never brought his lover with him when he came to see us, and Casper was a delightful man. You would have liked him, too."

"Mother would have known then?"

"Knowing how she felt . . ."

"Couldn't you talk to her . . . just the way you're talking to me?"

"I should have tried," David said. "I keep knowing that these are the conversations I should have had with her."

"Weren't you ever shocked?"

"No, not in the way you mean. I wasn't a very worldly young man. If I thought anything about homosexuality, I thought only extraordinary people were, like Shakespeare and Michelangelo."

"Shakespeare!"

"Some of the sonnets are written to a young man," David said. "When Diana came home with Constance, I was shocked to know they were in love, physically shocked. And maybe even a little jealous—of Diana or of Constance, I don't know. But D. was so extraordinarily happy and clear about going into medicine that it would have been stupid to question her choices. I found it hard to be around them, and not just because they made your mother uneasy. I envied them, I think, and I felt shut out. Before Diana left, I was the most important person in her life. We didn't have any gradual time to get used to the changes."

"So you never really had any doubt they were lovers, even at the beginning?"

"I didn't put it to myself in those terms," David said and then added, "until your mother did."

"Maybe she never knew how you really felt," Laura said. "How many years have I been married to Jack? And I didn't know until just the other night what an ignorant bigot he thought I was. Oh, he put it much more tactfully than that, but that's what he meant."

David shook his head.

"But I am," Laura insisted. "Except when anything touches me, I don't think for myself. I just soak up attitudes like a sponge."

"We all do that."

"You know," Laura said, "I don't even know how you vote."

David laughed. "I haven't voted for years."

"Mother always did."

"I know. That's why I didn't. I don't have strong political views. She did, and it seemed silly for me to cancel them. Anyway, closet socialists haven't a hope in our riding."

"That's exactly what Jack said you were!"

On the way home, David made a mental note to buy Laura some fresh crab for Christmas. It would be too smelly under the tree, but he could wrap it in Christmas paper and put it in the fridge. Men must almost forget what they don't like to eat, not having been served it all their married lives.

"What extraordinary creatures you women are," he said.

Laura glanced over at him quizzically, but he simply shook his head, not knowing quite how to put what he meant. Had Constance and Diana ever actually said they liked fish?

David grew nervous as Wednesday approached. He decided to make a halibut and cheese casserole ahead of time and then realized it would be too awkward to carry on the bus. Never mind, he'd take a cab. He didn't want in this first attempt to do anything complicated at the last minute nor anything that would make a great mess of his sister's kitchen. Broccoli and boiling potatoes would be good with the cheese sauce. He could take one of the bottles of plum wine Jack had given him, which would provide a natural opening for him to talk about that family. Dessert? He couldn't use frosted grapes because of the boycott. Would that surprise Laura, too? Patricia didn't believe in boycotts or picket lines, either.

David should explain to Laura that it wasn't that he didn't take Patricia's views seriously enough to disagree with her. It was his own views he usually didn't take seriously enough. But what about dessert? What had they served him? A strudle, he remembered, one of the sort you could get frozen at the store. Ice cream. That might melt. A melon. There were still melons in the store.

On Wednesday afternoon, when David had finished the casserole, he rummaged around in the storeroom and found an old picnic hamper they used to take down to the beach for supper when the girls were small. When everything was assembled, he folded his own chef's apron in on top, a bit of costume to give him comic courage for his part.

From the moment David walked through the door, he felt a different sort of space open up to him. Diana kissed him, as if casually, on the cheek, and there was a look of real recognition on Constance's lovely face. The living room seemed in warmer light, or perhaps the Mozart just finishing colored it, ordering even the fire to dance. Above the mantle a painting by Gordon Smith, which on past evenings David had tried to avoid looking at because of the weight of its images restrained by straight lines as taut as moorings, tonight seemed full of an energy to break free. He knew the room now and no longer had to sense his way around it to avoid those areas which belonged by custom to either Constance or Diana. At first the chair he now thought of as his own had also warned him away from occupancy, but by now whatever ghost of prior claim had been routed.

On his way by cab, he'd stopped at a liquor store; so he carried not only the heavy basket but a paper bag which contained a bottle of gin, a bottle of scotch, and a bottle of Frangelico, a liqueur the flavor of hazel nuts, and of lighter sweetness than most.

Diana went with him to the kitchen, a room he had not been in until now. He felt privileged to be introduced to the ample twenty-year-old appliances and relieved to see that the stove was old enough to speak English, "left front, right front," rather than the dots and squares of international sign language. And there was a dishwasher, freshly emptied and ready.

"Tell me what cooking things to get out," Diana said.

"Just two pots for the potatoes and broccoli."

"Do you want a steamer for the broccoli?"

"Excellent," David said, already fiddling with the oven control.

"It bakes hot," Diana warned him.

"The casserole isn't temperamental," David said as he placed it on top of the stove, ready when the oven was heated.

The bottles and glasses and ice bucket were already on the kitchen table, but David added his own contributions.

"All that wasn't necessary," Diana protested, but there was no rebuke in her tone, rather pleasure at his excesses.

"Why don't you make the drinks while I set this up?" David suggested.

The vegetables were already prepared for cooking. He only needed to ask for a dish for the raw vegetables he'd added at the last minute, thin carrot sticks, cherry tomatoes, small bursts of cauliflower, each in a separate plastic bag to make arranging quicker. The casserole was in the oven, and David had twenty minutes to enjoy his drink by the fire.

"I must say you're a very relaxed cook," Constance commented.

"Have you always cooked?" Diana asked.

"No," David said. "Patricia kept the kitchen pretty much to herself. I learned when she was ill. I wanted to keep her home from hospital as much as I could. And anytime she was up to it, we had friends over for dinner. I discovered I liked cooking. You have to keep enough of your mind on it to make it a real distraction, and it's such a nice, straightforward thing to do for people, to feed them."

"I don't mind it," Diana said, "but I have no flair for it."

"Oh, I don't either," David said. "Patricia said a man should only be allowed to cook if he was brilliant at it.

That was before she got sick. Then I demanded the right to be ordinarily good at it."

"I think I begin to see what you mean by 'ordinary,' " Diana said, smiling at him.

She hadn't flinched at the mention of Patricia, and now she conceded him a point before he was really aware of having made it. It was as if an emotional minesweeper had been through the room and left it free of all the dangers he'd worked so hard to avoid on other evenings when nearly everything he said had the potential for irritating Diana and confusing Constance.

They even *looked* festive, and David realized they had, in their own fashion, dressed up for the occasion, Constance in a bright red silk blouse which reflected in her intently lively face, trimly cut grey trousers with soft grey leather shoes to match. Diana wore over brown slacks a densely and darkly patterned long tunic which must have been made for her because it hung so becomingly over her ample body, giving her handsome authority. And even her brown shoes were not obviously orthopedic.

"You both look wonderful tonight," David said. "You should always wear red, Constance, and D., you look as if you might burst into song."

"Well, we decided we ought to clean up our act a bit for the occasion," Diana admitted.

"I've even got on earrings," Constance said in a tone of surprise, one hand at her ear.

"Shall I fix you another before I go into my act?" David asked, holding up his own glass.

He returned in his apron, and both women laughed as easily as he had hoped they would. There had been too little silliness in their relations so far.

"I'd think you were a professional if it weren't so

clean," Diana said.

"Oh, traces of blood and old soup would be overdoing it," David said.

His last act after he brought the food to the table and lighted the candles was to take off his apron and throw it over the back of a kitchen chair.

"This wine," David said, as he poured it first into Constance's and then into his sister's glass, "is made of plums by my son-in-law, Jack."

"Why, it's very good," Constance said, "not sweet at all, and it doesn't really taste of plums until after you've swallowed it."

"He's very proud of his wine," David said, as he began to dish up the food. "Actually, the whole family is because Laura and the boys all help. They pick the fruit, bash it up, and, when it comes time to rack it off and bottle it, they're on hand, too. Jack handles the chemicals and timing."

"It is good," Diana concurred. "You know, that's always been something I wanted to learn to do. Is it difficult?"

"I don't really know," David said. "I've often been down in the wine room to admire one stage or another; so I have some idea of how it's done, but I don't know how hard it is to make it good."

"Ask him," Diana said.

"This fish is marvelous," Constance said. "Who is this fine fellow? Did we hire him?"

"I'm David, Diana's brother," David said with the mock formality which he hoped conveyed his pleasure in introducing himself to Constance, as he did sometimes half a dozen times during an evening.

"Of course you are," Constance said, smiling at him in a way to make him wonder if it had been a joke at herself.

"I wonder," David said, not wanting to lose his opportunity, "if I could bring Jack and Laura over one evening for a drink. Then you could ask Jack yourself about wine making."

"I'm ready if you think they are," Diana answered much more directly than David had expected she would.

"I'm never ready for anything," Constance said. "Diana uses me as an excuse, you know, because I'm so unpredictable, but I'm not a bad bluff when I need to be, am I?"

Diana smiled at her. "You're very good at it if no one calls you on it."

"Let me remember something for you," David said. "When you had your gardening business, you did spring and fall cleanup for Jack and Laura. They have a house on Thirty-sixth Avenue near the bush. They already know you. Laura even remembers the board of seed packets you had in your truck to help you remember the names of the flowers."

"I remember that. You made it for me," Constance said, turning to Diana. "I remember things so much better than people."

"What does Jack do?" Diana asked.

"He's a chemist," David said, "attached to the university, but he doesn't teach very often. He seems mostly to be on loan to industry or government. At least part of what he does has to do with toxic wastes."

"Then perhaps he'll be able to tell me whether the Tory feds' taking thirty-five million out of the cleanup program is revenge for Ontario's returning a Liberal government," Diana said with some relish.

"Perhaps he can," David agreed. "He doesn't talk much about such things with me since I retired from the news."

"Do you really not even read a newspaper?"

"No," David said. "My excuse is my eyes, but I wouldn't if I could."

"Have they got that bad?"

"My doctor doesn't seem to think so, but I can't keep reading. What I miss is not being able to hole up on a winter day and waste it with a good novel."

"Have you tried talking books?" Constance suggested.

"Not yet, but it's time I started thinking about constructive solutions. It's so much easier to complain."

Diana asked for a second helping of fish, perhaps simply to please David, but it occurred to him that it must have been a long time since she'd tasted anything but her own cooking. They never went out to dinner. What they might have had sent in could be nothing but standard junk food. David had been so clearly directed by Diana's first letter not to think about the confinement of their life but of their contentment that he tried to turn his mind away from such speculations, but they came to him more and more regularly.

David found himself plotting as he loaded the dishwasher. If Jack and Laura were a success, Constance might grow accustomed enough to them . . . but he mustn't push ahead farther than he was. If Diana got the faintest whiff of anything afoot that smelled to her of liberation, they would all be banished. Whatever enriching of her life came to her through David must be seen as as much of a gift to Constance as to herself. And so it should be.

David could see for himself what real contentment they shared, and unlike David, Diana did read, evidence of that everywhere, not only on the bookshelves. There was always a book by her chair, and there was on top of the flour canister here in the kitchen. They were not novels. She read history and biography, and she also had a taste for those scientists like Loren Eisley who could make their fields intelligible to the general reader. Obviously Diana was used to turning to books rather than people for sustained thought. On the whole, books would be more satisfying, but it was too narrow a human world they had retreated into. As far as David could find out, they had very few friends.

He had to go on being careful and patient. Though he knew tonight marked a new acceptance of his place here, the reassurance must not make him reckless.

"Will you try Frangelico with coffee?" David asked when he'd finished cleaning up.

"Why not?" Constance said.

"But you mustn't get us into bad habits," Diana said.

"I don't think we'd make riproaring drunks," Constance said. "We'd be more inclined to stupor."

"By the way," David said as they sat enjoying their liqueurs, "I've got my own phone. Remind me to leave you the number."

On that phone David called Laura as soon as he got home.

"What night next week could you and Jack go with me to have a drink with Diana and Constance?"

"We can meet them?" Laura asked.

"That's right," David said.

"Oh, Daddie, I'm so pleased."

And she really did sound pleased. In his excitement, David heard himself telling her all over again what she already knew about Constance's peculiarities, about Diana's abruptness, all the while really wanting to sound reassuring.

"You're not going to scare me off, you know," Laura said. "I really do want to go, and so does Jack."

"It's just that it may be a little awkward at first, and I don't want that to discourage you."

"It won't," Laura assured him.

"Will you tell Mary you're going?"

"Oh, you know Mary. When she wants to know, she'll ask."

"I thought she'd decided against that line," David said.

"She had to try it on me first."

That was so like Mary. She had to try everything twice, even burning herself on the stove, to be sure the first experience wasn't a freak failure. In his calmer moments David could view it as a sort of persistent intelligence, but just now his patience with Mary was running thin.

David tried not to think about his younger daughter, her half-defiant, half-pious refusal to have anything to do with Diana as a new fact in her life. He should, he supposed, accept that. He acknowledged that Diana and Constance were potential obsessions for him, against whom he must not guard himself so much as them. They didn't, after all, view their life together as a banishment. They were not waiting to be forgiven and restored. David was the petitioner on behalf of himself and those members of his family who might be pleasing and even helpful to them. He couldn't take Mary out and buy her a brand new set of moral perceptions to make her presentable. And Ted, unlike Jack, had more personal ground to defend from Mary's encroaching will than he could handle without taking on the instruction of her as a potential niece to Diana. Perhaps David had all he could expect now from his younger daughter: a right to his privacy, her resigned acceptance of the fact that he had a sister and saw her.

Diana had agreed to receive Laura and Jack more to please David than to satisfy any curiosity of her own. And Mary's unwillingness would be a matter of indifference to

Diana, not the affront it was to David. While he knew that he had no right to expect what he did of either of his daughters, Laura's natural generosity of spirit made Mary's intractibility the more galling to him.

But why on earth would his perfectly intelligent child turn to magazines like *Chatelaine* for guidance, depend on gimmicks and clichés to avoid coming to some real understanding of herself? If David were an activist, he would begin by waging a campaign against women's hairdressers, for he knew that was where his own wife had weekly reconfirmed the moral structure of her universe in which the basic requirement of a good wife and a good mother was to be right. Mary had lost that mother with whom she had never really been able to make peace as Laura had. So willing to cross her mother in life, Mary was now mourning her with fierce, irrational loyalties to everything from garden shrubs to old grudges about which she knew and wanted to know nothing. In David's observation, time healed only very imperfectly a break not understood and set at the time.

David lay in bed, his mind too full of the women in his life, and turned for comfort, as he so often did, to that fantasy father and fantasy son, twins in young manhood, identical. His longing for them carried him into a betraying sleep with dreams as crowded with women as his life had always been.

David woke to the winter's first snow, the children up early and out in it, sent to clear the walks, no doubt, but Patsy and Tyler were throwing snowballs at each other while Christine stood dreaming into the whitened trees. David stood in his robe, watching them. Tyler, as a result of too mighty a pitch, lost his footing and went sliding down the steep pitch of lawn, feet first on his stomach. Patsy clenched round her laughter, clotted snow dripping from her hair, and even Christine's attention had been caught, her grown-up frown of disapproval giving way to a grin as Tyler stood up and shook a triumphant fist about his head as if that sliding fall had been the crown of his achievement. Ted came out to call them to breakfast, and the two younger ones threw respectfully mis-aimed balls in his direction before they followed him back into the house. Only Christine noticed her grandfather standing in his window watching. She gave him a friendly wave before she started back to the house. He was glad she gave no sign of feeling spied on. Perhaps she didn't realize her loneliness was so exposed, or perhaps she didn't mind his seeing it.

"Do you think it would embarrass Christine if I took her to the movies tomorrow night?" David asked Mary when she brought his mail down to him later in the morning.

"Not if you take her some place out of the neighborhood," Mary said. "I think she'd love it. Fifteen's awful, isn't it?"

"Do you remember being fifteen?"

"I certainly do. I was suicidal until I had my first date, and then he bored me. The only thing you know for certain at fifteen is that nobody, but nobody is ever going to marry you."

"I wonder why that's so important," David mused. "Is it hormones, do you suppose?"

"Well, I hope there's not a pill for it," Mary said. "Or what would be the incentive for washing your hair and watching the chocolate?"

"How would you like to go out to lunch today?"

"What for?" Mary asked, surprised.

"Just for fun," David answered, and he meant it, for he was tired of the ulterior motives which had held him distant from her for so many weeks and deprived him of the easy, funny companion she could be.

To his relief and pleasure, she accepted, recognizing it not as a trap but as the peace offering he intended it to be.

CHAPTER VI

Diana vacillated between a grouchy conviction that David's children would have to take her as they found her and the grouchier conviction that she owed David some effort for all those he'd been willing to make. Clothes had never interested her, and they'd been increasingly hard to find as she put on weight, but she'd never approved of the sterile lab coat, except in the sterile atmosphere of the operating theatre. In her office, her clothes had to be as competent and reassuring as her tone of voice. She had allowed herself one or two suits, but she had mainly worn dresses, simple in line, of expensive material in dark colors, even in summer. She had one good string of pearls and one diamond and gold Toni Calvelti pin, both of which Constance had given her, and she wore them alternately. Diana would not wear a ring or bracelet, not wanting anything to interfere with her diagnostic hands. Her only vanity had been her shoes, perhaps because, until the arthritis came, her feet had stayed slim and her legs shapely; she carried almost all her extra weight in her torso. But all those elegant pairs of shoes had gone to the Salvation Army years ago.

Constance had always loved clothes, but as costumes rather than social messages. And she loved her work boots and overalls as much as the full length skirts she liked to wear in the evening, which she often made for herself to have the bold colors which made her glow like a fire, to attract and give warning. Now, if Diana didn't set clothes out for her, choice overwhelmed her, and Diana would find her stalled at the closet door or wandering the house only half-dressed. So Diana chose for her and was aware that the flair had gone out of Constance's costumes as it had out of the meals they ate. It would have troubled Diana more if Constance had noticed, but she didn't.

Jack and Laura already knew Constance as the beautiful, eccentric little gardener with her hard-working, slavish crew of young women. Diana momentarily wished their guests were Constance's relatives, already charmed and no doubt delighted to lay new claim to her, but in the long run they'd be better off with Diana who, once she accepted any relationship, took her share of responsibility. Constance was like an exotic bird among the wrens, escaped from a cage surely, a prize to recapture and keep.

"What are you going to wear tonight? What am I going to wear?" Diana asked as they were eating their dinner.

Constance looked down at her memory board and frowned.

"Maybe I'll go to bed early?"

"Oh, don't desert me, darling, " Diana pleaded.

"I'm no earthly use to you," Constance said.

"You are. They already know you, after all. They've

never laid eyes on me, and who knows what David has said or hasn't said . . ."

"Dear love, you're the sort of person people trust on sight unless you've made up your mind to be rude, and even then . . ."

Diana didn't know what random scraps of memory Constance used for such generalizations, for they trailed off, like this one, before she ever offered any evidence. Was she thinking of Jill who had said in anger that she could depend on Diana more than she could on Constance? Constance had replied, 'Well, of course you can. I'm not Diana."

"Come and help me choose a dress," Diana said.

Dutifully Constance sat in her bedroom chair, shaking her head as Diana held up one dress after another.

"Tell me again. What is this for? Are you going to a funeral?"

Diana sighed.

"They look to me like someone else's clothes. Are you sure they're yours?"

"Yes, I'm sure," Diana said. "It's just that I haven't worn any of them for such a long time."

"Maybe you should get something new?"

"Constance, they're arriving in an hour."

Constance got up, moved Diana aside, and began to rummage in the closet herself. Finally she emerged with a dress Diana had bought and never worn, she wasn't sure why. It was a grey-blue wool, a little unprofessional perhaps, but these were not patients with appointments. She was supposed to look like an aunt, not a doctor.

"All right," Diana said. "Now let's find something for you."

But Constance had lost interest.

"I really do want to go to bed," she said.

There was no point in arguing with her. If she was doing this to make the evening easier for Diana, Diana wouldn't be able to convince her how reassuring her presence would be, whatever her state of mind. And perhaps she was simply tired, needing to avoid the difficulty of people.

Diana got out Constance's nightgown and robe, and Constance undressed while Diana changed from trousers and smock into the dress chosen for her, knowing her only pair of half-decent shoes, which were black, would be uncomfortable without being right. She added her pearls and combed her grey and indifferently cut hair.

"Oh dear," Constance said. "What am I doing in my nightgown when you're dressed like that?"

"You're going to bed, and I'm going downstairs to entertain my relatives," Diana said.

"You look like a relative," Constance decided. "That's the right color for your eyes, a bit smoky."

Diana could tell that David was both surprised and pleased by what he saw, and she was reassured as she hadn't been since she was a girl on her way to a party with him, knowing that he liked what she had on, that he liked her company.

"Come in, come in," she urged the small knot of people at the door. "You're Laura, and you must be Jack."

"Aunt Diana," Laura said, offering her cold cheek, which Diana touched briefly with her own.

"Dr. Crown," Jack said, offering a quickly ungloved hand.

"Diana," she corrected him, approving the kind intelligence in his face; he seemed substantially older than his wife or she young for her years.

They had brought their homemade wine, and Laura wondered if it would be all right to ask for a glass of that.

It certainly would—Diana had already sampled it and would like a glass herself. Would David? Of course he would, pleased to play host to show how much he was at home here.

"What a wonderful Gordon Smith," Jack said.

"Some people find it disturbing."

"It's full of hard energies," he answered.

As a scientist, he would greet them impersonally.

Diana would have asked her niece whether paintings interested her but for the blank eagerness on the young woman's face, that common mask worn even in Diana's office where she had to say, "Don't answer these questions to please me; tell me the truth."

"Where's Constance?" David asked as he came back into the room with a tray of drinks.

"She was too tired, she said," Diana answered. "But she may have thought this reunion would go more smoothly without her."

"I'm sorry," Laura said. "I was looking forward to seeing her again."

"People do," Diana said, smiling, but Laura looked uneasy then, as if she might have said the wrong thing.

"As a family," Jack said, moving nearer his wife, "we like to think of ourselves as workers, but Constance Crowley and her crew put us to shame twice a year."

"It's odd to have been so good at a thing, to take such pleasure in it and not remember," Diana said. "You'll have to remember for her when you do meet her."

"It must be very difficult for you . . . " Laura offered.

"I feel lucky to have her still," Diana said.

Laura glanced quickly at her father, made aware of his loss rather than her own. Turning back to Diana, she asked, "What was he like when he was a boy?"

Diana looked over at David. "Very like he is now. He

only looks made up to be old, doesn't he? Not like me.
I've taken growing old seriously. For him it's just an act."

"Take care," David warned. 'I'll take out my teeth!'"

"And Mother always used to say to him, 'Don't play
the fool,'" Diana said.

"I didn't take her advice, obviously," David said.

"The only thing you don't take seriously is yourself,
Daddie," Laura said.

"Well said," Diana nodded. "And I suspect you're a bit
like him in that."

"Oh no, I'm not good at laughing at myself at all,"
Laura said. "The only reason I don't take myself too
seriously is that I couldn't get away with it. My boys are
awful teases."

"Tell me about them," Diana said and watched her
niece grow certain of the gifts she had to offer, given
encouragement and detail by Jack and David, who teased
her, too, about her exaggerated sense of Ben's new maturity,
of Mike's sensitivity. What they all agreed on was the close
friendship between the boys.

"They've just never been rivals."

"Diana nearly killed me once," David said.

"Yes, I did," Diana agreed, but more seriously.

"Why?" Laura asked, shocked.

"He didn't like girls," Diana said, and some amusement
came back into her voice.

"She was a foot taller than I was, and I was supposed
to be superior."

Jack laughed. "No wonder you're such a superior
fellow. We all should have had twin sisters to knock some
sense into us early."

"Have you a sister, Jack?"

"Yes, but so much older than I that I never really knew
her well. I have a brother nearer my age, but we've never

had much in common except when we're on opposite sides of the same argument. I envy my boys sometimes, but I don't suppose their sort of closeness is common, and it's partly a matter of luck."

"Are you close to your sister, Laura?" Diana asked.

"Oh yes," Laura answered quickly, but she colored and added, "but we sometimes don't get along all that well."

"I call her Mount St. Mary," Jack confessed. "When she's not erupting, she greatly improves the view."

"A temper like mine, has she?"

"But she's never learned to control it," David said.

"Then it can't be as bad as mine, or she'd be in jail," Diana concluded.

"Do you think such things are inherited?" Jack asked.

"The tendencies are in the gene pool certainly," Diana said, "but that's far larger than we easily imagine. It's mostly vanity or guilt that makes us see ourselves in the next generation."

"Mary had a temper from day one," David said.

"They do," Diana nodded. "Without it they wouldn't survive."

"You must have seen such a lot of them," Laura said.

Diana nodded, but she turned to Jack. "Now tell me, how hard is to make wine as good as this?"

When Jack realized it was a serious question, he offered to take her to Wine Art and set her up with the basic equipment.

"Could you do that without me?" Diana asked. "I don't leave Constance alone if I can help it."

"Maybe I could come and be with Constance," Laura suggested.

"Or I?" David offered.

"Now the other thing I wanted to ask you," Diana said,

ignoring the offers, "is why so little is being done to get rid of toxic waste."

"Money," Jack said. "And disbelief. When I think how many years it took us to get something as simple as a stop sign on our corner, how many of our petitions were ignored even after countless accidents. It took two deaths to get a stop sign."

"So you think it's going to take local disasters," Diana said.

"We can't even get funding for properly educating people, and the media are very fickle help. But we do go on trying."

"Jack says you can't afford to get discouraged about something that important," Laura said.

"You can if you're old," David said.

"Well, you've done your share, Daddie."

"I can't get anyone in this family to believe I did nothing but read the news," David protested.

"I should think, some evenings, that took courage," Diana said.

"You simply concentrate on the correct pronunciation of proper nouns," David said wryly.

"In my field," Jack said, "it's very difficult to avoid doing harm; so people tend to stop thinking about it in the name of 'objectivity' or 'pure science.' "

"In mine," Diana said, "we do a great deal of harm in the name of morality."

"I'd be terrified of that kind of responsibility," Laura said. "Sometimes I think everything we're supposed to teach the children, from sharing their toys to telling the truth, is no use to them once they've grown up. I already have a sense that the boys keep things from me because I'd be shocked or wouldn't understand how it really is—what you really have to do to get along once you're out in the real world."

"Being a parent is the most terrifying kind of responsibility," David said. "It's the only one I've ever been able to take seriously. But I think it's probably true, Laura, that we raise kids to live in a world that doesn't exist any longer and maybe never did and maybe never should have."

"I think you're too hard on yourselves," Diana said. "The world you're talking about is childhood, and it's a gift of very great value to any child lucky enough to have one."

"And a fairly recent invention, I guess," Jack said, "by no means universal."

Diana would have been enjoying the conversation more if she had been less in charge of it. Without Constance's irreverent and irrelevant comments, Diana rode between fixed rails, ponderously benign. She could not, as Constance did quite naturally, charm her guests. She had to rely on reassuring them. Though Laura did not look quite so fixed in the headlights as she had when she arrived, her husband and father were more responsible for that than Diana was. Her years of kind impersonality in dealing with generations of women had eroded whatever skill she might have had to inspire affection. First she would have to feel it, as she increasingly did for David. But Diana was more mindful of the pain in her feet than she was of her warm manners as she saw her guests out the door.

Diana wanted to talk about her impression of Laura, in particular, but Constance was sleeping soundly. So Diana was left to her own thoughts as she got ready for bed. Of one thing she was certain. David had spoken to them about her relationship with Constance, and, though that would account for Laura's extreme nervousness, Diana was relieved that no sudden revelation lay before her. Laura did not seem to her a natural bigot so much as emotionally only half grown, one of those women so conscious of and responsible for other people's feelings that she had no time to discover and refine her own. She was aware, at least, that her children were in the process of leaving her behind in her nursery morality where she would be safe but increasingly lonely. So she had been willing, though mainly for her father's sake, to take the test Diana was for her and leave the grading in Diana's hands. Laura would be saying to Jack, "I'm not sure she liked me," and in that uncertainty Laura would be more astute than Jack who was too fond and protective of her to imagine anyone could find his wife less than charming.

David had brought his easy, his amenable daughter, but what of the other one, Mary? The blazing beauty of the family in Jack's judgment, with a temper David had little patience for. And it had been the subject of recent family concern, or Laura would not have blushed. Well, if David wanted to disrupt his family, it was his business. Yet, seeing him with his child, Diana knew that he had spoken the truth about himself as a serious father. Perhaps it was Diana's business to warn him that, in trying to make a bridge of himself, he could break his own back.

In the dark of early morning, Diana woke to find Constance not beside her. There was no light under the bathroom door. Diana snapped on her bedside light. The clothes she had laid out for Constance and her memory board were still on the chair. Perhaps she had gone downstairs to get something to drink or eat. Diana could not move quickly, cursed her bones as she struggled out of bed and found her robe, cursed the shoes that had turned her feet into sirens of pain as she made her slow way down the stairs. No lights had been turned on. At the touch of each switch, a new room bloomed into emptiness. The back door stood open, the kitchen stone cold. Diana turned on the outside light, but it illuminated nothing more than the back porch and steps leading down into the garden. Surely Constance wouldn't try to garden in the dark. Diana could see the car in the garage. Might Constance be in it? How long had she been gone?

Diana labored back through the house and dressed as quickly as she was able, hearing her own sobbing grunts as if they came from somewhere outside herself, for she had closed her mind down to anxiety. She would drive around the neighborhood for no more than twenty minutes. Then, if she hadn't found Constance, she would phone the police. After the police, the hospitals. In a confused state, Constance wouldn't know where she lived. Had she taken her handbag with her? Diana checked as she went through the kitchen. It was there on the counter where she always left it. No identification, and, if it wasn't Diana who found her, she would probably resist.

Why hadn't Diana gone ahead and put inside locks on all the doors? She hadn't wanted the house to seem a prison to Constance, and she'd never simply wandered off like this, except once or twice in a store before Diana stopped taking her shopping. Constance had been like an animal knowing the limits of her own territory, and Diana had put her trust in that, stupidly.

There was no point in trying to outguess Constance. Whatever motive had taken her out of the house would have been forgotten at the first corner. She might invent another, but that would not last more than a block or two. Diana's only hope was that confusion might have stopped Constance before she had gone too far.

As Diana started the car, she glanced at her watch. It was 5:30 a.m. She had until 5:50 to find Constance. First Diana circled their own block, hoping to catch sight of Constance, rooted like a tree, somewhere nearby. But there was no one out before dawn on this winter morning, no solitary jogger or dog walker Diana might have asked if they had seen a little white-haired woman in nightclothes wandering the streets. Diana widened the circle. There was no traffic; so she could hesitate at corners and peer down modestly lighted side streets. Here and there a light went on in an upper window. If only she could find her before day broke, before Constance had to be confronted by strangers. But the twenty minutes passed without sight of her, and Diana didn't give in to the temptation to look further. Any more delay in getting help could be dangerous.

In all the complex dealing with authority Diana had had to do for Constance over the years, she was grateful to have that key which unlocks all doors, her title; for as friend or lover Diana would have a difficult time even reporting that Constance was missing. She certainly wouldn't get access to her in hospital or in jail.

"It's all very well for you," Constance had said when she toyed with the idea of joining one of the early gay pride marches, "but what would I do if anything ever happened to you?"

"Our doctor is perfectly reasonable," Diana answered. "But you have to do what you have to do. For me, it's out of the question."

"If being a lesbian makes you sexually suspect with your patients, the only doctors dealing with them should be gay men or heterosexual women. Are there any heterosexual women doctors?"

"Of course there are," Diana said, and then added, "some. Do try to remember that sweet reason has no place in the real world."

"That's why I don't live in it," Constance said.

Constance decided not to go. She was only testing her right to. She had, at bottom, even less faith in changing the world than Diana did.

"This is Dr. Crown," Diana said when she reached the police, and "This is Dr. Crown" to each hospital switchboard for quick checks of recent admissions and emergency wards. Everyone was very helpful. If Constance turned up, they would notify her at once.

Diana wanted to go right out again, but she was now tied to the phone. It was 6:30. Constance could have been wandering in any direction for more than two hours. She could be miles away. To do nothing but sit was intolerable.

Diana picked up the phone again and dialed Jill's number. Jill answered on the first ring, a resonance in her voice Diana still recognized, even after all these years, as the tone of an interrupted lover.

"I'm sorry," Diana said, "but Constance is missing."

"I'll be right there," Jill said.

Diana put down the phone, full of simple gratitude that there was someone else she could trust to look for Constance without caring how great the odds against finding her had already become. But soon, surely, as people began to leave for work, someone would find her.

Automatically Diana plugged in the kettle. Then she thought to cook herself an egg. She had no appetite, but any chore would help to pass the time. She thought about breakfast for Jill, but Diana no more wanted Jill to take the time to eat than Jill herself would. Instead Diana made her a ham sandwich to take with her.

Dawn was breaking when Jill arrived.

"Any word yet?"

"No," Diana said.

"Has she ever done this before?"

"No."

"Any idea where she might have gone?"

"No."

"Then I'll just . . . look," Jill said.

"I made you a sandwich."

"Thank you," Jill said dismissively, but then she accepted it. "I'll call in about every half hour, all right?"

Diana nodded.

"We'll find her," Jill said, and she quickly kissed Diana before she left.

Diana watched her run down the path to her expensive sports car, her one luxury always. What a capable body she had to do Diana's bidding, but just watching her caused Diana physical pain. She should go back upstairs to make the bed, but her feet wouldn't hear of it. She sat down instead and poured herself another cup of tea while she waited for the phone which did not ring for forty minutes, and then it was Jill.

"I'm down by the beach," she said.

"She could be nearly anywhere by this time," Diana said.

"But on foot."

"Yes, she doesn't have any money with her."

The beach. Diana would not have thought to go there. Poor, romantic Jill. Was she, for lack of any real clues, going to places where she and Constance had gone before Jill moved in with them? For Diana to do that, she would have had to go back to London.

At nine o'clock the phone rang again. This time it was David. Diana had forgotten all about David.

"I wanted to thank you for last night," he began before he registered the strain in her greeting. "Is anything wrong?"

Diana explained.

"You should have phoned at once," David said. "What can I do?"

By now Diana realized the futility of Jill's driving aimlessly around the city, and, though Diana would have liked to alert the whole population of Vancouver, there was no point in sending her brother out to search.

"Would it help if I just came and waited with you?"

Would it? Diana supposed it would. She was learning to need her brother.

Before he arrived, Jill called in again.

"There's no real point, is there?" Diana asked.

"It beats sitting by the phone," Jill said.

"You must be due at the office."

"I'm just going to make the hospital rounds first."

David arrived by cab. It was silly of him not to have a car. He saw well enough to drive, but even as a boy he hadn't liked to. If they were by themselves, Diana always drove. Her distracted irritation with him vanished the moment he was beside her.

"If anything has happened to her, I'll never forgive myself," she heard herself saying, those rote love lines she had listened to so often.

"I'm sure she's all right," David answered, and she clung to that reassurance as if he had clairvoyant powers.

"The minute we've heard," David said, "I'm going to go out and get those locks for the doors, and I'll send Ben and Mike over to put them on. They're very good at things like that."

"I didn't want her to live in a prison," Diana said miserably.

"I know," David said, "but she'll understand. She'll know why."

The phone rang again.

"That will be Jill," Diana said. "She's out looking."

"Dr. Crown?"

"Yes?"

"This is Dr. Pilton at the General. We have a woman who answers the description you gave us."

"Oh, thank heaven! Is she all right?"

"I think she will be. She's suffering from exposure, and she's a bit scratched and bruised. She's very confused, but I gather that's to be expected. I'd like to keep her here for observation for a day or so, but I would be grateful if you or a relative could come down and identify her."

"Right away," Diana said.

"Shall I go with you?" David asked.

"Better not," she said, "but I'd be glad if you stayed until I got back. Unless it's more serious than it sounds, I'm going to see if I can bring her home. If you could wait for Jill to call. She's an old friend of ours, and I'd like her to know as soon as possible."

Jill was at the hospital waiting for Diana.

"The bastards won't let me in to see her!" Jill said. "Nobody but relatives or her 'doctor.' I told them I was her lawyer. They didn't believe me."

"You're far too elegant to be credible . . . as anything but a distraught lover," Diana said.

Jill looked at Diana and burst into relieved laughter.

"Dr. Pilton please," Diana said to the receptionist.

The young doctor explained, "We've had to sedate her. She should sleep for several hours."

Diana stood by the bed, looking down at Constance's sleeping face, which in that unconsciouis repose was simply old and vulnerable. Whatever she'd been through, she would not be able to remember it.

"Who brought her in?"

"We don't know. One of the nurses found her wandering

around early this morning. She thought she must be a patient. It took us some time to figure out that she wasn't, dressed as she was and so obviously disoriented."

When Diana had given Dr. Pilton the medical particulars, she explained that, in fact, she cared for Constance in her own home. She'd like to stay with Constance now and perhaps, when she woke, it might be best to take her home. Diana let the young intern raise objections, but, when she didn't counter them, he relented enough to say he would consider it. Diana had rarely had to challenge other people's authority to maintain her own.

Back in the waiting room, Diana reassured Jill and sent her back to her office or perhaps back home to deal with another distraught lover. Then she phoned David who said he would stay around and make himself some lunch.

Finally Diana was free to go to Constance and stay with her. As she sat down on the small, straight, uncomfortable chair which had been put by Constance's bed, Diana realized how exhausted she was. Move over, love, she thought to Constance, I'm getting too old for this. We all are.

Diana's head dropping forward jarred her awake to Constance's open beautiful eyes watching her.

"I haven't any idea where we are," Constance said, "but you're here."

"How long have you been awake?"

"I don't know."

Diana looked at her watch. It was 3:30 p.m.

"How do you feel?"

"As if I'd been slipped a mickey."

"You wandered off early this morning and turned up here—we're in the General—no one knows just how. Probably someone brought you here."

"Not even your hospital," Constance said wryly.

What odd bits of information floated up to the surface of her mind.

"There's some talk about leaving you here for observation. But, my hospital or not, I'm going to see if I can spring you."

"Nothing easier," Constance said. "We can just walk out."

"I don't think it's a good idea to make a habit of that."

Constance had sat up and swung her feet out of bed, making a jaunty show of her mobility. There was a large bruise on her right ankle.

"Where are my clothes?"

"You went out in what you've got on."

"All the easier then," Constance said. "Not even any slippers?"

"If you had them, you lost them."

"You know, if I didn't know you were a nearly reprehensibly honest person, I'd find it hard to believe some of the things you tell me."

"Well, try standing up," Diana suggested.

"I'm a bit stiff," Constance said, "and a bit lightheaded. But there's nothing wrong with me."

Dr. Pilton was not on duty, and the new intern, after a cursory check, agreed to release Constance into Diana's care. A nurse produced socks for Constance and a warm blanket before she was wheeled out to Diana's car.

"It's cold enough to snow," Constance said.

Diana fetched a blanket from the trunk of the car, a bit grassy and sandy from their various picnickings, and draped it over Constance's knees.

"David will be at the house," Diana said. "I may ask him to supper."

Constance nodded. She was looking around with a

curiosity other people reserved for new places. It had alarmed Diana that Constance rarely had the slightest sense of where she was, until Diana realized that Constance had learned to use it as a pleasure as long as she was securely in the car within reach of Diana.

When David came out of the house to greet them, Constance gave him a startled look and said, "Who in the world is that?"

"David, my brother."

"Hello, David," Constance called cheerfully, and she got out of the car and walked across to the house, unmindful of her nightgown and hospital blanket, unmindful of what she had just been through.

Diana took her up to their room, the bed still unmade, and suggested she have a shower and dress in the clothes laid out for her. While Diana waited, she lifted up the cellophane of the memory board to cancel the steps of a quiet day and wrote "Dinner with David."

"What happened to the rest of the day?" Constance asked.

Diana took Constance in her arms, held her close and said softly into her ear, "I erased it."

David was putting the chicken in the oven and the potatoes sat scrubbed on the counter when Diana came into the kitchen.

"An early dinner, I thought," David said. "The boys will be over around eight to fix the doors."

"I'm going to make Constance and me fruit juice for before dinner. She was sedated."

"Could you use something a little stronger right now?"

"No," Diana said, "I'm afraid it would do me in."

"She seems all right," David said.

"She's physically very tough," Diana said, "thank heaven!"

"You aren't going to see the boys through a mother's eyes," David said, "but they really are quite nice, useful kids."

Diana laid a hand on his arm. "A great-aunt's eye isn't apt to be jaundiced. I'm grateful to you, D. You know that."

Diana was not used to being alone with her brother, and she was only aware of it now because no guard went up in her. They moved around the kitchen quite peacefully together until they took drinks in to join Constance, who sat listening to Glenn Gould playing Bach.

"I could manage so much better if conversations were more like this," Constance said.

"Constance," Diana began, "tonight David's grandsons are going to come and put new locks on the doors. It means you'll have to ask me to open the door for you when you want to go out. We're doing it because you wandered out of the house around five this morning and were missing for some hours."

"Make your own home into a looney bin in just one easy step," Constance said brightly.

"I don't like it either," Diana said, "but you scared me out of my wits."

"Is that something new?" Constance asked.

"No," Diana admitted.

Constance turned away and did not speak again, even when she was spoken to, all through dinner, but she did eat eagerly, unaware that her appetite came from an inadvertent fast of twenty-four hours. David made conversation, but he also let silences fall. Diana sat mortified by Constance's implication that here was at last the excuse to lock her up as Diana had always wanted to do. How could she explain that in all the years of enduring Constance's freedom, Diana had come not only to accept but respect it, that locking her up now was as great a defeat for Diana as it was for Constance?

Over dessert, Constance suddenly said, "When I can't remember why I'm so angry, it's very difficult to stay angry. You'd better tell me whatever it is again."

"I'm locking you into the house," Diana answered bleakly.

"How fair she is!" Constance exclaimed. "In her place, would you have answered that question?"

"I'm not sure I would," David admitted with a smile, "but she knows you better than I do."

"It would be easier to be crazy," Constance said.

"No," Diana said, " you know it wouldn't."

"Do I?" It was a genuine question.

"Yes," Diana said.

"It's very peculiar having your memory located outside your own head. Diana is remarkably truthful, but it's still her version of the truth."

"Much of which I learned from you," Diana reminded her.

"And you still can't trust me?"

"I can't trust your memory."

"Well, neither can I, of course."

The boys arrived with a great stamping of feet on the front porch, the first indication to any of the occupants of the house that it had been snowing. David opened the door to them as they were taking off their boots, took their damp coats from them and slung them over the banister to dry. They came into the room behind him, tall, flushed young men, in stocking feet, smiling.

"This is your Great-Aunt Diana, and you already know Constance Crowley. Ben. Mike." David presented them with affectionate pride.

"Aunt Diana," Ben said, nodding. "Miss Crowley."

"Call me Constance, whoever you are."

"I'm Ben."

"My grandson," David added.

Mike stood back a little, imitating his brother's nod but not speaking.

"Do get them whatever they'd like to drink," Diana said to David.

"Should we work first?" Ben suggested. "Once we've done the locks, there's a bit of shoveling to do. We've brought our snow shovels. They're in the car."

"Good boys!" David said.

"They don't look a bit like jailers, do they?" Constance asked.

"They're not," Diana said.

"May we stoke up that fire?" Ben asked. "We have to keep the door open for a few minutes, and it may get a bit chilly."

Mike moved quickly to put another log on.

"Thank you," Diana said to him.

"When Ben says 'we,' he means me," Mike said, grinning.

"What a nice arrangement for Ben," Diana said.

"It is rather," Ben admitted, "but I'm second in command when it comes to anything difficult."

"That means he holds the tools and tells me what to do," Mike elaborated.

Diana was glad they went right to work. She wasn't sure, at the end of this bizarre day, that she could think what to say to these full-grown great-nephews suddenly available to her. And they were more comfortable, too, for offering practical help to a pair of frail old women.

"This front door is solid wood," Mike said with approval.

"I bought that," Constance called from the living room.

"Canada is a country of hollow doors."

"You've just given me the opening line for my next paper," Ben said, sticking his head around the hall archway.

"On what?" Constance asked.

"Well, it could lead just about anywhere, couldn't it?" Ben asked, pleased. "Literature? Economics? History?"

Where did she get the energy to rise to the occasion? With strangers Constance could catch such a scrap of memory and then dance with it wherever it went, the little missteps noticeable only to Diana who nevertheless could still be led on. The boys would report to their parents that, all rumors to the contrary, they were helping to lock up a perfectly sane, perfectly charming woman. Well, Constance had slept a good part of the day, and dinner had given her new energy. All Diana had from her own afternoon catnap was a stiff neck, which she longed to get into a hot shower. But, at least, when she went to bed, she could sleep in a house secured against this day's terror.

CHAPTER VII

People seem to assume Christmas is going to be here this year," Mary said to her father as she sorted the family's clothes in the laundry room.

"We shouldn't," David said.

"Well, it always has been. I suppose it goes with the territory."

The year before they had all gathered around David, both his daughters doing the planning and the cooking while David sat, too dazed with grief to be of use to anyone, only aware enough to know that he was both center and obstacle of the life that had to go on. Nothing could have made it clearer to him that Patricia, who had loved Christmas and risen to it as the culminating performance of the year, was dead and he was totally incapable of taking her place. It was soon after Christmas that David had made up his mind to offer the house to Mary and Ted.

"Have you spoken to your sister?" David asked.

"Not exactly. She just asked me what she could do to help."

"There's still time to rethink the whole holiday," David said. "The burden shouldn't fall on you."

"Christmas isn't exactly a burden," Mary said.

"You girls have learned your mother's lessons too well, always carrying on as if you had a staff of servants behind you. Christmas is a lot of plain hard work, and there isn't any reason why it should all fall on you."

"You know what bugs me?" Mary asked. "I really never did bend over backwards to please Mother, trying to do everything her way, until she died and we moved in here. Sometimes I feel as if I'm the maid to her ghost. And it doesn't help when Laura treats me as if I were."

"I don't think your sister would put it just that way. She may simply be trying not to pull rank. If you really talked about it, you might find out that everyone wanted to stay home."

"Out of the question," Mary said. "My kids wouldn't hear of Christmas without Ben and Mike. They couldn't even be bribed away with a ski trip. And what would we do with you, saw you in half?"

"I could make the rounds," David said, "ho-hoing first here, then there. I'm not suggesting it, Mary. I'm just suggesting that what we do at Christmas—or any other time for that matter—doesn't have to be carved in stone."

"Doesn't it? Mother always thought it did."

"Your mother liked tradition, but she invented her own. There's no reason why you shouldn't now."

"But now that she isn't here, what's the point of doing it any differently?" Mary asked.

"You're taking both sides, you know," David said, smiling at her.

"I know it," Mary said. "I've always thought I was a poor loser. It's discouraging to find out I'm even worse as a winner."

"Talk to Laura."

"All right, but I don't expect any surprises from her."

If Mary could only learn not to project her own doubts and self-criticism onto other people and then fight a war as if it weren't inside herself, some real emotional progress might be made. But perhaps she was gaining some ground. Patricia as a ghost might be more help to her daughter than she had been as an often exasperated parent. And to be fair to Mary, Patricia had crowded her sometimes unnecessarily. Patricia didn't think anyone had the right to take up more emotional space than other people, and she set her will against the fact that some people just do. Mary always had taken much space but not simply in anger. Her amusement and delight were more contagious, and what Patricia called "showing off" was often in Mary simply irrepressible high spirits, without which the family would have been the poorer.

All Mary needed now was to know she'd made up her own mind, and David didn't expect either of his daughters to want revolutions around Christmas, if only to keep peace with their own children, set in the conservative greed of the season.

David was writing a few Christmas notes to old friends, a task he hadn't been up to the year before. It must have been Laura who had notified everyone of Patricia's death. When he found himself wanting to write about his sister, he hesitated, for most of the people they had known weren't aware that he had a sister, and he was incapable of any explanation for her sudden reappearance in his life. Yet not to mention her was a part of that past behavior he wanted to be rid of. So he did mention her, and Constance, too, and how they spent evenings together being comic, old crocks. Let people think what they'd think.

Christine drifted in eating an apple.

"Is school out already?" David asked.

"It's four o'clock," Christine said.

"So it is."

"No one knows what to get you for Christmas," Christine announced. "Granny always just told them, and Mom said she couldn't just rummage around in your drawers to see if you need new socks or whatever. Aunt Laura was shocked you did your own laundry."

"Why should she be?" David asked.

"Well, she just thought that was the way Mother would know, you know?"

"So you've been sent down to rummage?"

"Not exactly. People always ask us what we want. Why shouldn't adults just say?"

"It's another place where the rules change. Greed is only attractive in children."

"We're not supposed to be greedy!" Christine protested, shocked.

"No, of course you're not, but you are allowed to ask for what you want."

"Not for what you really want," Christine said.

"What do you really want, Christine?"

"Oh, I don't know. To go to some really neat place for Christmas, like Mexico or some place, the way Carol always has, and come back with a winter tan and make everyone else jealous. But even Carol can't do that anymore."

"Can't she?"

"No, her dad had to take early retirement, but at least they don't have to sell their house. Ann's parents are going to have to sell theirs, even though her dad's still working.

They have to move some place cheaper. I'm really glad we live here."

"I'm glad you are."

"Patsy said at first it made her feel funny, to be living where all the really special things happen, as if every day should be somebody's birthday or Christmas. I wouldn't really want to be any place else for Christmas."

"Why don't we do some rummaging around in my drawers together and see what we can see?" David suggested.

"Sure, why not?"

David opened one drawer after another for his grand-daughter's critical inspection. She was uninhibited in her methods, undoing rolled up socks to check the heels, inspecting the collars of shirts. Patricia had taken such good care of his clothes that he had not had time, in a year and a half, to become a disgrace, but Christine did suggest pitching a thing or two, and he submitted to her judgment.

"One thing's sure," she said, when she had satisfied herself with the range of his wardrobe, "you haven't got anything that really goes with that new jacket. It's brown and practically everything else you have is blue."

"I suppose it is," David said.

"That's enough to be going on with," Christine decided.

Satisfied with herself, she went back upstairs to report her success to her mother.

It was not just in the supermarkets where baskets invited contributions to the free food banks or downtown where the unemployed lined up to receive the donations; it was in this relatively affluent neighborhood where the children could feel the recession dogging at everyone's heels, where more and more parents were facing a new truth, that they had taught their children to want what they couldn't any longer have.

David had never been anxious about money. As a child

he had never felt poor though he'd lived in a modest house in Kitsilano without a view and a good hike from the beach. He never thought to wonder where the money did come from that kept his mother from having to go to work. It was true that the expensive presents he and Diana sometimes received were never from their mother but from unknown grandparents, somewhere in the east, his father's people, but his mother never spoke about money. David hadn't associated his mother's growing attachment to Hugh Bacon as, at least in part, motivated by her anxiety about money. She told David only much later, when she was collecting her war widow's pension, that she had pretty well spent her first husband's insurance money and been as much of a burden as she'd dared on her own parents before she married Hugh. It had shamed David the more because he knew his mother was offering that information up as an apology, when David should have been on his knees to her to be forgiven for all he'd done to try to undermine her chance for security, and for his own mindless childhood and his sister's. At least Hugh had left her and his children modestly provided for. When David asked about his father's family, his mother said, "Well, they didn't really know me. They were always very generous with you children for your birthday and Christmas. And they had other children, closer to them."

David married, hardly realizing it at the time, into a family both affluent and so generous that Patricia didn't have to wait to inherit before she could live where she wanted to. David sometimes wondered if he might have been more ambitious without that help. Instead, he had taken his father-in-law's advice about investments and worried no more about being what seemed to him rich than he had about his mother's threatened poverty. With interest rates what they'd been recently, he was better off than ever. "The rich get richer, my boy," his father-in-law told him.

Ted worried. His law firm, in which he wasn't yet a partner, had let a few people go, and, though Ted himself didn't feel immediately threatened, he made uneasy jokes about its probably being a better world when fewer people had the money to sue each other. David knew what a relief it had been to Ted to get out from under his own fifteen percent mortgage, even though he'd lost money to get rid of their house. He knew the relatively modest rent he paid to David went into a trust fund for the children's education.

David was under no illusion that he and his family could survive, intact, in a general financial disaster. His own needs were so minimal that it hardly mattered to him, and Jack and Laura had so many survival skills that they'd enjoy the challenge. But Ted and Mary were another matter. David sometimes wondered if it had been sensible to move them into a house they could never have afforded instead of selling it and paying off their mortgage for them. He could not have lived with them there.

It had seemed practical, but David knew he was also fulfilling an idle fantasy in these rooms he had once so thoughtfully prepared for a student who would be a built-in babysitter. He had thought how simple and pleasant it would be to retire from the main floor of life, its requirements and alarms, its busy griefs, and, though he wasn't as detached as he had been in his imagination, he enjoyed his reduced space, its self-containment.

"Did you ever," David asked his sister on their now firmly established Wednesday evening, "think of us as poor before Mother married Hugh?"

"Not poor, no," Diana said, "but I remember being puzzled at how much she insisted we were dependent on him once she did marry him."

"She only told me after he died how nearly stone broke she had been."

"I know," Diana said. "It certainly confirmed the independent streak in me."

"It didn't have any effect on me at all," David said.

"We were poor as church mice," Constance offered. "When my father wouldn't marry my mother after my sister was born, she had me, thinking two would surely shame him into it. She always said I was just like him, and I'd pay for it. 'Why?' I'd ask her. 'He never did.' 'He was a man,' she'd say. Poor old Mum. She was a charwoman, and she used to steal food off the shelves of the people she worked for and tell us she was given it. After a while we realized she must be stealing because she changed places so often. Nobody ever called the police in, not for food; they'd just let her go."

It fascinated David how many great chunks of her past were sometimes available to Constance.

"Did she ever marry?" he asked.

"Mum? No. With two when she couldn't catch the father to feed them, she pretty well gave up. Now and then she found someone to buy her a pint; that's about all. She was a good soul, me Mum, but not what you'd call bright."

David would have liked to ask other questions, but he had learned to be careful with Constance in that regard. If he'd asked her where her ambition had come from to go into business herself, she could not have followed him there. He turned to his sister instead.

"What gave you the drive to do all the work of being a doctor?"

"I had the chance," Diana said, "and I suppose I had something to prove. To myself anyway."

"Going to college never occurred to me," David said.

"There wasn't the money for it, once Hugh went."

"I suppose I could have found a way, but I would have felt silly, even sillier than I did with so many other people in the war. I did read, but not the sorts of books you read," David said, nodding at the bookshelves. "I read novels and plays, occasionally even some poetry. I used to think that, if I'd gone on to study history and politics, I might have made something—for myself anyway—of that daily wash of disaster we call the news, and felt less simply drowned in it. But I didn't really have any faith in that notion, or not enough to make the effort. And I finally lost my respect for the fellows who were supposed to do the analyzing. Blarniers they were, all of them, and in the end I'm grateful that at least I wasn't one of them."

"The messenger is a rough part, isn't it?" Diana commented. "I used to turn on the radio and say 'Well, D., how about a bit of good news tonight?' As if you had some control over it."

"Well, I wasn't killed for it, which in simpler times I could have been, if those old plays are accurate."

"You can be killed for doing nearly anything," Constance said. "But most of us get killed for no bloody reason at all."

As if it were a clue, Diana got slowly up to put on a record.

"Let me do that for you, shall I?" David offered, hating to see the pain in her moving, so increasingly noticeable to him, perhaps because she made fewer pretenses about it now or because the winter was settling into her joints.

"No, thank you. It's good for me to move about; otherwise I set, like cement. I do miss getting down to the desert."

"Where did you used to go?" David asked.

"Various places: Phoenix, Palm Springs. Our favorite was a little place called Borrego Springs."

"Couldn't you go back?"

"She tells me I get lost in airports," Constance said with a show of irritability.

"It isn't just that," Diana said. "I'm as much past traveling as you are."

"Why couldn't we go down together?" David asked.

"David, it's one thing to deal with us on home ground, quite another when we're let loose in the world," Diana said.

"Think about it before you say no," David said. "We might go down for several weeks in January or February. If you know where to go, I don't know why I couldn't simplify the airport for you."

"I think you should think about it," Diana said.

"Is it warm in the desert?" Constance asked.

"Relatively . . . and *dry*," Diana answered.

"Sometimes we do things, don't we?" Constance asked. "We aren't always locked up in this house, are we?"

"No, not always," Diana said.

"Do you have the key?" Constance asked. "Or does he?"

"We both do," Diana said.

"Well, then. You can do anything you want."

"But being some place you don't recognize frightens you," Diana said.

"Not if you're there."

"Would you go swimming with me?" Diana asked.

"Are we a bit old for that sort of thing?"

"You're a wonderful swimmer," Diana said. "Let me remember that for you. You didn't learn until you got over here, and you were very proud of yourself."

"I may not remember," Constance said.

"I think you might," Diana said, smiling, as she turned to set the needle down on Vivaldi, a favorite obviously, for its opening was pocked.

A number of the records they listened to were noticeably worn, and David wondered if he might replace some of them for Christmas. It seemed in a way a dull gift, no duller than the years of potted plants, but he was under no constraint now.

He went to the Magic Flute on Fourth Avenue with that intention, having come up with nothing else.

Since he had left the CBC, David had paid scant attention to the technical gossip so familiar at his job. He knew some of the lingo from the half attention he paid to Clide Gilmore's patter between the records he played on Sunday CBC, terms like digital recording and compact disc. With his own modestly impaired hearing, he suspected that his only reaction to being directly exposed to this new technology would be the high shriek of his hearing aid. But when the clerk offered him an opportunity to listen, David, out of years of polite habit for the enthusiasms of his sound technicians, couldn't refuse.

His hearing aid did protest once, but that didn't interfere with his amazed pleasure at how much more he could hear than he ever had before, even in the presence of an orchestra, the voices of each instrument floating out on a base of true silence.

He left the store with all the literature on compact disc players, already certain that this would be his gift to Diana and Constance, with a modest selection of discs which he could add to on various occasions. His enthusiasm carried him so far that he also finally bought a player for each of his daughters' households with gift certificates for discs from the Magic Flute for each member of the family to choose a favorite. And he asked to have the mail order catalogue sent to his sister.

"You know," he confessed to Laura, "Christmas shopping could become an obsession."

"You've launched out on your own, have you?"

"I was looking for something for Diana and Constance, but what I found was so splendid I had to get it for everyone in the family."

"Jack's just taken the wine making stuff over to her. He said she seemed pleased. Daddie, we were wondering about Christmas. The boys quite liked their new great-aunt and her friend. Mike said, 'Why aren't they invited for Christmas?' I tried to explain about Constance, but they don't believe me. I haven't seen her again, of course, but from what they said, she's perfectly charming."

"She can be," David said.

That whole day had so newly colored his understanding of Constance, the boys' part in it so much the sad end result that he could hardly remember how she had been with them.

"Have you made any headway with Mary about them?"

"No, I haven't, but even if I had, the day wouldn't just be too much for Constance, it would be too much for Mary. Has she talked to you about Christmas?"

"Yes, and everybody, including Mary, wants it where it's always been. She told me you thought we ought to begin to make some of our own traditions, but the only radical departure we've thought of is pie rather than Christmas pudding."

David laughed. Christmas pudding was the only revenge Patricia had taken for seeing to it that they had what they liked to eat for the rest of the year. She actually liked it. No one else did.

"But shouldn't we do something about . . . with Aunt Diana?"

"Perhaps we might drop in some time over the holiday. Boxing Day?"

"Tactless. Constance is English, and she's bound to associate it with the servants."

"Do you really think so?" David asked, wondering if she would not find it comically appropriate, but he wasn't certain enough of Constance's humor to try to explain it to anyone else. "Well, what about Christmas Eve afternoon?"

"I've promised to do the pies with Mary. What about Christmas night? We'll have dinner at four. We'll have been together all day. Mary expects us to go home for a late supper."

"About seven for an hour or so?" David asked. "I'll see if that would suit them."

David decided he would also go alone on Christmas Eve afternoon. He didn't want to seem to disappear into the bosom of his family on this first Christmas of their reconciliation.

"But that's exactly what I'd hoped you'd do," Diana said to him when he phoned to make Christmas plans. "Constance and I are no good at Christmas."

"You don't have to be," David said. "Laura and her family just want to drop in, and on Christmas Eve I only want to stay long enough to set up your present."

"I hope it's nothing to do with wine making," Diana said. "That Jack's been here, turning the basement into a lab! I feel as if I had a couple of sick patients down there, needing their temperatures taken, needing tests run, wanting this yeast, that acid."

"Are you going to enjoy it?"

"You know, I think I am," Diana admitted. "Except

for the stairs. It makes me feel ever so slightly illegal, though I know I'm not. And I amuse Constance."

"Good," David said. "And no, it hasn't to do with wine making."

"D., I'm too old to be taunted with surprises. There's nothing I want."

"Only because you haven't been out to look around," David said, having learned to distinguish between her irritabilities, when she was actually pleased, when truly distressed.

David wanted to ask her if she'd thought any more about going to the desert, but he decided to leave that subject until after the holidays. She could be pushed only so far at a time.

David was busy wrapping presents when he recognized Mary's knock on the door. He looked around quickly to be sure there was nothing she shouldn't see and then called her welcome.

"I don't think I've ever in my life seen you wrap a present," Mary said.

"It isn't as generally a sex-specific activity as it has been in this house. I know lots of men who do it."

"Mother loved everything about Christmas," Mary sighed.

"Could you use help in this department?"

"No, I've set Christine to that. She's at loose ends now that school's out. Patsy and Tyler seem to have endless ideas about what to do with themselves. Not Chris."

Mary had settled herself in David's reading chair, an indication that she intended to stay for a while. David decided to go on with his wrapping until something she said required more than his casual attention.

"I've just had a long conversation with Aunt Sue," Mary said.

Sue was Patricia's oldest friend, a connection dating

back to their high school days, who had married a dull, good man with money. Though David fairly put himself under those adjectives as well, it did not prevent him from finding Sue's husband a bore. Kirk's social conversation sounded much like what David was paid to do, right down to the weather report, but Sue and Patricia never ran out of things to say to each other, and their passion for bridge allowed David to shift his boredom to a less personal activity than conversation.

"She's worried about you," Mary went on. "She thinks you're spending too much time alone. She knows for a fact that you've refused four Christmas parties."

"I can't stand big parties," David said. "I can't hear well enough to carry on an intelligible conversation. By now, all I can hear is my own and other people's hearing aids setting off their distress signals all over the room, like buoys in the bay: hard, inanimate object here, a threat to all navigation."

"You always used to be quite cheerful about them."

"I liked watching your mother have a good time."

"Sue says you've even stopped accepting invitations for bridge."

"Loyal as Sue is to your mother's memory, she can't resist a bit of matchmaking, and I'm well past that."

"Well, playing an evening's bridge occasionally certainly isn't grounds for a shotgun wedding," Mary said.

"At my age, it just might be. But here's another confession: I loathe bridge."

"Do you mean to say you let Mother drag you all those years . . ."

"She didn't have to drag," David corrected. "I liked to see her doing what she enjoyed. She went with me to a lot of parties with my CBC cronies agreeably enough, which she wouldn't have gone to by choice. You do those things:

the social world is set up for couples."

"And I think that's why Aunt Sue wants to fix you up with a nice widow, not to marry you off. She thinks you're in danger of simply falling through the cracks of old age."

"She always did turn a good phrase. But she should try it before she knocks it."

"You're perfectly happy?" Mary asked.

"That's a tall order," David said. "Is anyone?"

"But you're not lonely, missing old friends?"

"No," David said.

"I told her you were seeing a lot of your sister," Mary said in a neutral tone.

David went on cutting paper to wrap a shirt for Ted which Mary had aleady approved.

"She said, 'How awkward!', and hoped no one else in the family was being exposed."

David gave the scissors a final, violent snap.

"You don't really like Aunt Sue, do you?" Mary asked.

"She was your mother's oldest friend."

"Didn't you have *any* opinions of your own?"

Finally David put the scissors down and with a great effort at self-control turned to his younger daughter.

"You don't need to bait me to have this conversation, you know. I'm not willing to talk about Diana through Sue's eyes or even your mother's. The only reason you haven't been 'exposed' as Sue calls it is that you've made it perfectly clear you don't want to meet Diana or know anything about her. And no, I don't like Sue when she's reinforcing other people's prejudices, whether your mother's or your own."

"I don't much like her either," Mary said.

"Then why do you listen to her when you won't listen to me?"

"She doesn't wait for me to ask. If you didn't have

your damned private line, I could have buzzed you and made you cope with the old bitch. Why me? Why always me?"

Mary burst into tears, a child wanting her mother, no matter how often she'd fought to be free of her. But David could comfort her because he always had. He was far more familiar with her remorse than Patricia had ever been.

"Why don't you miss her the way I do?" Mary wailed.

"Because I was happier with her," David said quietly. "I don't feel guilty. I felt the way *you* do when my mother died."

"Laura doesn't."

"Laura was a better child than you and I were."

"I don't believe you weren't a good son. You're so good you sometimes make me sick!"

David smiled at her. It was the sort of thing Diana might say to him and mean it in the same way, both loving and furious.

"I won't get into a contest about it with you," he said.

"I'm just not ready for one thing more than I already have to cope with."

"Then ask for more help with what's already on your shoulders," David urged.

"I did love Mother," Mary said, and her tears started afresh.

"Of course you did, and she loved you."

"Why can't Ted understand what I'm going through?"

"He hasn't lost his mother," David said. "And I think he does understand, but you have to realize that it threatens him, too."

"Why should he be threatened?"

"It took me years to break down the walls your mother built after little David died. I didn't ever entirely succeed."

"I can't just stop feeling."

"You can stop a lot of other kinds of feeling, for Ted, for the children, and you're the center of their life."

"I've been wondering if I should see a shrink," Mary said, calmer again. "But I don't really want to be made into some other kind of person. I just want to like myself better."

David didn't speak.

"Do you think I ought to go?" Mary asked.

"Only if you think so."

David had a basic suspicion about psychiatrists. The people he knew who made a habit of them were more self-absorbed than ever.

"You think I shouldn't," Mary decided as she studied his face.

"I'm sure there are good ones," David said, "who know both how simple and at the same time how hard to see most human problems are. But a lot of them seem to break more than they mend, or at least that can be the result."

"You don't think I have a bunch of kinky hangups about Mother?"

"No," David said. "I think you're baffled by how to go on growing without her measure."

"But I never wanted her measure!"

"I know," David said.

"But I feel she's cheated me out of it or into it. I can't even figure out which."

"Should you be living in this house?" David asked.

"I sometimes think I couldn't manage without it," Mary confessed. "I know all its hiding places. And you're as good as a shrink, better. You know them, too."

Mary had taken the Kleenex David offered her, and while she mopped herself up, he went back to his wrapping. He felt the burden of her need like an anchor. It dragged at a heart he could wish freer.

David was glad he had involved himself so much in Christmas shopping. He felt much more in the spirit of the growing excitement. He was easily persuaded to go with Ted and the children to pick out a tree.

"Not the Salvation Army lot this year," David said to Ted before they left. "Let's support the Boy Scouts."

If he had been with Jack, David would have explained that the Salvation Army had been waging a battle against a homosexual rights bill in New Zealand, a piece of information David had picked up from reading a copy of *The Body Politic,* a gay newspaper from Toronto, which he discovered he could read, bit by bit, if he made the effort.

Grandfather and father gave the children the run of the lot to pick the tree for themselves, refusing to get caught up in each call of "What about this one?" Three were enough to quarrel and decide, a harmless way to expend some of the seasons's tense excitement.

"I'm a bit worried about Mary," Ted had the opportunity to say. "I finally told her the other night I thought it was time she pulled herself together over her mother's death and got back to ordinary living. And she decided that was grounds for divorce. God knows, I don't want to be insensitive, but don't you think she's beginning to overdo it?"

"Yes," David said, "but I'm not sure she's got herself to a place where she can help it. She did speak to me about going to a psychiatrist."

"Do you think she should?"

"I don't have much confidence in them," David said.

"Dad, I don't think I can handle much more of it," Ted said.

"Let's help her all we can with Christmas. I think she may be better when she's got through it."

"I used to like Christmas," Ted said miserably.

"You will again," David said, more sure of his ground than he would have been a year ago.

When the children had narrowed the choice to two, Patsy's and Tyler's, the men stepped in to help. Both trees qualified for realistic size, a first for that family. Tyler's was more symmetrical. Patsy's had more branches. Christine, who was hanging back from childish involvement, was assigned to choose.

"That's not fair," Tyler said. "She didn't even bother much about looking."

"She looked more than we did," Ted said.

Predictably, Christine chose Patsy's tree, and Tyler suffered, being both outnumbered and too small to fight for his rights.

"Why couldn't Ben and Mike be here?" he demanded. "They'd know a good tree when they saw one."

"They get to pick their own tree," Patsy said.

"Okay, Tyler," Ted said. "You can choose where we'll have lunch."

Both the girls groaned, and David sympathized with them. Ted and his son shared a taste for junk food, and Ted had figured out a way to avoid being outvoted. There was nothing at McDonald's David was happy about putting into his stomach. He assumed his granddaughters' protest was more social than dietetic; they were too old to be seen there in the company of older relatives. But it was all in the cause of keeping the family's demands on Mary to a minimum. Patsy succumbed to a belching contest with Tyler on the way home, which David could have joined with some relief, but he was sitting next to Christine, whose offended dignity was more important than relief from his indigestion.

David was glad to leave them to the chore of the tree. His duty as light stringer had been handed over to Ted along with all the other rituals as head of the house. Beyond that, it had been Patricia's pleasure, once the girls were grown, to spend a couple of hours at the decorating, and the elegant result always looked like something out of a magazine, to awe rather than to delight children. All of the homemade ornaments of the past had been thrown out. The only traditions that remained were the small, round-framed pictures of the children and grandchildren, which David had given her. This year the tree would be the children's own, and they'd be left to get on with it.

"Is that all right?" Mary had asked.

"Exactly right," David had assured her.

He went down to his own part of the house and collected the presents he had wrapped for Diana and Constance. He hadn't heard the sound of the compact disc player since the day he had bought three of them, and he was suddenly worried that there might not be so startling a difference when it was hooked up to Diana's good but certainly dated equipment. It seemed even more improbable when he realized that the player was small enough to slip into his coat pocket, and the half dozen discs he had bought made hardly a bigger package. Yet in a way, the smallness of the packages pleased him, one for each to open, no great display of Christmas to burst upon their quiet fireside.

It was four o'clock when David arrived, and he waited patiently for the greater length of time it took Diana to open the door, which now had to be unlocked from the inside first. David had keys of his own, but they were for an emergency, not for the privilege of letting himself into the house at his own convenience.

"There you are," Diana said with an eagerness of her own.

Constance stood right behind her with a smile whose brilliance still startled David.

"*We* have a surprise for *you*," she announced.

"Let him take off his coat," Diana said.

That took longer than he had anticipated, for the package which had slipped into the pocket so easily was more reluctant to come out. What would have been a cause for embarrassment some weeks ago now turned them into giggling children together as first David, then Constance, and finally Diana made attempts to extract it. Diana succeeded with damage to only one corner of the wrapping which exposed an anonymous black corner of the player.

"Whatever can it be?" Constance asked.

"Come along," Diana said. "David must see his first."

They led him into the living room, and there by the fire was a new high-backed armchair.

"We wanted you to have your own here," Diana explained.

It absurdly touched him, and only his vow never to lose control of his emotions in this room again kept his sudden tears from welling over.

"Try it," Constance urged.

Obediently he did.

"Is it comfortable?" Diana asked. "I had a man in the store who was about your size help me choose it."

"Perfect!" David pronounced, and it was.

"What I like about it," Constance said, "is that I keep forgetting it's new. It looks as if it's always been there."

Port and fruitcake had been set out on the coffee table, and Diana filled their glasses and passed the cake around

before she and Constance settled to open their presents,
Diana the player, Constance the discs.

"What do we have?" Diana asked, bewildered.

David took the player from her and plugged it into the
existing amplifier as he had been shown how to do at the
shop. He turned the selector switch to "other," opened one
of the discs, and placed it in the little player.

"It's really easier than a record," he said as he demon-
strated, "and it will never wear out."

Then out into the room came the strains of a double
violin concerto as pure and present as David had remembered
it. He looked from one to the other, watching the surprise
and growing delight on each of their faces. They did not
interrupt to exclaim. David sat down in his own chair and
gave himself up to the music. None of them moved or
spoke for a moment after the sound ceased. Then both
Constance and Diana spoke at once.

And David, gleeful, said, "I told you there was something you wanted."

Diana was looking at the discs.

"Can you just go into a store and buy them?" she
asked.

"That's right," David said, "and I've put you on the
Magic Flute mailing list for their newsletter; so you can just
phone and order if you like."

David had not thought of a present they might give to
him. The matching extravagance of their exchange spoke a
balance of care that they all wanted to make plain in a
season which invited but often failed to deliver such
messages.

"Now," he said, looking at his watch, "I've stayed
longer than I said I would by nearly an hour. It's time for
me to disappear into the bosom of my family."

Before he left, he showed them both how to use the

player, thanked them again for his chair, kissed them soundly and fled down the front steps before he made a fool of himself. He needed the length of his bus ride, shared tonight with exhausted late shoppers burdened with offerings, to put himself in a mood to deal quietly with the complexities of the day to come.

CHAPTER VIII

Cooking ham for their Christmas breakfast, Diana remembered, as she did every year, the first Christmas she had spent with Constance. Diana's mother had sent a tiny canned ham. Constance had two fresh eggs from a friend in the country, and the butcher had given her a bit of liver. How extravagant they felt in their London flat as they ate ham for breakfast, liver for lunch, and ham and eggs for dinner. They hadn't exchanged presents. It was a time when things led too much of a life and death of their own to hold personal meaning any longer. A teapot could as easily be found in the middle of the road as on a kitchen counter, a desk upside down in a back garden, and valuables could melt like snow in the heat of the fires. Constance's way of dealing with the loss of all her few belongings was not to care.

By eating each year what had been such a feast, they

kept Christmas as a private anniversary, something of a joke, and it had never been a time for exchanging important presents—this year a collapsible cane for Diana, for Constance a timer which she could hang around her neck to compensate for the loss of her inner clock. Diana could now add on the memory board the appropriate timing for each activity, and Constance could set the device for herself.

"Will it send me rushing to the stove?" Constance asked.

"I hope not," Diana answered.

Perhaps it was a silly idea, but Diana was always trying to figure out ways to give Constance a greater sense of independence. Rational as the decision had been to put those locks on the doors, they weighed as much on Diana's conscience as they played on Constance's nerves. She went to one door or another half a dozen times a day to test them, and each time she did, Diana had to explain again why they were locked.

"Never mind," Constance said, as if to comfort Diana, "my real prison is trusting you."

The phone rang.

"Merry Christmas," Diana said into a good deal of static.

"Merry Christmas to you," said a pleased Jill.

"Where are you?"

"In Mexico."

"Having a good time?" Diana asked, amused.

"Passable. How about you?"

"David gave us a new compact disc player."

"A what?"

"A new sort of record player. It's marvelous."

Constance came into the kitchen, drawn by the ringing of the phone.

"How's Constance?"

"Here she is to tell you herself," Diana said. "It's Jill in Mexico."

Jill was the only person Constance could be persuaded to talk to on the phone. Her side of the conversation didn't make consecutive sense, but Diana knew it was the sound of that voice, still with traces of a London accent, which Jill had phoned to hear, and she would contrive to make Constance laugh at least once.

Constance brought her amusement to the breakfast table, no longer aware of its source.

"Ham for breakfast? You'd think it was Christmas!"

"It is," Diana said.

"So it is," Constance said, consulting the heading on her memory board, and then she looked down at the timer hanging around her neck. "And I'm to go off at intervals all through the day."

"Well, try it anyway," Diana said, "but not today. You won't need it today."

Her real gift to Constance was to be with her all day and to treat the time as if it were as rare and special as it had been all those years ago when they had to spend so much time apart, when they were never without the anxiety that something might happen to either of them before they could meet again.

The compact disc player came as a new surprise to Constance. For Diana the sound, of such intense purity, recalled the first concerts she had gone to with Constance, music which seemed charged with erotic energy, as defiant and glorious as Diana felt herself in love. It was as if she had never before really listened or, for that matter, looked.

Poor as Constance's childhood had been, she had not been deprived as Diana had been, growing up at the pioneer edge of the world. The museums and libraries were free, concerts and theatres cheap.

"I seduced you with London," Constance had been fond of teasing.

"You didn't need London," Diana always replied.

There was nothing of London left for Constance now but hard chunks of her childhood. Sometimes it could feel to Diana as if she'd stolen it from Constance and had no way of giving it back. They had nothing together but the present, in which Constance lived in a poverty much more debilitating than anything her childhood had prepared her for.

Constance moved from her chair and sat on the floor leaning against Diana's knees. Her physical nearness closed the gap Diana had been staring into, and she began to listen again to what they did share now, her hand resting lightly on Constance's shining hair.

David and his family burst in on that Christmas solitude, and for a moment Constance cringed back in her chair. Nearly at once Jack took the boys to the basement to check the wine, and with only David and Laura in the living room Constance recovered herself enough to smile at David, sitting in his own new chair, to study the young woman with him, who sat on the edge of the couch, uneasily cheerful. Diana stood, wanting but unwilling to join the men in the basement because she didn't like to leave Constance with anyone she didn't know, even though David was now often familiar to her.

"You mustn't give any of us anything," Laura said to Diana. "We've done nothing but eat and drink all day long. Oh, you've got one of those, too!"

"I bought three altogether," David confessed.

"We've been listening to it most of the day," Diana said.

"So have we," Laura said. "Well, as much as you can listen to anything in a family mob. I can't wait to get ours hooked up at home."

"When do you expect your baby?" Constance asked.

"Baby?" Laura repeated. "I'm not pregnant. At least, I don't think I am. It must be the Christmas dinner showing."

"Laura's my niece," Diana said, "not a patient."

"Those great boys who went to the basement just now are my babies," Laura said.

"Grown men?" Constance asked.

"Nearly," Laura said. "I find it hard to believe myself."

"You're like your father," Diana said. "You don't know how to age."

Laura's blush must be a temptation her sons could rarely resist. It made her look even younger still and somehow old-fashioned, a throwback to their own generation before the war.

Jack and the boys could be heard coming up the basement stairs, and Constance threw Diana a look of frank alarm.

"It's all right," David assured her. "I know it sounds like the troops, but it's only my grandsons."

"It's coming along just fine," Jack announced. "We couldn't have done better ourselves. Next year we'll start soon enough for you to try fresh fruit."

"Isn't that a John Koerner in the back hall?" Mike asked.

"Yes," Diana said. "Are you interested in painting?"

"Sort of," Mike said. "I don't paint or anything."

"I don't think I'd ever looked at a picture when I was your age. I learned to in London during the war."

"Lots of doctors buy paintings, don't they?" Mike

asked. "Most of the paintings I see outside galleries are in doctors' offices . . . or dentists'."

"I suppose they do."

"Most people just don't buy paintings, real ones anyway," Mike said.

"They do cost an arm and a leg," Jack reminded his son.

"Well, no more than television, lots of them. I have this friend, Richard, who wants to be a painter, but he'll have to be a teacher or something else and just paint when he can."

"That's one of the reasons I like to buy paintings by artists around here, ones who are still alive," Diana said. "We have better ones than we deserve, that's certain."

"In western Canada the human form is yet to be sighted," Constance said.

"That's pretty true, I guess," Mike said.

"You know, I used the last opening line you gave me," Ben said to Constance. " 'Canada is a country of hollow doors.' "

Constance smiled at him attentively.

"I mean, you're terrific with opening lines," Ben said.

"They're all I have," Constance said. "I have to make them do."

"Could I come over some time and just look?" Mike asked.

"Of course you can," Diana said. "Would you like to bring your friend, Richard? We've got a fair collection scattered through the house."

"That would be wonderful."

"This really is an art gallery," Constance said. "That's why all the doors have to be locked."

Ben and Mike exchanged looks while David clumsily changed the subject to the new Vancouver Art Gallery, a handsome conversion of the old courthouse where he could still feel occasional ghosts of those on trial, an unfortunately accurate image for Constance's own dilemma. The others in the room seemed helpless to rescue him; perhaps he was too much in charge of this visit for anyone else to end it.

Finally Laura did say, "Dad, shouldn't we . . ."

"Be going," David finished for her, relief in his tone. "Yes."

Though the boys themselves had installed the locks, Diana felt self-conscious as she unlocked the door to let them all out. She had really looked forward to their visit, and both Ben and Mike had begun to open up a little. If it weren't for the damned locks, no one would have grown uneasy. They might have stayed a while longer and helped Diana fill the long evening. She had to admit to herself that a day, even Christmas day, alone with Constance without so much as an hour's break to read a book, was very long, and now there was nothing to do but watch the Christmas evening specials.

Constance had already found her way into the TV room and turned on the set. A flawless young blond was in the middle of a solo of "Silent Night," the camera all but shoved down his tenor throat. A dentist could have examined his teeth.

"Queer as Dick's hatband," Constance decided.

Finally the camera drew back and panned the choir, all eager young faces and clean hair, washed in the blood of the lamb they wanted it known, for what audience would be watching them but old Christian shut-ins, pining for the promised land.

"It's indecent for us to watch this," Diana said, getting up and switching from channel to channel. "There must be something fit for a couple of old pagans like us."

The only movie she could find was a war film. Flashing

guns and exploding bombs were even worse than all those sleigh bells in the snow.

"We don't have to watch," Constance said reasonably. "Turn it off and remember something for me."

Diana turned from switching off those alien images and said, "Christmas in Borrego Springs."

The name called up no recognition in Constance's face, but she waited, receptive.

"We flew down to San Diego and after a couple of days there, we rented a car and drove over to the desert. There was snow in the mountains, not enough to make driving difficult, just enough to whiten the trees. As we got further east, the trees and the snow disappeared, and then down below us in the bright sun there was the desert.

"You'd never seen the desert before, and I had to stop the car at the first cactus. You got out and set right off across the sand. It was warm. There was a dry breeze. Even I could walk and I did. We must have wandered around for an hour before we got back into the car and drove into the town to find a place to stay, a motel right in town that first time. We had an enormous bed, a tiny kitchen, and a big bare living room.

"We realized why there weren't any rugs. A little woman who talked to herself had to sweep out the sand every day. The wind never really stopped blowing. The tumbleweed piled up against the fences, and some days the wind blew so hard the deck furniture would slide right into the pool, but there were trails at the foot of the mountains where you could get out of the wind. One day we followed a little stream part way up the mountain and had a picnic sitting on a boulder looking out over the valley. You said the golf course looked like patches of spilled green ink in that great spread of dusty gold. And we could see the squares of date palm and grapefruit orchards.

"We ate those huge pink grapefruit at least twice a day. A dollar a bag for ten of them. And enormous moist dates. I didn't think I liked dates until you made me taste one, and then I couldn't stop eating them.

"There was a little Mexican restaurant that served the best chili rellenos I'd ever tasted, until you went right out into the kitchen and got the cook to teach you how to make them, and then yours were even better. You thought you might open a Mexican restaurant in Vancouver on the strength of those chilli rellenos.

"We even talked about buying something down there. We had a real estate woman take us around. We looked at condos for sale with gardens and pools and tennis courts and golf courses. We thought it was odd that most of them were for sale furnished, even the new ones, right to the pictures on the walls and the china in the cupboards. The only house we really liked was out on the desert by itself with its own orchard and pool, filled with what was obviously old family stuff, but the fellow was going to sell all that, too; he apologized about wanting to take one chair; it had been his mother's.

"But we didn't really want a place. Part of what we liked about Borrego Springs was having nothing we had to do."

"How could we ever have liked that?" Constance asked.

"We were very hard-working women in those days," Diana said.

"Do you think we could make up something we had to do now?" Constance asked.

"Most of the year, you have the garden," Diana reminded her.

"I'd like to go home," Constance said.

"Back to England, do you mean?"

"No, home. Where we worked."

"This is home, Constance. It's just that we've got old."

That night Diana lay awake, wondering what sort of work project she could think up which might give Constance some sense of accomplishment. The wine making didn't interest her, and, even if it had, there was nothing to do except rack it off a couple of times and finally bottle it. What Constance needed was something always there, as available to her as their always ongoing jigsaw puzzle but with some more accomplishing point to it. Neither of them had ever knitted, and the sewing Constance used to do was beyond her now. Anything that took planning or following directions was out of the question. Might Constance be interested in drawing or painting? Could that seem as idle to her as most of her other occupations? Diana had loved the medical drawing she had done in school. The accuracy required had commanded her attention, but also it was the pleasure of teaching her hand a new language without the impediments placed in her way when she had first tried to learn to write. No one questioned her use of her left hand, and with it she was as good as or better than her fellow students. Might they both try a little drawing?

Diana pictured them sitting together on canvas camp stools out in the desert sun, studying the thorny aura of a rounded little cactus which was as sensitive to enemies as a porcupine. It had taken Diana most of an afternoon to remove the thorns from Constance's hand after she had discovered that fact. Constance had always wanted to touch everything, food, fabric, leaves, people. Because she had so little sense of ownership, she dared. It wasn't only the cactus that sometimes misunderstood those sensuous gestures, but Constance was never overly concerned with the consequences. She assumed that what you learned from experience sometimes hurt without automatically assigning it moral significance.

Diana didn't suppose the desert would any longer be the healing miracle that it had once been. Her joints were too far gone for her to imagine that she could still hike out into the desert, but she might move about with less difficulty, not be roused several times in the night by pain.

If David were with them, if she never had to leave Constance alone, mightn't a change be good for her, too? If they could somehow minimize the risks as well as the terrors for Constance, then perhaps when she came home, she would feel more at home and accept the locked doors.

What Diana knew she also had to face was the spring when Constance would want to be out in the garden again. It would have to be fenced. If they were away while that was being done, perhaps Constance wouldn't be much aware of it when they got back.

In the morning, Diana admitted to herself that going to the desert was a pipe dream. The only useful idea she had had in the night was the fence, and it would be as hateful to Constance as the locks were. Never had it been clearer to Diana that the possessor is as trapped as the possessed, and there could be no lesson she needed less to learn in her old age, but her only other choice was to commit Constance, and Diana didn't have to learn the consequences of that either.

Constance was as cheerful that morning as Diana was bleak, a mood she gradually surrendered to Constance's affectionate teasing.

"I was remembering," Diana said with some confidence as they sat over a last cup of breakfast tea, "how much I used to enjoy drawing when I had to do some of it in medical school."

"Why aren't all doctors vegetarians? Flesh must be so real to them."

"Another of your great opening lines, as Ben calls

them," Diana said, smiling. "I wasn't thinking so much about medical drawing as just drawing."

"What would you draw?"

"I don't know," Diana said, "anything, I suppose—that bowl of mandarin oranges, for instance."

"I might want to eat one," Constance warned her.

"It might be something we could both do," Diana suggested.

Constance handed her a mandarin orange, and Diana knew she hadn't been misunderstood but was being teased. She accepted the orange, peeled it and offered half to Constance.

"Just the same," Diana said, "I'm going to try."

Even if it turned out to be like the wine, involving only herself, it was something she could do which didn't so clearly withdraw her attention as reading did. Or so she imagined until she began, first attempting the mandarins, then adding their teacups, her hand and eye beginning to remember that pleasure of cooperation which the act of drawing was.

Constance was drawing, too, sitting across the table from Diana as absorbed as she, not with mandarins and teacups, but with Diana herself.

They sat and worked for an hour.

"We should set your timer," Diana said, surprised at the time that had passed.

"It's a lot easier than trying to write," Constance said. "I can see what I've done."

Diana looked at the half dozen sheets of paper Constance had used to make crude caricatures of Diana, and she was reminded of a series of paintings she had seen, done by a disturbed child, depicting a huge female figure with ladders propped up on her, on which small children stood for the tasks of washing her face, combing her hair, feeding her.

There was no such reversal of role in Constance's sketches, but they could be captioned, *My real prison is trusting you.*

"You know," Constance said, looking at her sketches herself, "you need a good haircut."

"It's not as bad as that, is it?" Diana asked, studying the sketches more practically now.

"Well, I may have exaggerated a little," Constance admitted, "but I think I caught the essence of the difficulty. You could take this to a hairdresser and say, 'There, that's exactly how I don't want it to look.' "

"Why don't you learn to cut my hair?"

Constance took a fistful of it in her hand and drew Diana's face down to her own.

"I love even the things you can't do for me," Constance said and kissed her.

New Year's Day fell on a Wednesday, and David arrived early in the afternoon with a shopping cart full of supplies. Though he insisted on taking charge of the meal, he did let Diana do odd vegetable fixings and stirrings of sauces. She knew she gave him courage, for they were really very alike in their skills, competent without being adventuresome unless they had both encouragement and help. More than that, it was a time they could be alone together, for Constance had lost interest in the kitchen once she had lost it as a territory.

"I'm sending Mary and Ted off for a long weekend at Harrison Hotsprings," David confided as he worked to remove the membranes from freshly boiled sweet breads. "I'd like to send them farther away for longer, but Mary doesn't think I can last longer than three days with the kids."

"Can you?" Diana asked, amused.

"I don't really see why not. I began parental duties fairly early in life and got through my failures early."

"Failures?"

"How long has it been since you've seen Carl and Robert?"

"Not since Mother's funeral."

"Neither have I," David said. "I wasn't as hard on them as Hugh, but, once he left, I did lord it over them. I didn't want them to think they could run wild just because their father's belt went with him into the great war. They resented the fact that Mother let me play the role. They were obnoxious kids as they got older, and Mother was useless with discipline. I think one reason I couldn't stand them was that they reminded me of how obnoxious I was at their age. It didn't make me tolerant."

"In the last years Mother pretty well arranged it that none of us ever met," Diana said. "But by the time I got home, I didn't really know them or much want to. I never really felt close to them, but I remember how patient you were, even when they got into your things."

"When Hugh was still around, I used to feel sorry for them."

"Yes, I did, too, but I didn't feel really related to them. They just made it very clear to me how little I wanted children."

"It never occurred to me I'd have kids like that!" David said and laughed, but then he added more soberly, "It took me years to realize that the only thing really wrong with those kids was that I didn't love them, and by then they were grown men I didn't particularly like."

"Could we have loved them?" Diana asked.

"We should have."

"I don't know anything about that kind of love," Diana said. "For me it isn't voluntary."

"Isn't it?" David asked. "For me love isn't just voluntary, it's willful."

"For children ... if you're the father. But for the mother there's such a basic bonding, or if there isn't, it can't be helped. It becomes a matter of duty."

"We didn't have to love each other, did we?" David asked.

"I never felt any choice about it at all," Diana said. "I could have killed you, but I couldn't have stopped loving you. You were my 'given.' "

"Didn't you choose to love Constance?"

"No," Diana answered simply.

"You make love sound like fate."

"I think it is," Diana said.

"But that's impossibly romantic, D.!"

Diana smiled at him and said, "You're the romantic, not I."

"Well, I would have said so, too, but I didn't really feel fated to marry Patricia. I simply wanted to."

Diana wasn't tempted to reply, "Then you shouldn't have." She didn't mean anything like that. It could have happened that she'd never had the opportunity to live with Constance. It had happened that she hadn't seen David, except on their birthday, for years. Diana had taught herself not to suffer about it. She had even held herself aloof from him when he came back, but about loving him or loving Constance she had no choice at all, even when she had tried to think she did.

"I'm going to need those mushrooms in a minute," David said.

Diana gave a startled snort. She was getting as bad as Constance about forgetting what she was doing.

"If this is any good, I might try it on the kids this weekend," David said.

"A bit exotic for kids' tastes, I'd think," Diana said.

"I suppose it is. And no one wants a grandfather who's a showoff."

Diana finished the mushrooms and left him to find Constance at the jigsaw puzzle. The timer around her neck was ticking.

"You're early," Constance said, without looking up. "I've figured out what this thing is really for. It's to let *you* know when I'm done. But, if I want you, I can cheat. Look!"

Constance took hold of the timer and turned it abruptly to make it ring its bold ring.

"It's as good a use for it as any. You don't have to wear it, you know."

"I like it," Constance said. "It makes me feel edible."

"That's always been one of your dangers."

"You're not a cannibal," Constance said.

"One of my repressions," Diana admitted.

"You mustn't regret them, not now, at your age."

"I don't. I never have," Diana said.

They had always played verbal catch this way, only now Diana was often uncertain of how many exchanges back Constance could hold in her mind; but she had always thrown an occasional wild ball and had also occasionally dropped an easy catch. It was a game they had learned very early not to play in anger. Diana did not want to be wary now, but the anger often under Constance's bright playfulness was a danger to them both, for they shared it and were equally helpless before it.

"Don't you ever fight?" Jill had asked Diana.

"We've had all the ones that are useful," Diana had replied. "Once you know them by heart, there's not much point."

David asked, standing in the doorway, "Do you want

drinks in here, or shall I put them in the living room?"

"We'll come in," Diana said.

"Happy New Year," David said, lifting his glass to them.

"What year is it?" Constance asked.

"Nineteen eighty-six," David answered.

"What did you do last night?" Diana asked.

"I played Monopoly with the kids, and then we all made New Year's resolutions. The children were so serious about those that they made me think about pulling up my moral socks."

"Should we do that?" Constance asked.

"I suppose we should," Diana said.

"I resolve to stop feeling guilty that I'm alive," Constance said cheerfully.

"Now that's one that would help me," David said.

"Would it?" Constance asked, surprised.

"There were so many things Patricia still wanted to do," David said. "I squander the days and think about everything she might be doing."

"Patricia?"

"My wife. She died a year and a half ago."

"I think everyone I know must be dead, but I can't remember," Constance said. "I'd like to stop feeling guilty about that, too."

"I can't think of anyone who lives as well in the present as you do," David said.

"I'm not always sure that's what it is. You won't tell yours, will you, darling?" Constance said, turning to Diana. "You aren't really secretive, but you're very modest."

Diana laughed and then said, "I confess I'd rather live with fewer resolutions."

"That's because you remember yours," Constance said sympathetically.

It was not until after dinner that David broached the subject of New Year wishes.

"Mine," he said, "is to go to the desert for a couple of weeks with both of you, the sooner the better."

"Good!" Constance said.

"Nobody'd like it better than I would," Diana said, "but I think it's really out of the practical question."

"Not with me along, it isn't," David said. "I've given it a good deal of practical thought."

"If I go with him, you'll have to go," Constance said. "And I'm going with him."

Diana looked at David. Had he really been around them long enough to know what he might be letting himself in for? Did either of them have the right to act on Constance's cheerful resolve when she had no way of being responsible for it? Diana did long to go, not only for her bones but for her spirit, but, if it turned out to be too difficult for Constance . . .

"Do say you'll come, D.," David said. "I know we can manage it."

"You don't even like to travel."

"Flying down to the desert isn't exactly traveling," David said. "You can't get the good of the sun from reading about it or watching it on TV."

Why did she always imagine the worst? The airport would be hard for Constance, but with David to handle the problem of tickets and baggage, Diana could concentrate on reassuring Constance. The desert itself might be good for her.

"Let me think about it," Diana said.

"As long as you think positively," David said, "and I'm not sure you do when you're alone. I've already checked out flights. We can go directly to Palm Springs and rent a car to drive into Borrego."

"It's late to find a place there," Diana warned him.

"We can stay in Palm Springs if we can't get into Borrego."

Constance got up and started out of the room.

"Where are you going?" Diana asked.

"Upstairs to pack," Constance said.

"Darling, even if we go, it won't be tonight."

"What can I do about it then?" Constance demanded.

"One hard thing," David said. "The doors are going to have to be locked there, too. Otherwise Diana will be too frightened to go because, if you wandered off on the desert, we might never be able to find you."

Constance looked at Diana.

"He's right," Diana said. "I would be too frightened."

"I don't ever mean to frighten you."

"I know you don't, but I have to help you not to."

"I haven't lost my mind."

"I know you haven't, but you can lose your way."

"I understand the locks," Constance said.

"Well?" David challenged.

"We can't chew up rental doors the way we did here," Diana said.

"The boys are working on that problem."

"Oh, David, I'd love to go," Diana said.

"Then just leave it to me," David said.

Diana saw in his delight a flash of the boy, her brother, when they were about to escape the often tension-filled house for a party or a day at the beach. Her 'given' had been given back to her.

With such dividends! For Mike did call and ask to bring his friend Richard around to see the pictures. Not much over five feet tall, Richard could have been taken for a boy of twelve if there had been any softness in his face, but there were already strong lines bracketing his well-defined

mouth and the shadow of whiskers below prominent
cheekbones. He had thin black hair and eyes nearly as dark
behind glasses as thick as David's. His head was a political
cartoon on his small body.

It interested Diana that Mike, so paired with his
substantial brother Ben, would choose a friend so diminutive.
Tall as he was, Mike was still slight and coltish, with the
manner of one who admired and was indulged.

Constance inspected both the boys with bright severity
before she declined to join them on a tour of the house.
She went back to her jigsaw puzzle even as they inspected
the paintings in the TV room, only two of them because
the wall space there was mostly given over to books.

Diana had always known that most of the paintings she
chose were too declarative for domestic space. But in a
house that was so rarely and awkwardly accommodating to
people, Diana needed requiring presences on the walls. She
often bought a painting the artist was surprised to sell. It
was a refreshing change not to feel she should be apologetic
for their large intrusiveness.

Richard did comment from time to time, but his voice
was so low that only Mike benefitted from his opinions.
Diana learned from his small, gesturing hands, which told
her that, however judgmental he was being, he cared about
what he looked at.

When they reached the upstairs hall, whitely brightened
by two large early interior landscapes by Takao Tanabe,
Richard looked at Diana with surprise.

"They are Tanabes," she said, "but they're thirty years
old."

They had seemed to her when she first saw them
delicate in their lyricism, fields of white with scatterings of
red, ochre and black calligraphic images, but, set against the
monumental serenity of his more recent prairie landscapes

and the brooding weather of the Queen Charlotte Islands, this early work seemed crude and tentative. This judgment didn't revise her affection for them.

Only when she took the boys into the bedroom which she shared with Constance did Diana suddenly wonder at the propriety of it, the large bed with its twin bedside tables and reading lamps, the matching bureaus and double closets. Mike did glance around, but Richard went straight to a more recent Tanabe in reassured recognition.

Diana was glad she and the cleaning woman had so recently turfed out the other unused rooms. Diana had dusted again herself only this morning while Constance stood timidly at the threshold of rooms no longer familiar to her. In the guest room with its prim twin beds were two of Diana's favorite Koerners, one of the early coastal glitter series, another of his more recent African paintings, the one so full of familiar, cool light, the other hot enough to burst into flame.

The two rooms which had been Jill's, originally furnished as a bedroom and study, had been haphazardly filled with castoffs which would and should have been given away if there hadn't been these empty spaces to receive them. Here the walls were crowded with paintings, as daunting as a room full of noisy people. Mike stood back, but Richard plunged in, for here was treasure indeed, early Shadbolts, Gordon Smiths, Tanabes, Koerners, Molly and Bruno Bobaks.

"There's an Onley watercolor in the bathroom," Diana confessed, for he was a painter generally too remote for her taste.

"He's the guy who crashed his plane on the glacier, isn't he?" Mike asked.

"Yes, and threatened to burn his paintings unless the tax laws were changed," Diana said. "I wish his paintings were as colorful as he is."

"But he's good!" Richard said with such defensive urgency that Diana could finally hear him.

"Of course he is," Diana answered.

Richard's next remark didn't reach her.

"My aunt can't hear you, Richard," Mike said. "He says he wishes there would be more retrospectives. There's just nowhere you can see things like this."

"Why don't people care?" Richard asked, giving his voice volume as well as urgency.

"I think people do," Diana said. "Look at the new gallery."

"It's just a building," Richard said. "That opening B.C. show was awful, everything junked in together, everybody but Shadbolt stuck in one decade, buried there. It was like going to the funeral of B.C. art."

"Like going to the funeral of B.C. art," Mike repeated, for Richared had fallen again into a mutter.

"I didn't go," Diana admitted and wished very much for the first time that she had.

All Diana did now was sit at her desk and write out cheques for membership, for tickets, and then had to remember to send the tickets down to the art school or out to the university so that someone could make use of them. She had never stopped to imagine the students who might have used them, like this little gnome full of outrage and zeal.

As they arrived again in the front hall, Diana noticed that she had forgotten to relock the inside lock in her concern to make the boys welcome. Without explanation she left them abruptly and moved as quickly as she could into the TV room. There Constance sat, her timer ticking.

"Where have you been?" Constance asked. "I was about to cheat."

"I'm just seeing the boys out," Diana said.

As she did, she could hear faintly the buzzing ring of the timer. She stopped to relock the door before she went back in to Constance.

CHAPTER IX

"How can we go away for the weekend when Chrissie's going out on her first date?" Mary demanded of both her husband and father as they sat together in the living room Patricia had created and recreated over the years. "She'll feel abandoned."

"I think, if you asked her, she'd tell you she was relieved," Ted said mildly.

"Mary," David said, "there's always going to be something to keep you at home if you let it. When all the children are gone, there can still be house plants to water or a sick cat."

"We don't have a cat," Mary said.

Both men smiled.

David, as usual, was in conflict between his gut understanding of his daughter and his impatience with her. She reminded him so much of himself, trying to wriggle out of plans Patricia made for them, but Patricia had been firmer with him than Ted was with Mary, perhaps because David had never held the trump card of Mary's temper. Overwhelmed and inadequate as he had often felt, his own solution would have been to sleep round the clock. Patricia's answer to that was final: "That's no holiday for *me!*"

"Ted needs a break as much as you do," David said.

"He could still go."

"Right," said Ted, getting up out of his (David's ex) chair, "and I'm going."

Before Mary could answer him, he had left the room.

"That's what he does now," Mary said in exasperation. "He won't discuss anything. He just gets up and walks off."

"He's tired of fighting," David said.

"Fighting is about the only way I can get through to him," Mary said.

"Are you really not going to go?" David asked.

"Daddie, I'm afraid to go. What if, when we got there, we just really didn't have anything to say to each other?"

"The only serious mistake you can make about that is not to find out," David said.

Finally they went, Mary leaving David a list of instructions in case of such a variety of emergencies that it would have been funny if it hadn't also been such a confession of Mary's overtaxed imagination.

David's own list was quite different, a tending of a variety of masculine chores about the house which Ted lately had been too apathetic to notice. Half the taps needed new washers. Nearly every door squeaked. Two windows were too swollen to open. The curtain pull for the drapes at the large living room window had broken. How Patricia would have hated the grubby hand marks already visible where one hand or another had yanked the fabric to close them. He might try a bit of spot cleaner on those as well. But he had to be careful not to do anything very obvious. He didn't want to seem to be reclaiming the territory, nor did he want anything he did to be taken as a silent rebuke. Neither Ted nor Mary was apt to notice or if so only fleetingly, given their distracted states. But the children might give him away. So David did a lot of his chores on Friday while they were in school and was so preoccupied that he had to ask for help in the kitchen to get dinner ready on time.

The children had been well instructed, and the novelty of their grandfather's benign authority made them cheerful at their chores.

"Christine, you take your mother's place, and Tyler, you sit in your dad's," David suggested.

"Then you have to be the kid and clear the table," Tyler said gleefully to Patsy.

"I don't think Patsy and I are going to be kids tonight. We're going to be guests."

"So *you* have to clear the table," Tyler said, pointing to Christine.

"Dad sometimes clears the table," Patsy said.

David watched Tyler struggle between the pleasures and the burdens of his place of authority. But hunger nearly immediately overcame other considerations. Patsy, too, settled in to the demands of her stomach. Only Christine did more fiddling with her food than eating it.

"Not hungry tonight?" David asked her.

"Not really," Christine muttered, but she began to make an effort. "It's really good."

"Don't eat any more than you want," David said, not wanting his granddaughter to eat simply for the sake of his vanity.

"If you don't want your potato, I'll eat it," Tyler offered.

"Is Mom sick, Granddad?" Christine suddenly asked.

"Not sick. Just worn out from Christmas," David answered.

"Is that Dad's problem, too?" Tyler asked.

"Dad's just tired of Mom's being tired," Patsy said.

"But she didn't really want to go," Christine said. "She told me so."

"She'll enjoy herself once she gets there," David said to reassure them and himself.

He had wanted to say to Ted, "Make an effort." But, even if Ted didn't, Mary might at least have to look at how far unstuck her marriage had become and make an effort herself. All David had wanted to say to her was, "Have fun!" She had all her life been so good at it.

Tyler did help to clear the table because it gave him his father's privilege of dishing out the ice cream. His serving scandalized both of his sisters and nearly daunted Tyler, but he did finish it.

"Shall we go be more comfortable in the other room?" Tyler asked, making his child's voice as deep as he could, low in his throat, hollow with excess air.

Everyone laughed. It was Ted's line at the end of every meal.

In the living room Tyler reverted to himself, rolling around on the carpet, clutching his stomach in a parody of agony to act out his sisters' warnings.

"Listen, Tyler," Patsy said when she'd stopped laughing at him, "you're supposed to say what we have to talk about."

Ted liked to introduce a topic for discussion for a brief period after dinner before the children went off to do homework and Mary did the final cleaning up after the meal.

"Oh, I can't do that," Tyler said and explained again in

his fake voice, "I got home from the office too late to catch tonight's news."

"Then you have to," Patsy said to Christine.

"Me? No way. You have to, Granddad."

"I didn't catch the news either," David said, "but I never do. Why don't we try closer to home? Who would be your villain of the day at school or the most unpopular person around?"

"That's not hard," Tyler said.

"Is it a trick, Granddad?" Patsy asked.

"A trick?"

"I mean, Mother doesn't like us to say bad things about our teachers or other kids."

"Oh, I see," David said. "I didn't really mean that. If it is a trick—and maybe you could call it that—it's just that closer to home you can think about people who trouble you in a way that might make you understand them better."

"That's not so easy after all," Tyler decided. "I was going to show you how this weird kid in my class pulls out his hair and eats it."

Tyler took a tuft of his own hair and pulled.

"OW!" he shouted. "That really hurts, and I didn't even get any. This guy does it to himself all the time. He's even got bald patches, and he has to wear this cap, even inside, to remind him not to."

The pain obviously puzzled Tyler, jarring him out of mockery into a new place of speculation.

"Why would he want to hurt himself?" Tyler asked.

Patsy and Christine were quick with examples of their own, though none so dramatic, of self-inflicted pain. As they speculated on the various reasons for it, they remembered their own self-defeating gestures, and Tyler finally came to his own conclusion.

"He's mad at somebody he's scared to hurt."

David felt mildly subversive though he knew Ted and Mary would be as impressed with Tyler as he was. They both thought of themselves as tolerant people, but they didn't teach tolerance any more than he had though it might be the only lesson useful for their children to carry into adulthood.

"You know, Granddad," Christine said as he went into her room to say goodnight, "I wanted to say tonight that I thought I was the most unpopular girl I knew until Jerry asked me out to this movie. That's dumb, isn't it? Why should it make such a difference?"

"Maybe you'll find out it doesn't after it happens."

It was only sensible to be where the children could find him easily, but David had not wanted to agree to sleep in the master bedroom. He was quite simply afraid of it. He didn't know what part of the past he might find there. He had only learned to sleep well again after he had moved out, divorcing Patricia from the space where he rested alone.

Though the furniture greeted him—Patricia's chaise in the window nook where during the day she could look out over the sound to the north mountains whose remote serenity had comforted her, his low slung old armchair where he had sat with her to watch television, their bed, their matching bureaus—it was not the same room. Its smells were foreign to him, and none of the small, homely objects were for his comfort, though he could take comfort from them since they were pictures of his grandchildren, a book he had given to Ted for Christmas, a dressing table set Patricia had given Mary on an adolescent birthday. Nowhere else in the house was a room so fully and newly inhabited as here. Even the children's rooms had an unnatural neatness as if they were still guests in a grandparental house.

It was of Ted and Mary that he thought as he got ready for bed, and it was the tension of their unhappiness that he felt as he got between the familiar sheets. He was acutely embarrassed to find himself aware of his daughter as a sexual creature withholding herself from him/Ted as virginally as a girl in obedience to the fears of her mother.

Thus Patricia had shrunk from David for months after little David died. It was as if she were pregnant with a grief that would never be born, and she wanted to isolate herself just as she had when she was heavily pregnant with little David and could not bear the extra weight of his arm around her. To desire her filled David with unaccountable guilt, as if it were a taboo as strong as the one against lusting after mother or sister. Gradually he became impotent himself, and, though he had never invested much pride in himself as a sexual performer, it frightened him. It was against all instinct for their young bodies to close down against life like this, to lie together as if entombed.

Odd that he should take himself back there, not even in this room, for they hadn't moved here until after the girls were born. He had never been so lonely, not even in the weeks of Patricia's dying in hospital when he had come home alone, or after her death when the loss of her had unmoored him and left him afloat on the seas of meaningless time.

If he had not suffered so acute a sense of deprivation, David might never have had reason to puzzle over the nature of desire, why he had never felt its real force until he was without it. It was then that he thought of his father, dead at the moment of David's birth, and felt a peculiar kinship with him. At the same time David was appalled that he should be alive while both father and son lay dead. His child was a broken promise to that man. Only after there were other children could David gradually bring the two together in his mind, the secret male companions he had never sought out in life with whom he might claim common cause.

Peter Harkness was the only man David had ever felt close to. Peter had insisted on it, proffering friendship as other men didn't without conditions, never objecting to the conditions David had to put in place. Peter had that kind of sexual vitality David recognized in Constance the moment he met her. It had nothing to do with their homosexuality. It would and did frighten David in women who might be available to him, and it was often crudely predatory in heterosexual men he knew. But Peter was like the sun, his warmth indiscriminate and constant. David responded to it as passively as a plant and was nourished. He knew, if he had had a different moral nature, he could have been Peter's lover. He could feel the unthinkable. And it did not frighten him. Instead it gave him a new sense of potency, which stayed with him even after Peter and Casper moved to Toronto.

It made David more forebearing with a wife who could only intermittently desire him, and it was never a simple, joyful act as it had been before it was so clearly associated with birth and death. They were fallen creatures.

David wondered if all sexual love must be cast in such shadows. Perhaps it must if it was to survive. How could he speak with Mary about it except in the general platitudes he had already offered? Perhaps it was simply not his place to, but he mistrusted that idea. Like Laura, he increasingly felt he had taught his children too little that was useful to them in their adult lives.

David woke to sunrise and dressed in the cool, pale light of the winter morning, a troubled memory of his wife's pain-defined face hurrying him out of that room whose ghost had waited for the light of day.

Patsy and Tyler were ready for breakfast. Christine was old enough to sleep the morning away, and, though her mother had left instructions that she was not allowed to do so, David ignored them. It would pass the time better for Christine than a morning of nervous fiddling. An afternoon's waiting for her first date was long enough.

Tyler was off to play hockey. Patsy was meeting a friend to go skating down at Robson Square. So David was free to fool with windows, to oil doors. He enjoyed his chores. Here in the upper floors of the house rooms were filled with light. He might even, when he was done, try sitting to read a while.

Christine appeared just as David was contemplating lunch, her face still softly exhausted by sleep.

"The longer I sleep, the more I want to," she said.

"I know the feeling."

"Mom says, if I don't look out, I can sleep my life away."

"That's what your grandmother used to say to her."

"Mom never sleeps in," Christine said.

"No, women usually don't."

"I wish I could talk to Mom."

"Can't you?"

"No. She just gets mad."

"What about?" David asked.

"Oh, just about anything, you know, serious," Christine said, taking a bite of the sandwich David had made her.

They chewed for a moment in silence which David decided not to break.

"Like sex and stuff like that," Christine said. "I told her the other day what my friend Julie said her mother told her, that once she started going out with boys, she ought to be on the pill. I didn't mean I wanted to. I just wanted to discuss it. But Mom just went beserk!"

"What do you think about the pill?" David asked, the impropriety of his question so shocking to him that he felt unnaturally calm.

"Well, for one thing it isn't supposed to be very good for you," Christine said.

David nodded and tried to swallow a piece of sandwich that seemed to swell as he chewed it.

"But Julie said that's all boys want, and they'll work on you until they get it, or they'll just quit taking you out."

"That's true of some," David said, "but not all. How well do you know Jerry?"

"I don't know," Christine said, "but I can tell you this: if it turns out that that's all he wants, I'd rather stay home."

"Thank you," David said, smiling at her. "That will make my evening a good deal more peaceful."

"You don't have to wait up or anything."

"I certainly do."

That was one of Mary's instructions he would follow to the letter. He had always waited up for his own girls. Patricia was asleep on her feet by ten. He was naturally a night owl, and he tried to enjoy those hours alone, but one of the curses of his job was that it filled his head with wrecked cars. He had worried far more about road accidents than he had about his daughters' virtue. And that would be his concern tonight, he saw, when he greeted Jerry at the door. It was hard to believe he was old enough to drive a car, let alone be a seducer of innocent girls.

When David went back into the living room, he caught Tyler up on the couch in the living room window making kissing noises at the pair going down the steep walk to the street.

"That will do, Tyler," David said firmly. "You don't want to make a profession of being a nasty little brother. They only get bribed on television."

"All of a sudden she thinks she's somebody," Tyler said.

"She is somebody," David said. "She's your sister."

"I don't ever want to go out with a boy," Patsy announced.

"They improve as they age," David said. "You like your cousins well enough, don't you?"

"They're my cousins," Patsy said. "It's just so—I don't know—phony."

Christine, taking this giant step out of childhood, had embarrassed her brother and sister. How gratefully they surrendered to Monopoly and then the safety of their set bedtimes.

David sat down at the piano and played softly as he had always done, for this had always been for him a house of sleeping children.

Christine was home a full half hour before her deadline.

"Well, how was that?" David asked, getting up from the piano.,

"A while before I have to worry about the pill," she said with a grin. "He didn't even kiss me good night. But he did ask me to the Valentine dance at school."

"Wonderful!" David said.

If he had focused only on his young charges, David would have slept at once, but he instead thought of himself at fifteen with his sister, how much they had preferred each other's company, how gratefully they had inhibited and therefore postponed the sexual challenges in their lives. Everyone should be so twinned in adolescence. He must ask

Diana about this pill business. Surely mothers weren't marching their fifteen-year-olds off for a prescription! What kind of advice would she give? He had never really talked to her at all about her work, perhaps because talking about his own would have been entirely distasteful to him. Diana's life did not seem so much odd to him as without the perennial questions that went unanswered or badly answered from generation to generation, but of course she would have professional opinions. His wife would stir in her grave at the thought that David would value advice from *that* sister, particularly in sexual matters! But he trusted Diana far more than he had his wife or now his daughter, Mary, and not only because Diana was a doctor but because she had been true to her own desire.

The children were already in bed when Mary and Ted got home on Sunday night. Ted looked tired and a little seedy, but he was a man who had to shave twice a day and hadn't bothered. Mary's face wasn't as easy to read.

"We're beat," she said cheerfully.

"Too old for the high life," Ted admitted.

"We didn't last on the dance floor past eleven o'clock."

"And all Mary did in the pool was float."

"You and your heroic two lengths!" Mary said, laughing at him.

"Next time we're going to try a rest home," Ted said.

"You don't look any the worse for wear," Mary said to her father.

"I've had a fine time," David said.

"Oh, so did we, Daddie," Mary said, "and it's funny, but this is the first time since we moved here that it felt like coming home. Do you know what I mean?"

It was Ted who asked, "How did Chrissie get along?"

"Just fine. I'll let her give you the details."

He refused the drink Ted offered and went down to his

own quarters which felt to him, too, a little more like home. There on his desk were the airline tickets, and he had mailed a deposit cheque for a two-week stay at a place called The Road Runners' Club in Borrego Springs where there had been a cancellation. Now that Mary and Ted had been away, it would be less difficult for David to tell them about his own holiday. But it was with Diana and Constance he wanted to share the happy details.

"I called all the places you mentioned," David said. "But they were all full. Do you know this one?"

"Yes," Diana said. "We drove around it once. It's a mobile home park, but a really nice one with a golf course."

"They say it has a swimming pool," David said.

"Down there they all do."

"We're going to Borrego Springs, Constance," David said.

She gave him a smile of skeptical pleasure, brilliantly taunting, and he laughed.

"How was the weekend?" Diana asked.

"I'm not sure for Ted and Mary. Mary's inclined to say what I want to hear, but I think maybe she's beginning to get hold of herself. Maybe not having me around for a couple of weeks will be another good thing. I sometimes think I'm too good an audience for the five-year-old in her who still wants to have a good cry and curl up in a safe lap."

Constance's expression grew fixed. David was aware how difficult it was for her when he talked about his family, for, no matter how often he explained who they were, she had no place to store that information, and so it was the hardest kind of reminder to her of how shut off she was from ordinary human commerce.

"D., what did you do with teenaged girls who wanted contraceptives?" David asked.

"I thought you said this was Christine's first date!"

"She has a friend whose mother thinks any girl, once she gets interested in boys, should go on the pill."

"Yes, I've met my share of those," Diana said.

"What did you do?"

"Refused and then invited the mother into the waiting room while I had a talk with the daughter. I suppose some of them went elsewhere, but it's my experience that most girls don't want contraceptives. It takes away their last line of defense."

"What do you say to them?" David asked.

"She should tell them to give up men," Constance said, laughing, "but Diana is very broad-minded."

"I tell them not to have intercourse until they want to get pregnant. I ask them if they masturbate—a surprising number don't. I tell them how. I explain to them how a male reaches orgasm. I explain to them the number of ways there are for having sexual pleasure without penetration. And I tell them that any man who insists on it is basically a rapist."

"But not too broad-minded," Constance added.

"Is that fair?" David asked, "if the boys aren't given the same message?"

"They should be. I haven't had much to do with them, except as young fathers, a category I'm predisposed to. If I had a chance, however, I'd say to them that any girl who was willing was either stupid or manipulative, and either kind is expensive in ways most boys can't afford. There's an added dimension now. AIDS is spreading into the heterosexual population. If we don't teach children safe sexual practices, we face not only unwanted pregnancies and ordinary venereal diseases but a virus that kills."

"I've been reading about that in *The Body Politic,*" David said.

"What's that?"

"Canada's gay paper."

"Why would you read something like that?" Diana asked.

"I thought I might learn something from it, and I have," David said.

"About me?" Diana demanded.

"About your world," David said.

"I don't have a world, David, not in that sense," Diana said; her voice which had been clinically cool through this conversation was now simply frigid.

"If you're going to fight," Constance said, "I warn you, I'm on David's side."

"Why on earth would we have to fight?" David asked, entirely bewildered.

"Diana would rather sex was holy," Constance said.

"I would rather my brother didn't assume I speak from some kind of minority position!"

"I don't," David said, "except that you're in a minority of people who may know what you're talking about. I'm ignorant in ways that humiliate me."

"Reading about a homosexual subculture to understand me is insulting," Diana said coldly.

"Diana doesn't approve of parades," Constance said.

"They're beside the point," Diana said, speaking more sharply to Constance than David had ever heard her do.

"Do you simply accept all the injustice?" David asked.

"It has nothing to do with me."

"It could have ruined your career!" David protested. "People are still committing suicide when they're exposed!"

"So are pregnant girls," Diana said.

"Anyone can commit suicide," Constance seemed to agree.

"David, the point is that any number of things could have ruined my career, being a woman, being left-handed. If there hadn't been a war, I wouldn't have had the money to go to school. When people want to be unjust, any excuse will do."

"But it shouldn't be allowed," David argued.

"Changing things means killing people," Constance said, "whatever side you're on."

"You can't extend your sympathy to men arrested in public washrooms and think you're doing me any favor," Diana said.

"Do you think they *should* be arrested?"

"Of course not," Diana said, "but a lot of them will tell you it's God's will."

"Because they've been taught to feel ashamed."

"Everyone has been taught to feel ashamed about sex. Most of us outgrow it. I don't mean to sound unsympathetic about those who don't. But I do object to being lumped together with them as if I belonged to a meaningful minority. It isn't one."

"Then you don't see any point in amending the human rights legislation?" David asked.

"There are a hundred laws that should be changed. I'd sooner cast my lot with Morganthaller for abortion on demand if I had any political energy."

David felt emotionally and morally unhinged by this conversation. He was being confronted with whole areas of human experience about which he held no considered opinions. He knew Patricia's horror of abortion was part of her punitive grief, but it wasn't anything he'd ever thought about in a positive light. It shocked him to hear his sister so vehement in its support.

"I guess I have some moral reservations about that," he said.

"Men can afford to," Diana said.

He wanted to object to being so generalized, but it wasn't something he really wanted to argue about against her formidable experience and knowledge.

"Men are a meaningful minority, I suppose," Constance mused.

"When we're discussing things like terminating a pregnancy, I think so," Diana said.

And perhaps women were a meaningful majority when it came to self-righteousness, David pondered, as he rested on the bus from his battering. Was there any point in his attempt to reclaim the moral territory he had so long ago surrendered to Patricia if all he could do was surrender it to Diana? In relationship to women, men had the advantage only if they never took it; otherwise they were tyrants and rapists. David sighed and was given a sympathetic look by an old woman who was knitting a baby's sweater.

In his study, David picked up a copy of *The Body Politic* by which he had inadvertentlly offended his sister. She was the one who had brought up washroom sex. What he had been reading about was the blood-screening test for AIDS which might put numbers of people at political risk—not people, he had to admit, but homosexual males. But there was a story, too, about a lesbian couple who had won a custody case. And the photograph of Gale Wilhelm, a rediscovered novelist in her seventies, had the androgynous power that so often moved and sometimes intimidated him in his sister's face. What Diana would see, in the middle of the admittedly awful want ads, was a male nude, kneeling dreamily on a white bear rug with a bow and arrows in his hands. He looked vulnerable and silly, but, even as cupid, a hunter of hearts, he was "politically incorrect," part of the male romance with death. David had no more patience with that than Diana did, but he had tried to overlook such things in order to become familiar with the serious concerns of the gay community. It was crass of him to think of it as hers. Insulting even, yes. But, if David had to carry the burdens of his "meaningful minority" as Constance put it, how could Diana so completely dissociate from hers? It didn't exist, she said, at least not for her. David had no real male friends at all, no club, no bar, but that didn't let him claim he wasn't a man.

It was the label Diana objected to, as if by it he could dismiss her views as a lesbian plot against men's privilege and pleasure though they offered the young a good deal more freedom than he felt comfortable with, raised in a generation when below the belt was out of bounds for lovers as well as boxers.

How did one go about discussing such matters or even thinking about them without getting bogged down in personal defensiveness and inaccurate generalities? Diana, for all her medical candor, was really no better at it than he.

Jack never invited his father-in-law to lunch without a reason. David accepted, feeling he was responding to a summons. He mustn't let his apprehensions about Mary and her family spill over mindlessly onto Laura and hers, but he could not look forward simply to the pleasure he always took in his son-in-law's company, for whom he had never felt, as he did with Ted, the least bit fatherly. Jack was the only person with whom David felt an instinctive alliance, trusting his balance in this boat of family through all its weathers. It wasn't that they confided much in each other as that it was always an open possibility.

In the damp crush of students on the university bus, David mourned his old raincoat which, if it couldn't disguise him as one of them, might suggest he was a professor whose wife had taken the car for the day. He didn't even have a briefcase. How at home they all made themselves, eating their lunches, reading, a couple even trying to take notes as the bus swayed with new speed on Chancellor Boulevard. From the back of the bus came gusts of young male laughter, which did not distract the scholars at their work.

David didn't seriously regret his lack of a university education, but he did feel out of place as he stepped off the bus at the Faculty Club and walked up through the dead sticks of the winter rose garden. There were already plenty of signs of spring in his own garden. He knew where to look for Christmas roses, snow drops, early primroses, and everywhere daffodils poked strong green fingernails of leaves through the damp earth. But here on campus with its massed plantings of rhododendrons and roses, the show had not begun.

The winter mist hung so low over the water that only the deep laboring foghorn would alert a stranger to the fact that there was water, important water, just below the cliffs. Beyond it the invisible north mountains were as remote as spring.

David was early enough to hang up his coat and deposit his hat on the rack in the cloakroom before he went out into the central hall where he could warm himself by the great fire, a luxury he missed in his basement. It was a handsome building, a gift of a wealthy lumberman escaped from eastern Europe and determined to put a civilized face on this raw, young world. When it was first built, some of the faculty were embarrassed by it, used to a Quonset hut for a lunchroom, but only the most spartan among them failed to adjust to its opulence. By now it was an accepted establishment, even viewed with some nostalgia for those lost days of growing budgets and automatic raises in pay.

David saw Jack come through the main door with another man and thought for an unhappy moment that they might not be lunching alone, but Jack parted from his companion at the bottom of the stairs before he crossed over to greet David.

"Let's go into the dining room," Jack suggested. "It will be quieter there."

He had already reserved a window table which today could offer no more than an idea of a view. The menu the waiter handed to David had no list of prices; only Jack's would. David felt indulged. He could have a hot meal and not bother with anything more than a sandwich for supper. Jack signaled the wine steward.

"A double gin on the rocks and a soda water," he instructed and then said to David, "There's plenty of time for a drink, but the bar is jammed at lunch time."

David didn't protest. He liked the fact that Jack never pressed his abstemioius ways on other people.

"I caught sight of Ben on the way over," Jack said. "It still comes as a shock to me that I have a son old enough to be out here. Next year, both of them."

"He's settling in all right?"

"Well enough. He's restless about the size of all his classes. I'm sorry he has to be out here when we're not just cutting financial corners but gutting whole programs. The undergraduates are going through now like so many cans in a factory. But Ben's had more attention than was good for him. It's time he learned what matters to him whether he has an audience to play to or not. Mike is a different matter, but he'll have Ben."

The gin came. Its warmth in David's gut was as much a luxurious pleasure as the fire had been. Jack let him enjoy it. They grumbled together about how many years it would take the university and the CBC to recover from the deadly government blood-letting that seemed to go on and on. It was a topic they avoided around the family, not only because its details might not interest the others but because they didn't like to express their real apprehensions about the future in front of people whose well-being was in their hands.

"What we need is what Ontario's just got, a minority Liberal government dependent on the New Democratic Party. But we haven't a hope in hell of anything like that out here," Jack said.

David had nearly finished his lunch and had almost convinced himself that nothing was required of him beyond enjoying the food and Jack's company when Jack shifted position in his chair, signaling a shift of topic.

"Have you talked at all with Ted lately?" Jack asked.

"I don't really talk with Ted," David admitted. "He did say to me before Christmas that he was worried about Mary and losing patience with her, too. But that was before their weekend away. Since then, Mary seems to be on an evener keel."

"He's talking about leaving her," Jack said.

David might have been punched in the stomach. When the wave of nausea passed, he found himself shaking with rage.

"What kind of a silly bastard is he?" he shouted.

He was only faintly aware and totally indifferent to the stir his voice had caused at nearby tables.

"I'm sorry, David," Jack said and reached over to put a gentling hand on David's arm.

"But it's unthinkable!" David said, in a stage whisper nearly as audible as his shout had been.

David looked around him then, and the dining room full of contented feeders was suddenly intolerable to him.

"Could we get out of here?"

"Of course," Jack said.

When David had got his coat and hat and made his way out into the air, he was stalled in any further purpose. The mist was shifting. A cool, watery shaft of sunlight fell on the pavement at his feet.

"Why don't we go over to the Japanese garden?" Jack suggested.

They walked together in silence. David could hardly contain his fury at Jack, the one man who was supposed to be his ally, saying such a thing to him. Then he heard in his head, "Kill the bearer of bad news." But Jack shouldn't have allowed Ted to talk about it, even to entertain such an idea. It was not one of Ted's options, a man with a disturbed wife and three children.

They had gone through the gate of the gardens before Jack spoke again. "I'm sorry to upset you like this," he said. "But I think Ted needs your help. When I suggested he should talk to you, he said you'd simply kill him."

"He knows me better than I thought he did," David answered wryly.

They stood on the arching bridge over the pond, looking down at the carp nosing with a look of blind stupidity into the reeds at the bridge's foundation. Chinese symbol for wisdom, weren't they?

"It's the house, for one thing. Ted seems to think Mary's retreated back into childhood there."

"Sell the silly house," David said. "I should never have suggested the move."

"Mary won't hear of it. She says it's the only thing that is keeping her sane."

"It isn't Mary's decision to make," David said.

"Not technically, of course," Jack said. "I think there's some truth in what Ted has to say, but I think he's done some retreating back into childhood himself. He's stopped thinking about Mary and the children as entirely his responsibility. He said, if he tried to solve the problem by moving out and that didn't work, he'd be stuck with it, whereas if he leaves her there, she's at home, and you're there to look after her. He said, while they were away, you'd fixed everything in the house he'd been too depressed to deal with."

"To help!" David insisted.

"Of course," Jack said. "He's looking for ways to feel useless. If you hadn't done it, he'd use the burden of the house as an excuse."

"Well, what is to be done?" David pressed.

"Make him see he has other, better options."

David pictured Ted in all his masculine vanity with new and cold distaste.

"David, he's a basically good man. We all have times of being out of love with Mary."

Of course they had. What had created the absolute gulf between Ted and David was Ted's ability to contemplate leaving Mary. Marriage at its worst for David had been a prison term of solitary confinement, at its best the framing joy of his life. He had so little entertained the possibility of ever leaving Patricia that it even seemed his duty, against actuarial expectation, to outlive her. How could he have a rational discussion with a man who didn't know his wife was his own flesh?

He couldn't. His anger crippled him. Instead that

evening he served temporary notice to both his daughter and son-in-law.

"I'm going to Southern California for a couple of weeks on Monday."

"Monday?" Mary repeated in surprise.

"Yes, with my sister. We're taking our old bones to the sun."

"Two weeks?" Ted asked.

"That's right," David answered, giving Ted an appraising look from which he glanced away.

It was Mary who followed him down the stairs.

"I don't want you to go," she said.

"Why not?"

"I don't think I can manage . . ."

"Go back upstairs and have this conversation with Ted," David said sharply.

"With Ted?" she asked, puzzled.

"Your husband," David answered, as if he were speaking to Constance.

"Daddie . . ."

"Don't call me Daddie. You're a grown woman."

"Oh well, then, go!"she said, turned and left him.

CHAPTER X

"When Una Troubridge was asked how she and Radclyffe Hall, as Catholics, managed confession, she said they had nothing to confess."

Diana looked over at Constance, too used to these non sequiturs to be surprised. They were like messages in bottles washing up after years on the shores of her consciousness.

"Any Christian has a lot to rationalize," Diana said.

"You're like them," Constance said. "You want to be innocent. I don't care about being guilty."

"Nobody responsible can be innocent," Diana said. "I've made terrible mistakes. Loving you isn't one of them."

Constance smiled. The commercials were over. She punched the sound back on and returned her attention to the television. They were watching a movie Diana couldn't have recounted any better than Constance. Not for the first time, Diana had the impression that Constance was not watching the movie but reading Diana's mind.

Since David's last visit, Diana had been able to think about little else but their argument. No one but Constance and occasionally Jill had ever forced Diana into conversation about the value judgments out there in the ignorant and bigoted public mind. Constance flirted with opinions nearly as outrageously as she flirted with people, not because she had any intention of living with them but to see what they were like.

"How do I look, guilty?" she might ask, as if she were trying on a pantsuit in a shop.

"It just isn't you," Diana would answer.

Diana steadfastly refused to wear any label, and it horrified her now to hear of young women who called themselves not only lesbians but dykes, as if they took on the world's judgment of them and flaunted it. And now here was her brother, taking up the label and thinking he could sanitize it.

"You see?" says the moral dry-cleaner. "Spotless! Now won't you put it on and see how becoming it is after all?"

It was a uniform worn by a bunch of mercenaries pretending that their appetite to shock and horrify was instead a holy crusade. Or by the guilty, who smudged it on their foreheads as a penitence. Either stance went on contributing to the crucial and fundamental misunderstanding of the nature of sexuality which couldn't be isolated, labeled, and then judged by any system of real values. It was like trying to decide whether the power of speech was a gift from God or the devil.

But no matter which direction her argument took in her head, she came up against David's puzzlement at her fury, as if it weren't a topic about which she needed such righteous indignation to make herself clear. Why did something about which she was so sure come out sounding arrogant, snobbish and, yes, even fearful?

"This is drivel," Constance said. "It doesn't say 'bed' here, but everything else is crossed off."

"Jill's coming tomorrow with some new clothes for you to try on, for the desert. We're going next week," Diana said, after she had gratefully turned off the set. "And then she's going to spend the afternoon while I go hunt up some things for myself."

"Do I need new clothes?"

"We both do. We should really send everything we own to the Sally Ann and start all over again."

Jill had to make two trips from her small car.

"Sometimes a back seat would be handy," she admittted. "Marty put this sun hat on top of the pile so it would look like an overstuffed passenger."

Diana didn't have the figure for Marty's clothes on 10th Avenue, but in the old days Constance had often shopped there. Jill, with Marty's help, and chosen wonderfully well. The confusion of bright colors on the bed delighted Constance.

"I don't know where to begin!" she exclaimed.

"Try these white slacks," Jill suggested. "Then you can keep them on for various tops."

Diana and Jill sat on the two bedroom chairs in a conspiracy of pleasure. Constance stepped into the trim white slacks, then rummaged among the tops with increasing uncertainty.

"They all look too big," she confessed.

"The latest style," Jill reassured her, getting up to assist. "Look, try this one."

It was a brilliant watermelon pink, cut like a man's shirt with tails. Constance disappeared into it, her head emerging out of volumes of material.

"Push up the sleeves," Jill suggested, laughing.

"It's below my knees," Constance protested.

Diana laughed. "It's wonderful though. You've always been able to get away with anything!"

"Have I?"

Other women Constance's size would have looked lost, but her authoritative beauty along with the agile confidence with which she moved allowed her any style she wanted to take on.

"Decide before you take anything off whether you like it or not," Diana suggested, knowing Constance's capacity to choose was so limited that without clear help she could easily fail before the task.

When she'd succeeded in finding four tops and when a pair of lavender slacks had been added to the white, they paused for mid-morning coffee. Refreshed, Constance tried on jump suits, one terry cloth, one velour, a long white sweater, a raincoat, a robe. At the selection of bathing suits, she balked.

"We're going to the desert. There's a pool," Diana reminded her.

"I don't know how to swim."

"I think you'll remember," Diana encouraged.

"I'm too old," Constance said.

"Everyone's our age down there. If I can get into a suit, you can."

"Look," Jill said. "Here's one with a wrap to match."

Constance flung off her clothes. In nakedness she was trim-fleshed, her small breasts still clearly defined, but, when she stepped into the one-piece suit, her upper arms and her thighs were suddenly singled out and exposed, the slight flesh sagging under the draping skin. Jill quickly handed her the wrap. But she didn't put it on at once. She stood before the long mirror contemplating herself.

"I'm melting away," she said, an innocent bewilderment in her voice.

"You'll put the forty-year-olds to shame," Jill said gallantly. "Here, put this on."

Obediently Constance did, and the wrap restored her to herself.

"That's not too bad," she admitted.

When the task was finished, she had chosen nearly half the clothes Jill had brought, and they were all delighted. Silently Diana rebuked herself for having let Constance's wardrobe deteriorate over the last few years. She had cut more pleasures out of their life than was necessary, trying to protect Constance from confusion and fear. It had become an excuse, too, for things like shopping which Diana found difficult to do.

"Thank you," Diana said to Jill, embracing her, before Diana took up her new cane and went off on her own expedition.

"See you do as well for yourself," Jill admonished.

Diana didn't expect to, but she was much encouraged by the number of outsized garments in the stores. They may have been intended for slight teenagers, but they actually fit her. Finding a bathing suit was another matter, but there was a shop in Kerrisdale which specialized in swim wear, and it carried not only large sizes but suits for women who had lost breasts to cancer. Though Diana looked like a grotesquely blown up toy which a wrap only exaggerated, there were her still good legs. She shook her head at herself in the mirror. It was amazing what vanity could survive.

Her shoulders and neck ached from pulling things on and off over her head. Her feet hurt, but she did have time to stop on her way home for a haircut, and at least she could sit down for it. It was a good cut, shorter than usual, but shaped to a head that carried its authority of grey proudly.

"You look marvelous!" Constance exclaimed when Diana arrived home.

"Well," Diana said, dumping her packages on the couch, "I'm done in."

The pain she had learned to ignore at its lower levels burned down her back, shot through her feet, and her hands trembled with it.

"What you need is a drink," Jill suggested kindly.

"It's just what I don't need, ever, but I'd love one," Diana admitted.

Jill stayed to cook dinner, for which Diana was grateful. She sat with her drink, listening to a violin concerto, while Constance gently rubbed her neck. To be cared for and cherished in this kind of domestic harmony was something that perhaps couldn't be learned except in old age where the needs of the flesh, though humiliating, were rarely competitive. It was an accomplishment that came out of failure.

The late winter dawn was just lighting the low clouds when the doorbell sounded. She and Constance had been ready for half an hour though Ben and David were early. David sent Ben upstairs for the suitcases while he himself made a check of the kitchen, the basement, and finally the windows and doors on the ground floor.

"What is he looking for?" Constance asked.

"What I've forgotten to do," Diana answered, but she was glad of his thoroughness.

It had been years since Diana had put the house on hold and left it to its own mechanical life while she and Constance went off into the world. She let her domestic apprehensions occupy her mind so that she did not anticipate the fears of travel any more than she could help. And here was David willing to share even those with her.

She and Constance sat in the back seat. Ben drove with the alert confidence of the young, swinging them out into the traffic on Granville Street more quickly than Diana could have risked, but she felt quite safe in his hands. Next to him David looked less substantial, the back of his neck thin and vulnerable, his shoulders the hanger for his jacket without a sign of those functional muscles which played under Ben's sweater as he did a final shift of gears to the settled speed he would maintain until they got to the bridge which would lift them over the Fraser River. It was full of stored log booms this morning around which tugs must navigate carefully as they pulled enormous barges to the mouth of the river and then around Point Grey to the Vancouver docks.

Diana had taken no interest in local industry until she and Constance had come back after the war. Constance had been fascinated by the log booms, pulp mills, lumber mills, the working water of the inner harbor, and was full of questions Diana couldn't answer.

Now Constance did not look out the window. She stared down at her hands, softly humming, a sound Diana could just discern over the sound of the motor. She rested a hand on Constance's knee, not to shift her attention so much as to be part of it.

David had ordered a wheelchair for Diana. He settled her into it while Ben strapped the three suitcases onto a set of luggage wheels. Then David went round and opened the door for Constance.

"Where's Diana?" she asked, alarmed.

"Right over there, look," David showed her. "She won't have to do all that long walking. We're at the airport. We're going south."

Diana felt a moment of frustrated helplessness. How could she in this chair be reassuring to Constance? But her temptation to get out of it was unrealistic.

"You must help me," Diana called.

"Am I to push?" Constance asked, suddenly amused, "or ride in your lap?"

"Whichever you prefer," Diana answered.

Constance pushed Diana. Ben pushed the luggage right to the immigration and customs barrier and then took his quick leave.

"We should have brought him along," Diana said, sorry to see him go, leaving David with the luggage, the wheelchair, and Constance, when he also needed hands for tickets, customs declarations, boarding passes, all the paraphernalia that made boarding a plane so nerve-wracking.

Perhaps being so preoccupied with details took his mind off the flight itself. Diana knew that, because he'd spent his whole professional life aware of catastrophes, the word *plane* for him was automatically followed by *crash*. He wouldn't be aware, since he no longer listened to the news or read a paper, that two bombs had been planted in this airport only a few months ago, one to explode in Japan just before it was loaded onto a plane bound for India, the other exploding in mid-flight over Ireland, also on its way to India. Terrorists and hijackers were less likely to get on a plane flying to Palm Springs.

Diana wasn't privy in the same way to Constance's fears. Just now she seemed withdrawn as she had been in the car. Often being in the public world made her intro-spective, both acutely aware and confused. Perhaps having the wheelchair to hang on to gave her an anchor and responsiblity.

David went through customs ahead of them so that he could manage the suitcases which needed to be lifted up onto the ramp, cleared, and then carried to a moving belt which carried them out to the loading station. Diana managed to speak for both Constance and herself, willing the wheelchair into a throne from which she could command the customs officer's attention. Constance could have done it herself, but she stayed focused on getting Diana through.

Freed of luggage, David took over the chair when they got to the escalator where he turned it round and tipped it backwards onto the moving stairs. Constance stood and watched as they moved up away from her.

David, trapped behind Diana's chair, called out, "Con-stance!"

Diana, too, called out, "Constance, come with us!"

But Constance seemed unable to move.

At the top David shoved Diana abruptly away from the escalator exit and flung himself down the stationary stairs. Diana inexpertly turned herself around to see what was happening. In a moment, there were David and Constance making their way up the stairs.

"Bomb shelters," Constance said.

The escalator had obviously called up the memory of London tube stations used as bomb shelters during the war, but, restored to Diana's chair, Constance walked resolutely along until they got to their waiting area where they had the pick of the chairs.

"We're early," David said. "Well, so far, so good."

Diana's heart was still beating too quickly and she was as short of breath as if she had been the one who took those stairs two at a time to retrive Constance, but the most difficult maneuvers were over now. David chose a small bench isolated from the main waiting areas, big enough for himself and Constance with space for Diana's wheelchair. They sat and watched the lounge slowly fill with people, mostly old like themselves, learning to take advantage of their geriatric freedom. Once or twice Diana thought she could recognize a face from her school or college days. She was grateful that her own age disguised her so thoroughly. Only an ex-patient might recognize her, and too few would have reached this age to make it likely. David had lived his professional life invisible. Only Constance might be spotted, but she was in little danger of being approached. People had an aversion to acknowledging their gardener at the theatre or a concert, or on an expensive holiday like this one. Her presence tended to blur their sense of distinction.

Still, as an isolated little group, they attracted people's curiosity. Constance stayed so attached to the wheelchair she would appear to be Diana's attendant. Even when they were pre-boarded, Constance didn't surrender the chair to a cabinet attendant but pushed it herself, and David stayed carefully and protectively behind them not to be trapped again with the chair between him and Constance.

"Would you like the window seat?" Diana asked her.

"All right," Constance said.

"Let me be on the aisle," David suggested.

So Diana settled herself between them, a placing that would have made her faintly claustrophobic under any other circumstance, but with Constance in her seat belt and with David there on the other side, Diana could finally relax into excitement and remember how much she loved to travel.

As the plane taxied out onto the runway, Diana turned to David and said, "I love the takeoff."

"Do you?" he said, surprised.

"Don't you?"

"Well, I'm glad I'm not the pilot," David said.

He didn't seem nervous so much as resigned. Constance looked out the window. As the engines revved up, she reached over and took Diana's hand. Diana reached over and took David's.

"This is wonderful of you, you know," Diana said to him.

After his pre-lunch gin, David's mood lifted. He began naming the mountains for Constance. As he leaned across Diana in order to see, sometimes using her shoulder for balance as he half-stood, she recognized the casual physical intimacy from her girlhood which made such absolute claim, making no claim at all. Her own gesture had had to be deliberate.

"What a silly picnic," Constance said, as they sat in a row with their elbows carefully tucked in at their sides, "everything is either too hot or too cold."

It wasn't good food, but both Diana and David ate every bit of it, down to the packet of cheese and crackers which Constance slipped into her handbag and would come upon weeks later if Diana didn't remember to remove it.

Hardly had the trays been cleared away when Diana could feel the beginning of the long descent into Palm Springs. Constance twisted restlessly in her seat.

"It's your ears," Diana said. "We're starting down to the landing."

"Will you stay with me?" Constance asked.

"Of course," Diana said. "We're getting a car at the airport, and then we'll drive over to Borrego Springs in the desert. We've been there before, and you've always loved it."

Diana had packed Constance's memory board as one more thing to carry and perhaps lose, but she realized how much in limbo Constance was without it unless she kept being reminded of where she was and what lay ahead. It was at the top of the suitcase. She would get it before they loaded the suitcases into the car.

Diana could feel David's different nervousness on her other side as he checked luggage claim tickets, car authorization, the road map, the little map of the Road Runner's Club which showed them which house was to be theirs. Diana was glad she would do the driving to take at least that burden from him.

Neither of the other two sat as patiently as Diana did while the plane emptied of its other passengers.

"Here we go," David finally said with some relief. "I said you could manage the stairs if there was a wheelchair waiting at the bottom."

Dry, Diana gratefully thought, as she slowly descended the stairs onto the tarmac where the chair waited.

"Well," David said after he'd stowed the last of the suitcases and got himself into the back seat of their rented car.

Diana had the memory board propped against the steering wheel and was writing the names of the desert towns they would pass through.

"Now, we can go on today or stop here if you think this has been enough," David said.

"It's only about an hour and a half, and it's easy driving," Diana said.

David sat with the map spread out across his knees, but at the first decision requiring a turn, when Diana glanced into the rear view mirror, she saw that her navigator was asleep. She knew the turnings; there weren't many. Soon they were on highway 86, a long straight two-lane road, the railroad on their left, great shaggy date-palm groves on their right, on their way to Salton Sea.

"I must have had a dream like this," Constance said, "or else I'm dreaming."

"You're awake," Diana said. "Feel the air."

Dry and warm and faintly dusty, it had already worked its magic on Diana's joints. She could turn her head farther and more easily. There was no pain in her shoulders, and her knees did her easy bidding.

When they finally made the right-hand turn that took them into the badlands, Diana spoke to David and watched him start awake.

"I don't want you to miss this part," she said.

"I *must* be dreaming," Constance said.

"We all must be," David said.

For the landscape now was bleakly beautiful, only the road indicating the human way through it, a fragile way which dipped into dry flat beds, marked each time by a small sign WATCH FOR FLASH FLOODS and rose again into dunes, sparsely figured with giant cacti.

"I must have watched too many of those awful movies with the kids," David said. "I keep expecting a giant lizard to lumber over the crest of a hill. It's dinosaur country."

"Does it ever rain here?" Constance asked.

"Half an inch can wash out the road. One year we had to wait a couple of extra days to get out," Diana said. "But you can see the storms coming out of the west over those mountains."

"Do we cross those?" David asked.

"No, Borrego Springs is this side of them," Diana said.

Child of the rain forest, Diana never ceased to be surprised at how at home she felt on this desert, how it answered some longing in her spirit for bold simplicity. She was touched, too, by its fragility. And knew Constance felt she dreamed it because it was so like her, timeless and changing at the will of the weather, wind and water uprooting and transfiguring in the circling seasons.

Suddenly they dropped out of the badlands onto the flat floor of the desert and sped along a more substantial road past an airport maintained mainly for private planes, and then there was the green oasis of The Road Runner Club with its palm-lined drive that led directly to the clubhouse and pool.

For Diana all the landmarks were familiar. The other two peered out of the slowly moving car with suspicious curiosity. As instructed by the map, they drove to the house assigned them. They wouldn't have to check in at the office until the next morning.

"We're in luck!" Diana exclaimed, as she turned into the carport.

The house, a mobile home like all the others, its license plate tacked to the side wall, was imbedded in concrete. The side which faced the road had a screened porch the full length of the house, which gave them an unobstructed view of the western mountains, and it was well furnished with comfortable chairs and a table for eating on or for setting up a puzzle. The living room had a dining ell that faced south. The narrow kitchen was well-equipped with dishwasher and microwave as well as an ordinary stove and refrigerator. The larger of the two bedrooms had a dressing room and bath, the other bathroom opened onto the hall next to the smaller bedroom.

"This is really very nice," David said. "I've never been

in one of these before."

"I'm just going to drive into town and get some groceries before the store closes," Diana said. "I won't be more than half an hour."

It was too abrupt a way to leave Constance, but Diana had no choice. David didn't yet know the town, and she doubted that he wanted to drive the car though he might not mind once he saw for himself how wide the roads were, how little the traffic and easy the parking. And nearly everyone behind the wheel would make him look like a boy.

There was the little Mexican restaurant still. Might they even be able to go out for dinner? Diana swung the car around Christmas Circle and was in the little town with its shabby, high-priced market and its several competing liquor stores. There would be gin tonight for David, scotch for herself and Constance.

Diana could harldy believe how agile she was as she got out of the car and nearly strode into the store. Her liberated body was still connected to Constance by a taut string, but she was a kite in the sweet desert air, not a fish straining into the hurting dark. She could hurry. She could be extravagant.

The valley lay in the shadow of the mountains as she made her way home. It did feel like going home. David and Constance came out to help carry things in.

"You're all unpacked," David announced, "though Constance keeps telling me we must have claimed the wrong luggage because she doesn't recognize a single thing of either hers or yours."

"They're all new, that's why," Diana said, kissing Constance.

"Whole suitcases full?" Constance asked.

"Look at the size of that gin bottle!" David said. "Can I drink that in two weeks?"

"Well, be careful of it," Diana said. "American drink is stronger than ours."

"Do you know how to use a microwave oven?" David asked.

"I'm too old for that sort of thing."

"But I do," David said. "Both the girls have them. Bacon, good. I can do you wonderful bacon for breakfast."

"I got it for chicken livers tonight," Diana said. "Something quick after this long day."

But she didn't really feel tired, and David was obviously refreshed from his nap in the car. Only Constance showed the strain of the trip, a dark brightness in her eyes which was her will straining against her fearful uncertainty. Though she couldn't really help in the kitchen, she stayed there in the way until all the groceries were settled and they could go into the living room together for their drinks. Then she sat on the couch, needing Diana to sit beside her.

Diana put her arm around Constance and said, "You're marvelous. You did it, all the way from Vancouver."

"Here's to our holiday," David said, raising his glass.

"You're going to stay with me?" Constance asked.

"Of course we are," Diana said.

"Are we locked in?"

"Not yet," David said, "but I'm going to fix the doors tonight so that we'll all be safe."

"We're never safe," Constance said.

"As safe as we need to be," David answered.

He insisted on cooking this first meal by himself, claiming the kitchen too narrow for two people to work, and Diana let him. She needed to stay quiet with Constance, to give her time to be reassured. Because Diana was so full

of promises to herself, of swimming, of walking out onto
the desert, of driving out to the grapefruit groves, she
might have offered those things to Constance if Diana had
not known it was too soon for them to sound like anything
but impossible demands. There was time. They could live
the days slowly. Right now it seemed the greatest of riches
to be sitting here with Constance, looking out beyond the
screened porch to the last light on the ridge of the western
mountains.

Diana woke hearing voices very near, right beyond their
open bedroom window.

"Who are they?" Constance asked. "Where are we?"

"Golfers," Diana decided. "They're up with the sun.
We're on the desert."

She smelled bacon.

"David's playing with the microwave."

Constance was like a cat in a new place, hesitant at
every threshold, head up, listening, sniffing, but she understood the workings of the shower and had to show Diana
how to turn it on, and she was pleased with the white
slacks, oversized pink shirt and white, velcro-fastening
shoes.

If Constance was catlike, David bounded around like an
over-excited dog. He'd already been out for a look around,
had found two lemons lying in the road, fallen from an
immodestly bearing tree.

Because the birds feasting on berries just beneath the
south window didn't startle away when the three of them
sat down for breakfast, they realized they must be looking
through one-way glass. Not only could they be secretly

intimate with the birds, they could watch the parade of people without being watched themselves.

"It must be men's day on the golf course," Diana said.

David was comically alarmed at the golfers' attire. Old men went by in bright pink, egg yolk yellow, and lime-green trousers with garishly patterned shirts, sporting billed caps from the major tractor companies of the nation.

"They must all be prairie farmers," David said.

"Did you bring a sun hat?" Diana asked.

"Yes, and I've even got prescription sunglasses. Oh, I'm prepared all right, but I'm not going to look like it."

"I seem to be the latest thing," Constance said, looking down at herself, "but I'm sure I've got on Diana's shirt."

"There's quite a good men's shop in town," Diana said to David. "You'll have to get yourself something outlandish."

She expected him to protest, but he didn't. He looked tempted.

After breakfast they went for a walk around the settlement. Though all of the some three hundred houses were mobile units, most of them double like their own, they didn't look alike. Sidings and roofs varied, and each landscaping of their tiny front yards was distinctive. Most people had accepted the desert and had chosen from a large variety of cacti at home in this climate, set out on crushed rock of various colors, but one garden they passed could have been found in southern England. Constance paused before it for some minutes.

"My mother had a sister in Sussex," she said.

As they turned into the most northerly road, they felt the wind, degrees colder than the sunny still air they had been sheltering in, and they saw the tumbleweed speeding across the open desert to be stopped by a wire fence where it was piled nearly six feet high.

A roadrunner, looking as ridiculous as it did on ashtrays and cocktail napkins, dashed across their path, appraising them with one startling red, white, and blue eye.

"The owner?" David asked.

"They're all over," Diana said. "People feed them ground beef."

They circled round, sometimes stopping to watch golfers tee off on the little course that wound around the settlement, admiring great patches of desert daisies, trees lit with grapefruit and oranges and lemons, until they reached the pool enclosure. No one was in the pool, but two women sat amiably visiting in the Jacuzzi.

"I do want to try that," David said.

Constance was persuaded into her suit and wrap, but she eyed Diana with critical scepticism.

"We're really going out like this?"

"Everyone does. It's only across the road. Come on."

David waited for them on the screened porch, his thin hairy legs exposed below his short terry cloth robe. Constance burst into laughter.

"Come on," he said in his turn, taking Constance firmly by the arm. "We'll be beauty and the beast."

Constance would have nothing to do with the water. She sat in the sunny shelter against a wall, inscrutable behind dark glasses. Diana was glad the two women who had been there were gone. Even by themselves, she felt self-conscious as she took a firm hold of the railing and stepped down into the pool. The water was warm. For a moment she forgot the mocking Constance and her brother behind her, watching that misshapen old body, exposed. The water took her weight from her, and she swam the length of the pool and back.

"Bravo!" David shouted.

"It's wonderful. Come in."

Purposefully, Diana turned away as he took off his robe, and then he was in the water with her, still with his glasses and white sun hat on, swimming the breaststroke like a stately turtle.

When they got out and went into the Jacuzzi Constance was persuaded to sit on the edge and dabble her feet, but she wouldn't actually join them.

"I could live in this," David said.

"No more than five minutes," Diana warned, but her medical good sense vied with the pleasure she took in the heat.

A pair of men, discussing golf scores, came into the enclosure. Before they could join Diana and David, the sister and brother in unspoken agreement got out, put on their robes and took Constance back to the house.

Constance did not want her puzzle set up on the porch.

"I'd feel like an animal in the zoo," she said.

It discouraged Diana that even here Constance couldn't escape the sense of imprisonment, but Diana didn't argue. She cleared the coffee table in the living room instead and set out a puzzle of flowers Jill had found.

David also chose to stay indoors, for the glare of the sun troubled his eyes. He read for a few minutes and then sighed. Constance looked over at him.

"Old as I am," he said, "I'm still looking for miracles. I just can't read."

"Do you want me to read to you?" Constance asked.

It was a solution that hadn't occurred to Diana.

"Would you?" David asked. "I haven't got very far. We could start at the beginning again."

"It makes no difference to me," Constance said wryly.

She took the book from him and began on the page where he had lost patience with his difficulty. Diana went into the kitchen to fix lunch. Her own uncertain hearing let her know only that what Constance read must be a novel. Diana had never been a novel reader, but Constance had. Though she wouldn't be able to keep the story line in mind, she'd probably enjoy it scene by scene. Far more important, of course, was that she was doing something for David. It wasn't a trumped up activity like sketching to fill empty time.

Diana could now sit on the porch or go into their bedroom to read her own books, or she could go into town to shop, knowing she left them contented. She could even sketch if she wanted to. There *were* miracles, and maybe they were easier to recognize when everything else began to fail.

Constance wouldn't remember how much she liked American cottage cheese and San Francisco salami, but she could still taste and enjoy them. Diana was beginning to learn her brother's tastes, too. It didn't matter to her that he wouldn't notice either, having lived a life in which he was catered to. Real contentment shouldn't often be disturbed by gratitude.

Constance went to bed early that night. David and Diana took nightcaps out onto the porch and sat in the dark so that they could see the desert sky, bright with stars as their northern sky rarely was.

"What a lovely place," David said, "and it's so good for you, D."

"To think I didn't believe we'd ever get here again."

"You ought to live in this climate," David said.

"It would be nice if we could import it."

"Haven't you ever considered living down here, in the winter anyway?"

"I used to, but even before travel got so difficult, I realized I'm too political a creature to stand the American climate for any length of time."

"There are a lot of flags about," David said.

"And probably nearly half the people are Canadian," Diana said, "but the rest are retired American military who think it's unpatriotic to discuss politics."

"I'd get along with them nicely," David confessed.

"You're too amiable," Diana said, smiling.

"It's not that I don't have the courage of my convictions. I just don't have very many."

"Perhaps you'll teach me to shed some of mine," Diana said.

"Do you think Constance has forgotten how to swim?"

"I don't know," Diana said. "If she'd learned when she was a child, I'd feel surer about encouraging her. I never know whether I trust her instincts too much or not enough."

"She's amazing," David said.

"Yes," Diana agreed and was tempted to add, so are you, but the silence felt more comfortable.

They sat for some minutes before Diana reluctantly gave in to the sleep threatening to overcome her. Out of habit, she braced herself to get up and nearly catapulted herself out of the chair. She laughed, surprised.

"I'm so agile, I'm going to have to be careful not to break a leg!"

David did not go in with her. He probably needed a little time to himself, and she must see that he got it through the day as well. For her, having someone else to think about and be with was a relief. For David, taking on the responsibility of two peculiar old women must be exhausting. Diana had the sense to know that, of the two, she presented him with the greater difficulty.

"Who is it?" Constance cried and sat up.

"Me," Diana answered, gathering Constance into her arms.

"Oh, you," Constance said, relaxing into the embrace.

It will be all right, Diana thought to her, I promise you, it will be all right.

CHAPTER XI

David declined the use of the car and set out on foot into the little town. It was only a mile away, and it was a cool, windless morning. He needed the exercise, for he was nearly apprehensive with happiness. The components of it were obvious: they had managed the trip without serious incident and arrived in a comic little paradise which overnight had transformed his sister from a near cripple into an athlete, and, though Constance was still tense with uncertainty, she was comfortable enough with him to read to him. But what pleased him most, what he could not have said he wanted beforehand, was his sense of being one of three people equally engaged in the routines and pleasures of the day. He had not ever expected to get over feeling alone, only hoped gradually to be more resigned to it. But now for two weeks he was going to be one of three, and his being alone, walking along the desert road toward the town, toward the mountains, only seemed to emphasize the connectedness he felt.

He was, he supposed, in some quite simple way in love with Constance. Perhaps he had always been. He certainly remembered the first day he had met her, the shock of her loveliness so beyond his ambition as a lover. He had also known, without articulating it to himself, that his sister was in love with Constance. When Patricia put an ugly name to it, he was stunned at first and then a little in awe of them. When he made his yearly birthday visit, he had the irrational sense that he was the one who was banished, that his ordinary life didn't qualify him for any intimacy with them.

David still sometimes felt that Diana had gone too far beyond him for him ever to stand with her as he had once stood, her twin. That self knowledge which had made her left-handed had also freed her to love Constance, had given her the direction to become a doctor, sure that her life was her life while his seemed fixed by accident, shaped by other people. But those differences assumed less importance now. As he got to know his sister again, who she was, rather than what she had accomplished, engaged him. And she was very recognizably his sister, old. She needed more courage than he did because she was basically shyer, because she was proud. Pride had always been a defense in her rather than a fault. Perhaps his amiability was in him too. Their temperaments had balanced when they were young. Why shouldn't they now?

"I am not as young as I feel right now," David said to himself. Being old made that possible.

He looked up at the barren hides of the mountains. Though they were very different from the lushly green mountains he was used to, they were mountains all the same, and he felt at home with their defining presence.

He came to the grocery store and did not go in. He wanted to walk the town first. He discovered the shopping mall with its expensive shops, its art gallery, its banks, like a chunk of suburbia tacked onto this little desert town for the money-spending tourists. He was glad to turn back away from the new condominiums beyond the mall and find himself again in the more authentic street. He looked in at a bar, a large U shape with high stools where several locals in dusty work clothes were having a morning beer. Around the corner he found a country hardware store and then a little library.

Constance would read to him. He went in. Seating space seemed designed for children, and he was glad to think that not everyone in the valley was over sixty-five. Somewhere there must be ordinary houses, a school. He browsed through the small adult collection, not quite as glutted with mysteries, science fiction and romance as he'd feared it would be. There was even a shelf of poetry.

Might poems be more of a pleasure to Constance? David picked up a volume of Auden. Then he found a collection of Eudora Welty's short stories. If he could find a good biography, maybe Diana would sometimes join them, but perhaps not a literary biography. He would ask her first. She needed the time to herself.

Back in the grocery store, David peered at the various offerings of Mexican food. Would it all be too hot for their aging digestions? He made a note of what meats were available. The prices seemed reasonable until he remembered they were in American dollars. He picked up the chicken Diana thought might be good for dinner.

The sun was warmer now as David walked back down the road, but the dry heat of it on his shoulders was as welcome as a back rub. The chicken and the books weighed a little more heavily before he got back to the house, and he was thirsty.

"Did I see beer when we were unpacking last night?" he asked.

"You did," Diana called to him from the living room. "Would either of you like anything?"

"Iced water," Constance called.

"I was about to get us some lunch," Diana said, coming into the kitchen. "How did you like the town?"

"I found the library," David said, holding up the books.

The fruit salad Diana made for them had a taste so distinctive to David that for a moment he was sitting at his mother's table.

"What is it?" he asked. "What did you put in the salad?"

"Miracle Whip," Diana said.

David laughed. It was one of the few arguments about food which he'd had with Patricia, and she had won it, he was embrrassed to remember, by saying that no one with any refinement of taste ate Miracle Whip, that she would be embarrassed to have it in her refrigerator. She either made her own mayonnaise or used Best Foods, and the tangy sweetness of sandwiches and salads had been removed from his palate for over forty years. He couldn't really say that he liked it any longer, only that its taste recalled his childhood.

"Don't you like it?" Diana asked.

"It's delicious," he lied, believing it might be again as he got used to it.

"Constance used to make her own," Diana said.

"Did I?" Constance asked.

"Do some tastes make you remember?" David asked.

"Smells," Constance said, "but I think I've been away from home all my life, haven't I?"

"Yes," Diana said.

"Is home a house or a landscape or a country?" David asked.

"All those," Constance said. "And people. If I'm alone and look at my board and it says, for instance, 'lunch,' it's easier for me to expect to sit down with my mother and sister than to remember it will be Diana there. I remember the forks. I remember the pattern on the dishes, the shape of the teapot. At this table I don't recognize anything familiar."

"There isn't," Diana said. "We just got here."

"Do you remember those cheese glasses we used to drink orange juice from in the morning?" David asked his sister.

"Yes," she said, smiling, "and I swore I'd never save a cheese glass again."

"And I wish I still had one," David said.

"Why don't the birds know we're here?" Constance asked.

"One-way glass," David said. "They can't see us."

"Would you like to move the table?" Diana asked.

"No," Constance said. "It's like remembering, isn't it? You can see so clearly, but you can't make them see you. Knock on that glass. It wouldn't help. They'd simply fly away."

David washed the taste of childhood out of his mouth with a long drink of iced tea.

"It says," Constance said, looking at her board, " 'Read to David' with a question mark. What does that mean?"

"If he's in the mood," Diana said, "and you are."

"I like that," Constance said. "There should be more question marks. Why couldn't everything be question-marked?"

"It could," Diana said.

"Would you like to be read to?" Constance asked.

"I would," David said. "Do you like poetry?"

"I don't know. It doesn't matter."

How bright she could be and how quickly that brightness could fade! David wanted to snatch back the question that had discouraged her, snatch back the brightness. As soon trap the sunlight. He must trust it like the sunlight, not of the sort that shone with such consistency here on the desert but that more elusive light of his own climate.

Diana took her own book out onto the porch, which had already become her territory since Constance refused to go there, Diana's and David's in the late evening if Constance went early to bed.

Instead of the library books, David chose to have Constance continue to read from the book he had been reading at for weeks in such snatches he couldn't really keep the characters straight. It was Virginia Woolf's *The Voyage Out* which he hadn't read before, and he wanted to listen to it long enough to decide what in that young voice she had discarded and why.

The faint London accent in Constance's voice did not suit the priviledged cast of characters, but, when they actually spoke, Constance seemed to hear them, to be able to recall and mimic those voices as her working-class mother might have done, coming home with her filched food.

What an uproar of emotion the lovers seemed to be in, vacillating for pages in extremities of feeling. Had David ever experienced such extended periods of indecision? Or so acute a sense of the division of the sexes? On the contrary, he had struggled to discover his own male superiority as if his life had depended on it, passed through puberty and finally, even three inches taller than his sister, admitted failure with a sense of wondering relief. He hadn't courted Patricia as these young men seemed to court these young women. Peacock-brained, these young men seemed to have been, strutting their learning to dazzle, to intimidate and then blind.

David had never wondered if he was making a terrible mistake. What nagged his young conscience was not his unworthiness of Patricia, but his need to escape Hugh's sons and therefore his own mother, to leave her to suffer the error of her ways, and begin his own life. He was deserting Diana, too. It was not until she came home with Constance that David understood she had not intended him to wait for her, keeping their androgynous, virginal life intact for her. What separated them was not the gulf between the sexes but sex itself. She had chosen her own. He had accepted what was expected of him.

"Are you listening?" Constance asked suddenly, interrupting her reading.

"In a way," David answered. "Can you?"

"I don't try," Constance said. "If I did, I'd snag on a word and be gone."

"I don't remember anguishing so," David said, "about love and marriage anyway."

"Such traps," Constance said.

"Oh, no more than life is," David said somewhat impatiently. "You're born into it. You live it. Why not?"

"There are choices nobody has to make," Constance said.

"But do, for lack of better," David said.

He tried to listen more attentively as Constance returned to the book, tried to impose the lush hot damp of the jungle on the dry desert out beyond the window, its sky dusted with palm trees. It must be like this for Constance, the present something being read to her imposing itself when it could on a consciousness no longer caught up in the flow of time, as surprised and dissociated from the emotions and events as if they were no more than a story in a book. I am someone for her, he thought, invented by Diana, and Constance has as much difficulty remembering who I am as I do trying to place St. John or Susan or any of the others at Virginia Woolf's hotel.

The story intensified as Rachel fell ill. The sentences took on almost hypnotic rhythm, and now the characters vaccilated not between being in love and intense repulsion but between terrible concern and indifference. Facing the possibilty of Rachel's death, they seemed to grow old overnight, and David could believe it. Once death cut at the heart of any life, youth was over.

David had as much difficulty as Constance must in trying to return to the place he actually was. Even her presence surprised him as she closed the book. He had been St. John, sprawled in a chair, letting the other guests at the hotel flow by him. We park our bodies like cars, David thought, and walk off into books, memories, dreams, and the more intense the experience is the harder it is to find our way back into our fleshly means of transport. Where was Constance now as she sat there in the room with him? Certainly not in any part of the story she had just read out, for she had paid no attention to it.

How easy it was to detect Constance's young face, there like an afterimage, so that loving her, he could be aware of always having loved her, this time with her therefore a gift that seemed to him as natural as it was amazing.

"Are you ready for a swim?" Diana asked, coming in off the porch. "I seem to have slept over my book for nearly an hour. Maybe the water will wake me up."

Constance was reluctant about the water as she had been the day before. Diana's pleasure in it was so intense that David chose not to swim with her. He was with Constance instead so that Diana did not have to check again and again to be sure Constance hadn't suddenly wandered off.

"Aren't you going to swim?" Constance asked.

"In a while," David said.

"She doesn't look like herself in the water," Constance said.

David didn't say that Diana looked more like herself to him, the shape of her head in her swimming cap, the power in her arms to pull herself through the water, and, though she kicked only enough to keep her legs from sinking, they were recognizably the same legs she'd had as a girl, long and shapely. Odd how bodies which took on weight rarely did it uniformly. Diana carried nearly all of hers on her torso. Patricia's weight had settled in her hips and legs, which then wasted like fruit which had refused to ripen, the flesh softening under the skin, then falling away. Bones meant to support and heal the flesh finally cast off that burden and emerged with deathly authority.

David felt Constance take his hand. He turned to her with an odd sense that she could read his mind and he wanted to excuse himself for his morbidity.

"Are you going to try it today?" he asked, smiling at her.

From behind her dark glasses she said, "I haven't enough flesh. I'd sink like a stone."

"Well, I haven't much, and I manage," he said.

"You know how to swim?"

"Well enough, and Diana thinks you do, too."

"Isn't there any limit to trusting Diana?" Constance asked.

At that moment Diana emerged from the pool, leaving behind that easy authority of body, a fat, wet old woman on dry land.

"There you are!" Constance called, laughing.

Diana returned her laugh, all shaking flesh, her pleasure a joke to be shared not against herself but against likelihood.

"Come into the jacuzzi with me," Diana called.

Constance again agreed only to dangle her feet in the hot water, freeing David to go into the pool, more familiar to him today, and he didn't mind when two other swimmers joined him from the half dozen sun-bathers at the far end of the pool. They exchanged pleasantries in passing, but David did not stop to talk. He had no desire to make causal acquaintances who might in any way infringe on his holiday with Diana and Constance.

Diana did not let them lie long in the sun, even with sun block cream. Through the cool air, David could feel its power even on this winter day.

"You can tell," Diana said, "it's only the tourists here who lie in the sun. The locals know better."

David surrendered himself easily to his sister's direction, whether about how long to sit in the sun or when to eat dinner. He sensed in her a need to establish a routine quickly, to make the days ordinary for Constance while at the same time not wanting him to be bored, urging him off on his own to take desert walks, to stay for lunch in town if he would enjoy it. She herself took only limited times of independence when she drove into town to shop or out to the local grove for grapefruit they all ate at both breakfast and dinner. She did not suggest taking Constance farther than evening walks around the compound until they had been there a week.

David was certain that the place came as a surprise to Constance not only every morning when she woke but every afternoon when they swam, every evening when they walked. She surely recognized only Diana though she did take David now increasingly on faith. He tried to discover what about him might really have become familiar to her and decided with mild chagrin that she often identified him by his hat when they were out of doors. But he also noticed that his voice was more familiar to her than his physical presence. If he saw her look at him strangely across the room, he spoke to her, and she relaxed, smiling. She had, like Diana, been listening to his voice for years.

David found himself wondering if wearing a distinctive after-shave lotion would help. Certainly the smell of someone wearing Patricia's perfume could still make her absence palpable to him. And there was one woman, often at the pool when they were there, who had stolen one note of Patricia's laugh. He would have liked to thank her, for on that one note he was learning to travel back before the long months of her dying when she did laugh at the antics of a grandchild, at David's clowning. He needed to remember what a happy grandmother she had been, how much she had healed before her dying.

He and Diana were beginning to make a game of some of the regulars at the pool, some they habitually met on their evening walks. One woman they called "Oh, Larry!" because she must call to her husband at the sight of anything from a bird to a golf ball. "She's trying to own his eyes," Constance said, but surely there was no flesh here to tempt poor Larry away from his wife's enthusiasms. "The royal babies" were a solemn couple who toured the grounds on a pair of enormous tricycles, once in the morning, once in the evening, he with a cigar in his mouth, she chewing gum. A single man, perhaps ten years younger than most of the other residents, dressed in sweat-stained white, wearing a headband, ran the day long. David christened him Orestes, pursued by his invisible furies.

Whenever David saw something really interesting enough to share with Diana and Constance, he would cry out, "Oh, Larry!" at female pitch. Beyond the joke, it made him realize how much harmony among people consisted in not trying to own their eyes or ears, to be companionably silent so that Constance could become acquainted with the trees and flowers, so that Diana could divide her attention among the creatures, whether human, feathered or furred. If he did not pull at their attention, he could be quietly absorbed with them. For himself, he often watched the sky, so large here in the open desert it was possible to watch the journey of one cloud from the time it appeared in the west over the mountains to its vanishing point on the eastern horizon.

"Shall we drive over to the mountain trail this morning?" Diana finally asked as they sat at breakfast, eating in the company of the ravenous birds.

The cane, which had stayed collapsed on the hall table since they arrived, Diana flicked to its stiff length to be taken along, only as a precaution David decided, for Diana had been walking easily for days. They equipped themselves with hats, a pair of binoculars, and a plastic bottle of water, the last more a flamboyant gesture than a necessity. Diana had explained to David that they were taking what she called "an invalid's walk," carefully designed by the park rangers for the ordinary tourist in this valley who had heart trouble or arthritis or failing eyesight or all three.

Constance, cheerful enough at the outset, cowered a little as Diana pulled into the parking lot half full of cars, their car followed by two more which disgorged their elderly passengers, noisily and unnecessarily organizing themselves for an assault on the little path that wound gently back and forth across a mountain stream, water as tame as any found in an English poem.

"Where are we going?" Constance asked dubiously.

"On a short walk," Diana said, obviously herself disappointed by the number of other people.

David got out of the back seat and opened Constance's door, offering her his hand and remembering to speak his encouragement. She got reluctantly out of the car, but once they were out of the parking lot, the clumps of people had strung out and began to disappear among the boulders. There was no one visible before or behind them when they set out. Only occasionally a light breeze that played against the base of the mountain carried voices back to them, and now and then they caught a glimpse of walkers on the alternative return route.

Here and there Diana used her cane for negotiating her balance up a steep rock step or over a little bridge, but more often she used it as a pointer to show David the tiny desert flowers he could not have found for himself. Diana led the way, and David brought up the rear, aware that they formed a guard for Constance which could not help inhibiting as well as protecting her, for she was far more agile even than David.

They all stopped to look up at a hawk, solitary and intent in the high air, waiting for rodent or lizard to give itself away. When David took the binoculars from his eyes, he saw, too, the hawk's shadow skim across the side of the mountain, a warning.

Constance was gone.

David and Diana looked at each other, faces drained of color. Then she turned forward and he turned back, but the path was so narrow it seemed inconceivable that she could have slipped past either of them. On the right they were blocked by a sheer cliff. On the left rough rocks dropped down to the stream, treacherous only because its bed was a rubble of unstable rock no one could easily cross.

"Constance!" Diana shouted up ahead of him.

"Constance!" he repeated, throwing his strong, known

voice into the air.

If she had fallen—but how could she fall?—they would have heard her. She must have climbed, but where? David scanned the ten feet of trail between where he and Diana had been standing. She must have gone down toward the stream, but how did she go so quickly? And which way, downstream or up? She would have to get up onto the trail again eventually.

"Diana?" he called.

She came back to him around a bend.

"You follow the trail back down," David said. "I'll go on up. Keep watching the stream. She'll have to get back onto the trail eventually. It's too hard going down there."

Diana nodded and set off the way they had come. Other walkers had already begun to pass them awkwardly.

"Anything wrong?" a balding, shallowly breathing man asked David.

"We're missing one of our party," David said. "A slight short woman with very white hair. She just disappeared off the path."

"You'd have to be a mountain goat," the man said.

"Well, she is," David said, as they walked along, his eyes so intent on the stream that he stumbled and almost fell, would have if his new companion hadn't offered a steadying hand.

"Thank you," David said.

"She can't have gone far, can she? Maybe she's just up ahead of us."

They hurried on until David realized he had set too fast a pace and stopped to let the other man catch his breath.

"You needn't . . ." David said.

"You go on then," the man answered with difficulty through his struggling breath. "But I'll keep looking."

David came to the end of the trail, a sudden oasis of

palms sheltering a waterfall, backed by impassable cliffs.

Several walkers were resting there. He asked if they had seen a small woman with unusually white hair. They hadn't but they would look for her on the way down.

He started down the return trail, less sure than he had been that he would see her around each next turning of the path. For a moment he stopped. It wasn't an accident, or anyway hadn't started out to be. Whatever had happened, Constance had chosen to disappear. If he hadn't found her by the time he got back to the parking lot, he'd go back to the place she had disappeared and figure out how she could have managed it. Why had she wanted to, fearful as she was of everything away from Diana? Constance hadn't complained of locked doors since they'd been on the desert, David had thought because in a strange place they had spelled security more than imprisonment, but she did hate the screened porch, the cage as she called it. Did the simple desire for freedom finally overcome fear? Was that why, in Vancouver, she had wandered away?

David arrived in the parking lot to find Diana walking back from the car toward him.

"Not a sign," Diana said. "I don't see what to do but go to the rangers."

"That's a good idea," David said. "You go over to the station. I'll have another look myself."

As he set out again, he saw a woman running down the path.

"What is it?" he called to her.

"A man," she called back, hardly slowing her pace, "I think he's had a heart attack."

What were any of them, all old fools, doing out in this godforsaken place? For the landscape now seemed to David nothing but bleak rubble, the little man-made signs next to various points of interest lures into the trap for the magpie-brained who couldn't resist collecting useless bits of information, blind to the real risks. He was suddenly frightened of crossing a sturdy little bridge, aware that he could lose his balance, fall, and then where would they all be? He tried to steady himself, to calm down. He had a perfectly good body, except for his eyes, and he was not about to make a mistake, like his damned father, like his damned son. David was crying a tributary of tears to join the sweat leaking out of his hair.

"Constance!" he shouted. "Constance!"

He arrived back at the point where she had disappeared. He forced himself to remember. They were all—or at least he and Diana were—looking up at a hunting hawk, and he had seen its shadow moving toward them across the face of the mountain. Had Constance been afraid? Instead of calling her name again, David stepped carefully and quietly off the path toward the stream. He edged around a boulder twice his own height. He didn't see Constance until he nearly stumbled over her, crouching up against the rock, absolutely still. She stared at him with eyes blank with terror.

David caught his breath in a fear of his own at this wild creature trapped at his feet, cowering in his shadow. He was the hawk, she the prey. He crouched down beside her out of the sun so that she could see his face.

"Constance," he said softly, "it's David, Diana's brother."

She trembled violently.

"You're all right," he said.

He was close enough to her to take her in his arms, but he dared not touch her. She could die of fright. He could think of nothing to do but stay there beside her, murmuring reassurances until somehow his voice might push through her fear and she would recognize him.

David heard quickly running steps on the path above them. He thought of calling out for help, but the sound had sent new violent waves of trembling through Constance's body, and she had closed her eyes.

"Constance," he said quietly, "you're all right. As soon as you're ready, I'm going to take you back to Diana. She's worried about you. She doesn't know where you are. Constance, open your eyes. Look at me. I'm David, Diana's brother."

By now he was trembling himself from the strain of his crouched position. He was relieved enough to have found her, to be with her, that he began to feel silly, hidden there behind a boulder. He shifted his weight and sent a scattering of pebbles down to the stream. Constance glared at him for such an error which might give them away. So she at least knew that they were hiding together and he was no more than her clumsy accomplice.

"This is silly," David said gently. "Diana doesn't even know we're playing hide-and-seek. Come on. We need to find her."

David stood up, careful not to get between Constance and the sun, hot now as it reached toward noon. He held out a hand to her and waited. She offered hers to him, and he nearly lifted her to her feet. He let her stand a moment, and then they began to edge back around the boulder. Just as he was about to urge her onto the path, he heard steady footsteps coming down toward them. Constance tried to draw away from him, but he did not let her. Instead he stepped back into the shadow of the rock and waited.

Two rangers with a stretcher passed within five feet without noticing them. On the stretcher was the man who had hurried up the path with David, looking for Constance. David could not tell, in that brief glimpse of him, whether he was still alive.

"Come on," he said to Constance, his tone almost harsh.

She obeyed him meekly. Though it was awkward, he held her hand firmly all the way down. David saw Diana, sitting on the shady side of the car with all the windows and doors open.

"Diana!" he shouted. "Here she is!"

Constance smiled at her. It was as if nothing had happened. David looked down at Constance and realized that for her nothing had. Diana knew that, and she let no shadow of concern play over her greeting face.

The sister and brother sat in the dark out on the porch. Only now was there an opportunity for David to tell Diana what had happened.

"Has she ever looked at you like that?" David asked, "as if you were the hawk?"

"Yes," Diana answered, "when I dug her out of the rubble."

Where had David heard of a tribe of people who wouldn't come to each other's rescue because to save a person's life was to be responsible for that person from that time onward? He felt himself a new sense of require-ment, as if, having persuaded Constance that there was nothing to be frightened of, he was obliged to prove it.

"We do prey on her," Diana said. "That's the pity of it."

"You mustn't begin to think in her terms," David protested.

"I have to," Diana replied. "I have to know how it is for her. I always have. She was never like us, David. She always said she'd die in a cage. She was never at home in one the way most people are."

"A cage?"

"She never wanted to be owned, to belong to anyone. She had to be free, whatever the cost. But I own her now. What else can I do?"

"She wasn't trying to run away," David said. "She was frightened. She was hiding."

"Oh, D., I did want you to have a good time, too."

"I am having a good time, a wonderful time, in fact," David said. "This morning she *did* recognize me. She *did* trust me. I think it's my voice."

"I'm sure it is," Diana said.

David could see Diana only in outline, and it struck him that this intimacy was more possible for her because she also recognized his voice which had been with her through all the years of their separation. In the light she would still be growing used to accepting this old man as her brother, as he puzzled, too, to find his sister in that aging flesh.

"I want her to trust me," David said. "I want you both to trust me."

Diana reached over and put a hand on David's knee.

"I'm not sure I know any longer what that means," she said. "I do love you, D."

He understood that she was speaking without reluctance.

"You've got to trust yourself," he said.

"It never used to seem so difficult."

It was as hard for David to see that strength in his sister waver as it was to see her lame and in pain. The sun was doing its good work on her bones. If David could share the responsibility of the accidents and mistakes, perhaps Diana could learn not to see each one as a defeat. There was a virtue in Constance's failure to remember any of them. She might feel unaccountably tired tomorrow, but she would have nothing to forgive them for.

David walked the straight road into town in the morning, having said he would stay to have his lunch there. He wanted them to have an ordinary morning together, for Diana's sake as much as for Constance's. He never felt with them, as he had expected to, times when he was an intrusion. He cherished their solitude more than they did, their sharing it with him so that he became part of it. He did like these times to himself but mainly because he felt their presence behind him, there to welcome him back. His sister loved him. Constance knew who he was.

David looked up at a car coming toward him. He noticed no more than the bald head of the driver. He suddenly remembered the man on the stretcher. It was a part of the story he hadn't told Diana. What if that man died as a result of being hurried up the path in search of Constance? The thought angered David. If someone knew he had heart trouble, why had he been so careless as to try to lay his own death on a stranger's conscience?

"It wasn't my fault," David said aloud.

He had spoken in a child's voice, speaking the guilt of a child who knew his father had died rushing to the hospital to attend his birth. All his adult life he had tried to believe in taking care, in making everything safe, but it hadn't prevented his own son from dying. Really, it was a bit of luck to have found Constance. It was a bit of bad luck if the man had died. Or not, for him. But perhaps he had a wife . . . a man should have the courtesy to outlive his wife.

David's gentle mother had outlived two husbands, and of the three sons only David had felt briefly obligated to play a stand-in part as the man of the family. During all those war years he had had too much of being cast in roles nobody really thought him worthy of. He was a war substitute not only at home but at work and with a number of young women for whom he was not only too young but not good enough, having been unable to put on a uniform. Not much of a man, no, he hadn't been, but he had outlived his wife.

And he was now setting himself up to outlive Constance? Either he or Diana would have to. David wasn't sure what Diana had meant when she said Constance could not live in a cage, for she wasn't speaking just about locked doors, the fence that was even now going up around their house if Ben and Mike were on schedule. Those two women had lived together for over forty years, and that seemed to him no less a commitment than marriage which was, he supposed, sometimes something of a cage, but it was also so much else in positive requirement that to use that image seemed to him perverse. Oh, he understood Diana's distress, her grief for Constance in her increasing dependence, but at least there were things Diana could do about it. She was not yet reduced to sitting helplessly, day after day. If all David had had to do to keep Patricia safe was build a fence around the property—bars at all the windows would have seemed a small price—but he was committing the sin of claiming superior suffering, which comforted neither himself nor his sister.

David had arrived in the little town without having watched the sky or been much aware of the sun's kind warmth on his back. Why had he let what amounted to nothing more than a briefly frightening episode turn him inward where he discovered no insight worth the name, a mournful irritability rather which he disliked in himself? He was thirsty. He would go to the horseshoe bar and drink a beer with the locals.

The bartender this morning was a woman of toughened age, still dyeing her hair and painting her face in a caricature of desirability. She was talking to a woman sitting alone halfway down the bar, younger, more tentatively hopeful. On the other side of the U three men nearly identically dressed in khaki seemed camouflaged for the desert. Even their hair and skin were the color of dust. They seemed to stare at without really seeing the two women. All eyes had shifted to David when he walked in and shifted immediately away, except for the bartender's. She left her companion promptly, swiped the already clean counter in front of David and smiled at him.

"What'll it be this morning?"

"Have you draft beer?"

"Sure do."

He drank it gratefully, realizing how rarely he had been really thirsty; the pleasure of a drink intensified as it answered a need. It was like being with Diana and Constance where even the most inconsequential and, with Constance, sometimes odd exchange slaked a loneliness in him he had accepted as his condition. How different it was from the two conversations at the bar, the men in mock modesty really bragging about how much they could afford to lose, how many machines they owned which could break down. One man had just had his damned plane in for an overhaul. Another complained about the faulty air conditioning in his tractor, and they all competed to claim the prize lemon of a car they had at one time or another been crazy enough to buy. The women did not talk to be overheard, but David could hear them in a reversal of the usual roles, the bartender telling her troubles to her customer.

"I told her, 'Don't think getting knocked up will change anything.' Where do kids get these ideas, off the tube?"

"You don't look around when you're a kid. You think you're different. You think it's going to be different for you," said the customer.

David thought of Christine, who was afraid of being different, who wished she had a mother who would talk with her. How primly he expected she would draw back, faced with the experience these women might offer up. Sheltered. All their women were sheltered, Jack said. Ben and Mike were already in league with their father to keep the less savory truth about the real world from Laura. And they were there building the fence to protect Constance.

David would not have taken any of the women of his family into this bar, yet it was his own choice. The places he had dropped in to for a drink in his own city were also the sort he thought of as out of bounds, not for women but for his women. Yet he could imagine sitting here with Constance or Diana. Only those with illusions could be disillusioned. Constance had never been sheltered in her marginal childhood in London, in the war, and Diana had chosen to work in the world. He would not have called either of them a masculine woman. They were worldly women, as his wife and daughters were not.

David was tempted to order another beer, but Patricia would consider two "drinking in the morning," and she had a point. The three men, into another round, had deteriorated from bragging to telling dirty stories at which the bartender and her friend were expected to laugh. David stood up.

"Getting a little rough for you, are they?" the bartender asked, kindly. "You want another? I'll tell those apes to clean up their act."

"No, no thanks," David said.

"You come and see us again, now."

It wasn't a forced friendliness but natural to the climate, and the tourists who stayed long enough learned to speak not only to the locals who served them but to each other with the same shy awkwardness of people learning to speak a new language. Even Diana nodded curt acknowledgment to people they encountered by the pool or on their walks. On good days, Constance spoke and smiled. Sometimes she walked with her head down, refusing to see anyone.

David wandered over to the shopping mall. His Christmas shopping experience had given him a new confidence about going into stores. He had liked the bright tents he saw so many of the women wearing out on their screened porches, and he wondered if he could find any for Constance and Diana. In the window of one shop he saw one that would be exactly right for his sister, the colors darker, the pattern smaller and more complex than most he had seen.

"One size fits all," the clerk assured him as she held it out for him.

"All" which could include his outsized sister obviously didn't include the small, elegant Constance. With the present for his sister under his arm, he was puzzled by the difficulty of Constance's size. He finally found a robe in bright orange with a Chinese collar and frogs, which fell straight to the floor, in a size he thought would do, though it might be a little long.

David wanted to buy something for himself to amuse them. But in the men's shop, his courage failed before the loud plaids and garish flowers. Then his eye caught on a brown jogging suit. He heard Christine say, "Everything else you have is blue." Everything else he had had been chosen by Patricia until this Christmas when he was given shirts to go with his new jacket. He liked brown.

"Don't buy it without trying it on, sir."

"No, I suppose not," David said.

Once he had it on, he didn't want to take it off. Would he be too hot in it walking back across the desert? If Diana was sitting on the porch, he would run the last hundred yards.

There she was, and David broke into a sprint.

"Oh, D.!" she shouted. "Constance, do you see what we've got."

"Yes, do," David said, jogging across the porch and into the house.

"But your *shoes!*" Diana protested.

David looked down at his brown leather shoes.

"I hadn't thought about that," he said.

Constance and Diana stood laughing at him, and he looked up at them, glaring vengefully.

"Wait until you see what I've got for *you,*" he threatened.

"Not jogging suits, I hope," Diana said.

"Oh, look," Constance said, as she took her robe out of the bag. "It really is for me."

"You had one very like that years ago," Diana said.

"I know," Constance said.

She put a hand on David's shoulder, and he bent down to receive her kiss.

Diana was more simply delighted with hers, and they both went off immediately to try their new clothes on. David looked again at his shoes and decided they had been the most effective part of his act, but he was suddenly very tired. He flung himself down on the couch and let himself breathe.

Constance came out first.

"I do love you in bright colors!" David exclaimed.

"It's mine," she said.

And then there was his sister, regal as she could be whenever she was robed in rich, dark colors.

"You look like a queen from the south seas," David decided.

"You look like a silly tourist," Diana said.

"Always dress the part," David agreed.

"You must buy him a proper pair of shoes," Constance said.

"Would I look any less silly?"

"You're quite good-looking, for a man," Constance said, amusement glittering in those eyes which only yesterday had been blank with animal fear.

Constance's prejudice against men never rankled as his sister's did. David enjoyed Constance's back-handed compliments. He was exempted by them rather than reduced, as he sometimes was by his sister, to a category. Diana never admitted prejudice as Constance candidly did.

It was their last day. Both David and Diana put off the packing, wanting to savor the time as long as they could.

"You have a real tan," Diana said to him as the three of them walked over to the pool.

"A farmer's tan," David said. "You two look pretty fine yourselves."

Constance always did. The change was more noticeable in his sister whose body was firmer now and less bloated, whose face had been smoothed by rest and pleasure. David regretted that he hadn't opted for at least three weeks, but he had needed to be conservative on this first adventure.

Constance took up her usual place by the sheltering wall, and David sat down with her to watch Diana swim. He wondered if he could persuade his sister to take up

swimming at home. He was far more aware of her imprisonment than he was of Constance's and wondered if Diana's
disproportionate guilt was in part a way of not blaming
Constance for their isolated circumstance.

When Diana got out of the pool, she came over to
Constance and said, "Won't you try if I stay right with
you?"

Constance looked at David as if he might offer some
protection from this suggestion.

"I'll go in, too," he offered.

Reluctantly Constance took off her wrap and walked
with them to the steps at the shallow end. The warmth of
the water surprised and pleased her, but it took her time to
go down from one step to another. The water, when she
finally stood on the bottom, covered her breasts, and David
realized, as he stood only waist deep, that already she'd
feel possessed by the water. He and Diana stood on either
side of her, neither making any suggestions. Slowly Constance walked to the side of the pool, and Diana walked with
her. David remained where he was, watching. Constance
turned back to him.

"Shall I swim?" she asked Diana.

"I think you can."

Already Constance's feet were off the bottom as she
hung on to the side of the pool. She pushed off, her face
in the water, and swam to David who caught her by the
hands to support her while she found her footing.

"Well," she said. "This is a very wet experience."

She set off from David and swam back to Diana who
stood there at the edge of the pool, laughing.

"I'm quite good at this," Constance said, recovering
herself.

She set off again, this time swimming past David to the
other edge of the pool.

"There's really nothing to it," she said.

David could not even regret that it had taken her two weeks to gather up her courage. That she was swimming was enough to vindicate them in the risks they had been taking for all their sakes. David swam off himself, wearing his hat and sunglasses, smug old turtle under the desert sun.

CHAPTER XII

They set out across the badlands in a benign morning. There had been no great wind or rainstorms throughout their stay. Diana was grateful for that though she suspected David would have enjoyed either.

"For your sake," she said over her shoulder to her brother in the back seat, "I'm sorry there hasn't been any Shakespearean weather."

"Another time," David said. "I've become addicted to this sky, you know."

Diana had been thinking of it as their last trip, and perhaps it would be, but it was far better to be of David's optimistic turn of mind even if it brought disappointments with it. She had lost the habit of looking forward except as a way to prevent potential disasters, of which Constance's wandering away was really no more than a metaphor. The episodes Diana couldn't avoid took place in Constance's mind, electrical storms Diana could read only in her eyes without knowing what centers had been struck.

Constance pointed to one of the large desert rabbits, whose large, translucent ears were as curious to them as the red, white, and blue eyes of the roadrunners. Diana saw off to the left the shadow of a hawk and did not call it to anyone's attention, glad they were in a car which could outrun that rabbity destiny.

"Oh, Larry!" David called in falsetto from the back seat, for he had spotted an ocotillo in fuller bloom than any they had seen before, the tips of its spidery branches in a delicate red flame of flowers.

Diana was sorry to turn out of the badlands onto a road with traffic enough so that all she would now see were the large trucks which blocked her view ahead and bore down on her from behind. She drove in their vise for nearly an hour, and her passengers were silent in their different apprehensions. David's timidities, when they weren't an inconvenience, often touched Diana, for they had been among his first offerings of trust after their long childhood estrangement. She could feel both her passengers ease a little as she turned onto the big highway though it was really more difficult driving for her with its too many options.

"How long have you lived with us?" Constance suddenly turned and asked David.

"Two weeks," David said.

"That's hardly any time at all," Constance said, mildly surprised.

"Has it seemed an eternity?" David asked, teasing.

"No," she said, "but I feel used to you."

Diana realized that Constance was the only one of them who did not know that within a few hours this happy arrangement would be over, and, once they were home again, she would forget to mind. Not for the first time, Diana was tempted to suggest that it didn't have to end. Increasingly through the holiday, she had imagined David settled with his own things in the rooms that used to be Jill's. They would offer him about as much private space as he had at home now, as well as giving him the run of the house. But every time she thought of it, she knew that what his living with them really meant was taking on a burden intolerable without love, occasionally intolerable even so. Those rooms, when the time came, should be nurse's quarters.

It wasn't as if they were losing him when they got home. He'd still come every Wednesday for dinner, and perhaps young Mike and his odd, intense little friend would drop in occasionally. That whole family, for that matter, might gradually grow accustomed to two peculiar old women who had been offered up to them after all these years. Diana wanted to warm to Laura, and perhaps she could when they were more familiar to each other. Or if she couldn't, Constance might. Diana wasn't sure she hadn't used Constance's confusion and fear as an excuse to cut her off from the long habit of diverse intimacies. Constance had, after all, got used to David, as she put it.

At the little Palm Springs airport, they turned in their car and had time for lunch before they had to board their flight back to Vancouver.

"I don't need to be pre-boarded here," Diana said. "It's an easy walk for me now."

"But in Vancouver you'll need help," David said.

"Oh, I suppose so," she said regretfully. "I hate to give up the desert illusion that I'm not an old cripple after all."

Constance seemed less troubled now being surrounded by strangers. She looked about her with natural curiosity and even smiled at the waitress who took their order.

"Do you remember that little place in Bloomsbury where we used to go for scotch woodcock?" Constance asked.

"I do," Diana said, "those awful watery powdered eggs which tasted so good," and she wondered what about this airport eating area could have reminded Constance of that little shoebox of a restaurant.

"I had a mad passion for the waitress there," Constance confided to David.

Diana was relieved to see that David was amused rather than shocked. She looked more carefully at their waitress and could see nothing in her that would trigger Constance's interest, but Diana rarely had seen what Constance saw to desire, her own so clearly locked in place.

They boarded the plane easily. Obviously for Constance, walking out across the tarmack and climbing the steps into the plane was less disorienting than being funneled into it by windowless corridor. It was an experience that could snag memories far enough back to be accessible to her and reassure her that she understood what she was doing.

They settled as they had on the way down, Constance at the window, David on the aisle, Diana comfortably centered between them. She was not really even apprehensive about the Vancouver airport where Ben would be waiting beyond the customs barrier to help David with the luggage.

"I find I'm suddenly dreading going home," David said.

"Why?" Diana asked, surprised at the energy in his statement.

"I've left it all so easily behind," David said. "Before we left, I thought I'd brood about it, burden you with it, but until now it's hardly crossed my mind."

"What is it about Mary?" Diana asked, feeling by now so comfortable with her brother that nothing he might say about this daughter would trouble her.

"She's so taken up with her own problems, she doesn't see how many she's creating around her which are going to become hers as well," David said, "or they may already have by now. Jack told me Ted was talking about leaving her."

Diana heard the shock and anger in David's voice. She didn't say anything. She waited.

"I don't understand that," David said after a moment. "What do young people these days think they mean by 'for better or worse, for richer or poorer'?"

"Girly woods," Constance said.

Diana grinned at her. David looked puzzled.

" 'With all my girly woods I thee endow,' " Constance elaborated with a satisfied chuckle.

"A young doctor friend of ours," Diana explained, "married an English girl at the end of the war. He was so nervous, that's the vow he took."

This irreverent diversion, so many of which David enjoyed, threw him uncomfortably off balance, and, though Diana was sorry for him, she thought Constance's war against anyone inclined to pompous piety a good one.

"Constance," David demanded, "why are you so set against marriage when you have been virtually married for forty years?"

"I have?" Constance asked. "Oh, surely not. To whom?"

Diana laughed, shaking her head. "Must the whole world live on your terms, D.?"

"They're not *my* terms," David said with some irritation. "Ted wasn't forced to marry Mary, quite the contrary. She had plenty of young men to choose from, and she took her time."

"He won a prize," Diana mused. "So he thinks he has a right to be happy."

"Happiness is beside the point," Constance said, "except

for Americans."

Diana remembered a story Constance had told her
about a young American lover who couldn't see the
conflict between liberty and the pursuit of happiness for
herself but had a good deal of difficulty with it in other
people.

"Jack wanted me to have a talk with Ted before I left.
I was just too angry with him to risk it," David said. "I
don't blame him for being low and discouraged. Mary isn't
easy to live with at the best of times, and these haven't
been the best of times for her. But I can't understand his
ever entertaining the idea of leaving her."

"You do understand, don't you?" Diana asked gently.
"What you mean is that you disapprove of it."

"Of course I disapprove of it."

"Are you a judge?" Constance asked.

"No," David said, answering her as if it were an
interruption in the conversation he was having with his
sister, "I was a radio announcer."

"Second marriages are often better than first," Diana
said. "People are more realistic."

"Mary has *three* children," David protested.

"Her chances aren't that good then?" Diana asked.

"Oh, I don't know about that," David said. "I've
sometimes thought there is no end to the number of ships
she could wreck if she wanted to. She isn't considerate of
Ted's feelings. Her own take up all the room these days,
but surely there are ways of making her understand that,
short of leaving her."

"Did you really give Mary away?" Diana asked.

"I certainly did, and I don't want her back," David
said.

"But you already have her back, don't you?"

David sighed.

"Ted does know what you think surely," Diana went on.

"Oh, yes. He told Jack he couldn't talk to me because I'd kill him."

"What if you let him talk? What if you listened?"

"I don't think I could," David said. "And I don't see what good it would do to let him think about leaving her, let alone talk about it."

"But, if he already is, not listening to him doesn't stop him," Diana said. "Does he have a father?"

"Not one he can talk to," David said. "Ted's always been much more comfortable in our family than he ever has been in his own. He's been like a son to me really. And maybe that isn't as good a thing as I thought it was. I never feel fatherly about Jack."

"If Ted were your own son?" Diana asked.

"No son of mine would behave like that!" David asserted. "Oh, am I such an awful prig? I feel as if I simply don't know how to be a parent to grown children. Why do they need parents?"

The flight attendant stopped at their row. David ordered gin. Diana and Constance asked for tea.

"Am I to think that having Mary and the three children on my hands is a real option?" he asked.

"I suppose it's one of them," Diana said, "if you want it to be."

"I don't, but unlike that young wretch I don't believe even a father has a right to desert a woman with three dependent children. When it comes down to that, what I want hasn't much to do with it."

Diana saw David burdened with the guilt of all the men who had left women and children to fend inadequately for themselves, whether the men got themselves killed on the road as their father had, or were wracked up in a foreign war as Hugh had been, or simply wandered off in pursuit of their own happiness as Ted contemplated. For three generations David had been trying to put it right.

She was sorry to suspect that David was part of the problem between Ted and Mary and that this might be why he so readily assumed he'd have to be the solution. She didn't know them. Who was she to argue him out of his sense of responsibility when she had nothing but the worst of motives, needing him to be free enough only to be saddled with more of her needs and Constance's? He needed Diana to be just what she was telling him he should be, a disinterested listener.

"Why am I putting an early end to all our fun?" he asked.

"Because that isn't all we share," Diana said. "Anyway it isn't over. It's just beginning."

Diana felt so strengthened by what they together had been able to make happen that she was sure it could go on, in any number of forms, however they came about.

"Where are we going now?" Constance asked.

"Home," Diana said, pointing to the word on Constance's memory board.

Constance frowned. Home, for the moment, was nothing but a word, written in Diana's difficult hand.

Ben stood on the other side of the barrier waiting for them as David pushed the luggage and Constance pushed Diana through the automatic glazed glass doors.

"I've got the car right outside," Ben said, taking the luggage from his grandfather.

When everyone was settled in the car, David asked, "So how is everyone?"

"Well, okay, I guess," Ben said, "except that Aunt Mary seems to have moved in with us."

"With the children?" David asked.

"No, they're still at home with Uncle Ted. Dad doesn't seem to think it's that serious. As a matter of fact, he thinks it's funny."

"But who's looking after the children?" David asked.

"Uncle Ted is ... and making heavy weather of it, I can tell you. He can't wait to have you come home!"

"That's a new wrinkle," Diana said.

"Aunt Mary's great at giving people new wrinkles," Ben said. "The situation doesn't really amuse Mother."

"I'll bet it doesn't!" David said.

"We finished the fence," Ben said.

Diana glanced at Constance, but she wasn't following the conversation. She was looking out at the landscape as they drove toward the city.

"Are those our mountains?" Constance asked.

"They are," Diana said, relieved to know that they hadn't deprived Constance of the few landmarks that remained for her by taking her away from them for two weeks; she did, in general, know where she was.

"We went a bit farther than we should have, maybe," Ben said.

"How is that?" David asked.

"We put a new door off the breakfast room, one that won't have to be locked. We thought Constance would like to be able to get out into the garden."

"What a wonderful idea!" Diana said. "I'd never have thought of it."

"We felt bad, not checking it out first, but it seemed like such a good idea, and we had the time; so we just did it. It doesn't look too bad really."

The cedar fence had a raw new look, but at least it didn't look like a cage. Constance didn't take any notice of it. She went into the house and looked about her curiously.

"This is home, is it?" she asked Diana.

"Yes, look, let me show you,' Diana said, taking Constance by the arm and leading her through the house, reintroducing her to familiar objects, places she was used to sitting, and gradually Constance's face began to clear.

Only after the tour did Diana go to have a look at the new door which, unlike the fence, looked as if it had always been there.

"Look at this," she said to Constance. "This is new. It's your own door. It won't be locked. You can go out into the garden any time you like."

"I always do," Constance said, "but it's very nice. Thank you."

"What do you think?" Ben asked, coming up behind them.

"It's wonderful," Diana said.

"It was really Mike's idea. I wasn't going to say unless you really liked it."

"Shall we try it?" Diana suggested.

It was dusk. The air was damp and cold, and Diana was very grateful for the firm rail in place on the new steps down into the garden. It did look to her very different, enclosed by the new fence, but Constance hardly noticed it, her eyes on the ground where she found hundreds of bulbs pushing up through the earth and where the tiny buds of snow drops glowed white in the last light.

"Mother's sent over a casserole for your dinner," Ben said. "It's in the oven. There's enough for Granddad, too, but everyone hopes he'll come home with me to dinner."

"I'm sure they do," Diana said. "After all, we've had him to ourselves for two weeks."

"What's this?" David asked, coming out to join them. "Isn't it cold!"

Ben said to him, "You could have dinner here or with

us. Oh, and there's stuff in the fridge, Aunt Diana, for the morning."

"How thoughtful you all are!" Diana exclaimed. "Much as I hate to let you go, D., I think you'd better, don't you?"

David gave her a rueful look before he went over to where Constance was musing over her bulbs.

"I'm off now, Constance."

"Off where?"

"To dinner with my family and then home to my basement suite."

"Don't you live with us now?" Constance asked.

"Off and on," David said, and he bent down to kiss her good-bye.

Diana watched them and then turned to Ben to send her greetings and thanks back to his family with him.

"Good-bye, D.," David said. "It's been wonderful. I'll see you Wednesday night."

"Or before," she said, kissing him. "At least phone. I'll want to hear the news."

Diana left Constance in the garden to see the men out and then checked supplies and the casserole before she called Constance in.

"I must say it's nice to be home," Diana said, as they sat down in their accustomed chairs after she had fixed them drinks and lighted an already laid fire.

"You're a homebody," Constance said.

She didn't, of course, know they'd been away, but Diana no longer felt such despair at that thought, for the trip had been good for Constance, and, if it couldn't nourish her in memory, it could nourish Diana, counter the settled pain in her bones with the knowledge that somewhere she could still stride out, swim; and in her luggage, which she would unpack after dinner, there were several small sketches she had made of the desert in precious hours to herself with no one around to make references to Grandma Moses. There had been only Constance's voice back in the house, reading to David.

How hard it was to put away all those new clothes, which would be useless now until summer, but Diana might be able to wear the muumuu David had bought her occasionally on evenings a little later in the spring.

"There's my robe!" Constance said, holding up the bright orange garment with recognizing pleasure.

Diana could learn from that happy accident to look for clothes which reminded her of what Constance had worn years ago in hope that it might happen again and Constance wouldn't persistently feel that she had no belongings of her own but was, instead, mysteriously provided for from other people's wardrobes.

When the phone rang at ten the next morning, Diana answered it with confidence that it would be David, full of the drama Mary had created in his absence.

"Aunt Diana?" the young male voice inquired. "This is Mike."

"Oh, Mike, how glad I am to hear your voice. Did Ben tell you what a miracle that door is? Constance doesn't even realize it hasn't always been here, and she's out in the garden right now, checking on her bulbs. And the fence, too, it's all just wonderful."

"I'm glad," Mike said, in a tone which made Diana realize that she'd deflected him from another purpose.

"What's on your mind?" she asked.

"I wondered if I could come to see you," Mike said.

"Of course, and bring your friend if you'd like," Diana said, not at that moment able to remember his name.

"I'd like to do that again," Mike said, "but this time I'll come alone. Could I come about four o'clock?"

"Today?"

"If that's okay."

"Four is just fine," Diana said.

She hung up knowing that Mike had something hard on his mind. She did not know him well enough to think in which direction to worry. An emotional problem? Money? Mike had so many people to turn to—his beloved brother, his parents, his grandfather—Diana couldn't think what she might particularly offer. Fond of him, grateful to him, she hoped whatever help he thought she could give would be within her capacity to offer.

The phone rang again, and again Diana picked it up expecting to hear her brother's voice. This time it was Jill.

"Well," Jill said, "I can hear by the tone of your voice that you didn't lose her on the desert."

"Only briefly," Diana answered, found herself telling the story as a comic incident, and ended by adding, "And she went swimming."

"How are you?" Jill asked.

"Oh, back to myself just about, but it was a wonderful two weeks. Constance got quite used to David."

There was a silence on the other end of the phone.

"She's just learning to give the devil his due," Diana added quickly, for of course Jill could still wish that, if there were to be three, she might be the third. "Let me call her for you."

Constance had by then come in from her brief tour of the garden, for it was very cold, and, even if she did not remember that she'd spent the last two weeks in the hot desert sun, her body sent its messages.

"Come talk with Jill," Diana said. "We've just been away for two weeks on the desert, and she wants to welcome you back."

Constance took the phone.

"Diana says we've been away, but the only news I have is that we're living with a man. At least, I think we are, but I can't seem to find him anywhere, and he isn't on my memory board."

Constance listened again and then laughed. "Nobody has to remind me of *that,* love. I'm senile, but I'm not crazy."

Diana moved away, deciding to check the wine in the basement. She and Jill felt sorry for each other, Jill because she knew she couldn't have done for Constance what Diana was doing and therefore assumed it was impossible, Diana because Jill couldn't share Constance's life, even second-hand, because Constance could not remember it to tell her, and that sort of estrangement from Constance would have been intolerable for Diana.

The wine had stopped working. It should be racked off one more time, according to Jack's instructions, and then bottled. Perhaps they could all come over for dinner and then have a bottling party in a few weeks' time.

Back upstairs she found Constance at her jigsaw puzzle. There on the shelf with all the puzzles was Constance's timer, which Diana had left behind, thinking the buzzer might get on David's nerves or embarrass Constance.

"Here's your timer," she said. "Would you like to try it again?"

"If you tell me what it's for."

The phone rang again.

"Will it never stop!" Diana complained, already twice disappointed.

This time it was David.

"It's a curious state of affairs," David said. "I'm dealing with an irate husband who says it's unheard of for a wife to desert a husband and three children. When I asked him if he hadn't been thinking along those lines himself, he said, of course, he supposed everyone thought of it now and then when things got tough, but thinking about it, even talking about it, was a very different thing from *doing* it. After all, he loved Mary. He was married to her, wasn't he?"

"What does Mary have to say?" Diana asked.

"She says she hasn't left him, yet. She's just taking some time to think. She's perfectly willing to have the children stop by for a while after school, and any time Ted wants to talk reasonably, she's willing to talk, but not to shout. She's tired of shouting, and so she should be, since she's the one who does most of it."

"How long has it been going on?"

"Five days," David said. "You know, it's a great deal easier to listen to Ted than I thought it would be."

"He isn't saying the things you were afraid he'd say," Diana said.

"No, not at the moment anyway. I find his injured innocence a little silly under the circumstances, but I've been too similarly silly myself on occasion not to feel sympathetic. I do feel sorry for Laura. Mary being all sweet reason is even tougher to take than Mary in a rage. The glassware and china are safer, but you can think you're losing your mind."

"I'm sometimes tempted to say I'd like to meet Mary," Diana said, chuckling.

"Sometimes I think it's inevitable," David answered. "Sometimes I think you may be spared. The kids are taking it very well so far. I think they've known something was going to have to give, and their father is a far more dependable martyr than their mother. He's letting them be injured parties with him, something that would never occur to Mary. On the whole, her approach is probably the better one, but not so immediately satisfying."

David was relishing this conversation, Diana could tell, for with her he could be as ironic as he pleased, in danger of hurting no one's feelings. She could also sense that he felt a good deal more hopeful than he had been on the plane.

"David, in all this drama, I don't suppose you've picked up anything about Mike. He called me this morning and is coming over to talk at four this afternoon."

"No," David said, "I can't say that I have. Come to think of it, he was very quiet at dinner last night, but I assumed it was sensible self-protection. Ben talks too much when he's nervous. Mike shuts up. Even his jokes dry up. His sweet, long-suffering aunt, as full of sighs as Ophelia, is enough to give even an adolescent stomach indigestion."

So Diana wouldn't be forewarned, but with Mike she didn't need to be forearmed.

"Who was that?" Constance asked. "You were on the phone for twenty minutes. I timed you. I like this little gadget."

"The man you think we live with, David, my brother."

"Well, when is he coming home?"

"He didn't say," Diana answered. "His children need him for now, but he'll be over soon to see us. Will you go to the store with me? We need food."

Diana had baked brownies and put a part of a leg of lamb in the oven by the time Mike arrived. The plate of dark chocolate squares and the pitcher of cold milk momentarily cleared his troubled young face.

"You better not make a habit of this," he said, "or I'll be here every afternoon after school."

Diana watched him as he ate. He had David's slight build and would be able to eat into old age without worrying about his weight. But he looked like his father, had his auburn eyes and hair and would have his father's kind strength when the boyish softness had gone from his face, though he would perhaps stay more vulnerable, not a matter of bone structure so much as his position in the family, the cherished one. Even his brother cherished him.

"It's about Richard," Mike began, when he'd finished a second brownie and downed a glass of milk. "I don't know how to talk to anybody about it, but I thought you're a doctor, and you're . . . you live with Constance . . ."

Diana was grateful that her professional training had taught her not to stiffen at anything, but far below the surface, where it couldn't be read, her guard had gone up.

"Richard found out last week that he's got AIDS," Mike said and then released a trembling sigh.

Diana didn't say anything. She waited for him to recover enough to go on.

"He had to tell his parents, his mother and his stepdad, and they told him to get out. He doesn't really have anywhere to go . . ."

"Hasn't he been in touch with the AIDS people?" Diana asked.

"I don't know," Mike said. "I think he's just sort of freaked out."

"Where is he now?"

"He knows this other painter, an older guy, who is letting him sleep in his studio, but Richard said, if the guy knew, he'd throw him out. Everybody would."

"Are you involved with Richard, Mike?" Diana asked gently.

"Sure . . . oh, do you mean, am I gay? No, but Richard, if you don't count Ben, is my best friend. People can't just treat him like a leper. It isn't even dangerous for people to help him, is it?"

"No," Diana said.

"Could you, maybe, talk to him?" Mike asked. "Could

you, maybe, tell him what to do?"

"Of course I will," Diana said. "How soon can you get him here?"

"Tonight," Mike said. "Is it stupid? I don't want him to kill himself."

"It's not stupid."

"He's going to die, isn't he?"

"Almost certainly, if it's the correct diagnosis, but Mike, we all are."

"Yeah, but he's not even twenty years old, and he knows what he wants. He's one of the very few people I know who really knows what he wants."

"He can have five years to be what he wants, or five months. Let's see what we can do to help," Diana said.

"Do you know why he's going to die?" Mike asked, a bitter anger in his voice, "because he's funny looking, that's why, because he's short and ugly."

"There isn't any reason, Mike," Diana said, "anymore than there is that some people live to be as old as I am."

"You're not that old," Mike said.

"Well, I'm five years out of practice, and, if I'm going to be useful, I have some phone calls to make as well as dinner to cook before Richard gets here. About eight?"

"Do you have enough for me?" Mike asked.

"I think I probably do," Diana answered, surprised at his directness, like a child asking for a cookie.

"It's just that it's so rough at home at the moment and so stupid . . ."

"Ah, your Aunt Mary."

"I could help. I could set the table. I can peel potatoes well enough to join the army. While you phone."

"What a good idea," Diana said, more accustomed, now that David had been around for so long, to help.

"Constance," she said, stopping by the TV room on her

way to the kitchen, "we're having a guest for dinner, Mike, David's grandson, my great-nephew. You've met him before."

By the time Diana had spoken to several people on the phone, she was encouraged by how adequate a support system had been set up, not at the instigation of her profession, though there were responsible doctors involved, but by volunteers who referred to themselves as members of the gay community or friends of the gay community, knowledgeable and personally concerned. These were the people whose existence she had always denied, who believed, as she never had, that they were members of a real minority and responsible to it. Dealing with them behind her professional mask, she was aware of it now for the first time as a mask, but the guard at the center of herself had locked her behind it. This was a medical problem to be dealt with like all medical problems with dispassionate confidence. Mike had come to her because she was a doctor.

At dinner, Diana explained to Constance that Richard would be here at eight, and he might be very upset because he'd just found out he had AIDS. Did she know what AIDS was? Constance shook her head.

"It's a disease which attacks the immune system for which there is no known cure. On this continent the large majority of the victims are sexually active homosexual males."

"This Richard is queer?"

Diana saw Mike flush at the word.

"It's only our generation's slang," Diana said to him, and then to Constance, "Yes, he is. And his parents have refused to help him."

"I'd like to speak to them," Constance said brightly.

"I'll bet you would," Diana said, smiling.

"Where is David? You're too young to be David,"

Constance said to Mike.

"He won't be here tonight. Only Richard's coming," Diana said.

"I'm no help, you see," Constance said to Mike, "but have I ever been? I don't know how to worry about what other people worry about."

"That's the greatest help in the world," Diana said.

"Well, tonight I'm going to read to David whether he's here or not."

"You could read to me," Mike suggested. "Richard really needs to talk to Aunt Diana by himself."

"Would you like that?" Constance asked uncertainly.

"Sure," Mike said. "Would you mind reading me some of my homework?"

"I don't care what I read."

Diana wondered where both her nephews had learned the ease they had with Constance. Their parents were like most people she'd known, uneasy in the dislocations Constance made in any conversation, polite, sympathetic, but self-conscious, unable to avoid condescension. The boys treated Constance's lack of memory as a problem for her rather than for themselves, and they went about talking with her as practically as they went about putting locks on doors, building fences, making her a safe door she could open.

"Did you come over on your bike?" Diana asked Mike. "Do you want to take my car?"

"No, I've got Granddad's ... Ben's," Mike said. "I won't be long."

"Are you developing a taste for boys in your old age?" Constance asked as Mike went out the door.

"For relatives, I think," Diana said, smiling. "At least some relatives, and they do seem to be male."

She picked up Constance's board and wrote, "Read Mike his homework."

"Mike," Constance said, looking at it.

Diana had just time to clear away the dinner things before Mike came back with Richard. Once again Diana was struck by the contrast between Richard's head and his body and wondered what it was that attracted so many cartoonists to such distortions. He wasn't "funny-looking." He might have come from some great king's court, a wise fool, the role her brother cherished above all others. A tragic fool.

Once they were alone, Richard sat with his large head bowed, his small hands clasped between his knees.

"I want you to tell me everything you've been told by your doctor," Diana said. "And you must speak up and speak slowly because I don't hear as well as I used to."

He raised his head and looked at her through glasses that magnified his black eyes. Then, making an effort to speak clearly, he described his symptoms, the tests he'd been given and the results. His doctor had been matter-of-fact about it, but he had told Richard there was nothing he could do. He had referred Richard to a doctor who was treating AIDS patients.

"Have you seen him yet?" Diana asked.

"No," Richard said.

"Why not?"

"There's nothing he can do. There's nothing anyone can do."

"He can't cure you, that's true," Diana said, "but he can help you. There are people with AIDS who have lived for five years, a lot of the time well enough to work."

"Work?" Richard asked. "I'm only in my first year of college. I'm not qualified to do anything."

"You want to paint."

He made a bitter sound, perhaps it was even a word caught in his throat.

"Are you thinking of killing yourself?" Diana asked.

Richard didn't answer.

"I want you to talk to me about it."

Richard pushed his child's hands up to his eyes under his glasses and shook with the same violence Diana had witnessed in Constance, sourced in similar terror and despair. Diana had no difficulty in going to him, in putting her arms around that small body, of holding that large, really handsomely shaped head against her. She held him so for perhaps fifteen minutes until the violent shaking had subsided, until he was still enough to be asleep but for the irregularity of his breathing. Finally he sat up, cleaned his glasses and put them back on. Diana didn't move away from him.

"I really don't want to die," he said, "except as a way of hurting my parents, and I wouldn't be there to get the satisfaction. It might even turn out to be a relief to them. Why aren't you afraid of touching me?"

"Nobody should be afraid of touching you."

Again he made that bitter sound.

"Do you believe in God?" he asked suddenly.

"No," Diana replied.

"How do you explain it then? They call it the gay plague."

"When there was a polio epidemic—you're too young to remember—"

"My stepdad is lame from that."

"Is he? Then it's a better parallel than ever. When doctors suspected it could be transmitted in swimming pools, they closed the public pools, but nobody suggested that polio was God's punishment of swimmers; nobody even suggested there was something sinful about swimming."

"I don't feel innocent," Richard said.

"Nobody does," Diana said. "There are a hundred reasons why any of us should be struck dead at any time."

"I feel filthy," Richard said. "I never expected to get sick. I expected to get beaten to death or jailed."

"I expected to be killed by a bomb in the second World War."

"Because you were gay?" Richard asked.

From behind that deep barrier, the real person of Diana was silent. "Because I was there," she said. "I want you to make an appointment with the doctor you were referred to. And I want you to phone the AIDS support people. This is the number. You have to find a place to live. They can help you. You have to have money. They can help you with that, too."

"Why should *you* want me to do anything?"

"Because you're Mike's good friend, because you need the help there is. Your life isn't over, Richard. The most important part of it may just be beginning. And you know you don't have endless time to get on with it."

"This last week has been as long as my whole life."

"Make that a good thing," Diana said.

"Could I ... look at some of your paintings again now?"

"Of course," Diana said. "You know where they all are."

Diana watched him leave the room, his defeated young body suddenly full of quick eagerness. Richard did have a great love, he did know what he wanted, not some time in a far-off future but now, and he might learn to live in the present because of it. But how much harder it was to counsel such a boy than it had been to help a pregnant girl, deserted, disgraced, ready to kill herself. She could be delivered, one way or another. Even bad cases of venereal disease confronted women with sterility but rarely death, their own anyway. One such patient had killed her husband, and for years Diana had sent books to her in prison. Willing victims, they were called, and the right-to-lifers were bombing abortion clinics in the name of Christ and the unborn. They clamored now to shut down the bars and baths, but really they didn't have to do anything. They could even put away their labeling guns and let the disease run its fatal course, except that the general populaiton was at increasing risk from bad blood transfusions, from bisexual men infecting their wives. Without a cure, education was the only hope, and the bottom line of that was to persuade boys like Richard that he did have a right to live.

In one sense Mike was right. Richard was dying because he was short and ugly. Of course it was little or no comfort to say to someone that young, we die in any case, sex the mortal bomb, used, abused, neglected, it didn't matter, set at our conception to tick away until it triggered the spewing of seed on barren or fertile ground, it didn't matter, set finally to fail in any case, that crucial failure in the complex and intricate design of a system meant to self-destruct.

She heard Constance's reading voice faintly behind the closed door of the TV room, then a burst of male laughter.

"What's going on in here?" Diana asked, opening the door.

"I didn't realize *Romeo and Juliet* was so full of real jokes," Mike said.

"I've read this one before," Constance said. "In school, was it?"

"Very likely," Diana said.

"Where's Richard?" Mike asked, his attention quickly shifting away from his own concerns.

"Upstairs looking at paintings," Diana said.

"Could you . . . help him?"

"I hope so. I want him to go to his new doctor and get in touch with the AIDS people. He has the number. You must encourage him to get all the help there is."

Mike nodded.

"That was really fun, Constance," he said. "Thank you."

"Any time," Constance said, smiling.

"And thank you, Aunt Diana."

"Let me know how it goes," Diana said.

"I will."

Richard came back downstairs, the pleasure in his face temporarily overcoming the grim set of his mouth.

"Do you ever sketch, Richard?" Diana asked.

"All the time. I guess I'm old-fashioned. There are really big painters now who never learned how, but for me it's basic."

"I had to learn something about it in medical school," Diana said. "It was certainly basic there."

"The body," Richard said.

Perhaps precisely because it does fail, Diana thought, it is worthy of our various obsessions with it.

"I'd like to see some of your sketches," Diana said.

Richard looked at her with his magnified eyes, as if trying to measure that interest.

"Thank you," he said simply.

"Do as I tell you," Diana said then, putting a hand on his shoulder.

To that instruction he simply nodded.

"Did you know *Romeo and Juliet* was full of jokes?" Diana heard Mike ask as she shut the door behind them and locked it.

Constance sat watching television, her face in pale

repose, the skin almost transparent, the mask of her will set aside. A boy's laugh could touch her only for the moment while the effort to call it up left its longer lasting mark. Still, it was true for Constance, as it was for Richard, for them all, to live as long as they could in the moment. In the moment, dread could fall away. On the way of it even *Romeo and Juliet,* that tale of mortal desire, was funny, and for Diana Mike's laughter lingered in the room.

CHAPTER XIII

"Dad, this can't go on too many more days," Laura said.

They were sitting drinking coffee in what David tried to think of as Mary's kitchen, but now that she had absented herself, it had reverted to Patricia's, and he felt her absence more acutely than he had in months.

"The boys aren't turning up for meals, and even I think of every excuse I can to get out of the house. Jack has scared up a consultant's job in Prince George for a week. My family is just vanishing before my eyes."

A rehearsal for the real event, David thought. He remembered how often at first he and Patricia had sat blankly when Mary was gone, unable to function in the quiet climate of their own relationship after so many years of emotional upheavals. They had had to learn to talk all over again and to be companionably silent.

"She says she has to stay away long enough for Ted to know what breaking up the marriage would really be, and she doesn't seem to have any clear idea of how long that will be," Laura went on.

"I don't think Ted believes, in the real crunch, she would leave the children," David said.

"Has she talked to you about it?"

"No," David said.

"Well, she has to me. She says since Tyler's the youngest, and a boy, he should be with his father, and she doesn't believe in splitting up the children; so the girls would have to stay, too. They all need a strong, positive male model, Tyler for growing up to be a decent human being, the girls for choosing good husbands. I asked her about a positive female role model, and she said they were surrounded with them. Anyway, children really needed their mother only when they were small."

"Is she serious?" David asked.

"Well, I think maybe she's just practicing a speech for Ted when he agrees to be reasonable enough to listen. She certainly isn't thinking anything about what on earth she'd do with her life if they did split up."

"I've thought what she has really been hankering for is a good row with her mother. And maybe that's what this really is."

"What use is it?" Laura asked. "I said to her, 'What if Ted doesn't want the children, can't handle them by himself?' " She said, "Don't be silly. Daddie's there to help."

"Well, I can clear that up for her!" David said energetically.

The thought of taking on the responsibility of Mary and the children had been depressing to him, but he had felt required by that possibility. He did not feel required to

continue batching with his distressed son-in-law and inadequately reassuring the bewildered children.

"I can't just tell her the time's up," Laura said. "She's
my sister after all."

"I'll try to see what I can do," David said.

"Now?"

"Why not?" David said.

"Would you mind if I stayed here?" Laura asked. "It
feels more like home than my own home at the moment."

"If I'm not back by noon, maybe you could make
some sandwiches for the kids. They've taken to coming
home every day for lunch, I suppose to see that it's still
here even if their mother isn't."

"Of course," Laura said. "Do you want me to drive
you?"

"No," David said, and he smiled at his daughter. "I
need the time the bus takes."

He did not use it to think of his confrontation with
Mary. He thought instead about his other life, tomorrow
night's dinner with Constance and Diana. Diana was preparing it, and after dinner Constance would read to him a
while.

"This is such a funny, empty house," Mary said as she
welcomed him in. "Nobody ever seems to be home, not
even Laura. She's been gone all morning."

"Peaceful for you," David said.

"How can anything be peaceful for me?" Mary sighed.

"I left Laura at the house to make lunch for the kids."

"Why aren't they in school?" Mary asked in sudden real
concern.

"They are, but they come home for lunch now. I think
they keep hoping you'll be there."

"Oh, they're old enough to make their own lunch,"

Mary said impatiently. "What was Laura doing there anyway?"

"Mary, you're holding everybody hostage, and it's time you declared your terms."

"Well, everyone was holding me hostage before," Mary said, "Ted talking about leaving me, you going off without any thought of what it was like for me. It's about time you had a little of your own back, all of you, Laura, too."

"Why Laura?"

"Oh, she's just so smug!" Mary declared "and I'm going to tell her she's got no business in my house making lunch for my children."

"I asked her to."

"Well, what right is it of yours?"

"Every right in the world," David said, "beginning with legalities, going on to a quite natural concern for my grandchildren."

"What about me? What about how I feel?"

"I'm here," David said, "but I'm here to serve notice. I haven't any intention of living with Ted and your children. If you're not going to come home to look after them, other arrangements are going to have to be made."

"What do you mean?"

"I'm going to sell the house," David stated. "I may sell it in any case. It seems to me it's made nothing but trouble between you and Ted."

"Oh, Daddie, the house has nothing to do with it!" Mary wailed.

"You'll have to convince me of that," David said. "Maybe you would have needed to have this last, long fight with your mother wherever you were, but being on home territory hasn't helped. Everybody has scores to settle with the dead. It's part of the grieving process. But you've let this go on long enough to threaten to wreck your own life, and that doesn't settle any score at all. You don't have any time left now."

Mary stared away from him for a moment.

"You aren't giving me any choice," she said.

"I hope not a real one for you. I'm not going to say anything to anyone about this conversation," David said, using that old formula between them that gave Mary some measure of pride in negotiating peace with her mother. "I want you home by tomorrow morning, ready to deal with your difficulties with Ted, ready to take care of your children. You have made your point. I think Ted's learned from it as much as he can. There's still time to take advantage of that. But you've got to get out of black to do it. Your mother's dead, long since."

David kept his promise with difficulty. He was so nearly sure that Mary would be back that he wanted to share that hope with Ted and the children who had worn themselves out with indignation and self-pity and now simply drifted together disconsolately. At eight o'clock in the evening the phone rang, and fortunately Ted answered it. He listened, answered in one syllable, listened again, answered again briefly. When he hung up the phone, he stood looking at it for a moment. Then he turned to his children.

"I'm going to get your mother," he said. "She's ready to come home."

Their instinct to cheer with relief was checked by the permission their father had given them to feel hard done by.

"Look," Ted said. "We've all been mad at her, but maybe she just had to do this, and anyway it's over. So be sure you let her know you're glad she's home."

When Ted had gone, David said, "Well, it's time for me to go back downstairs."

"Granddad?" Christine asked, "will she be better?"

"I think so," David said.

"I'm still sort of mad at her," Tyler said.

"We haven't always been such perfect children," Patsy said, the most self-contained, the least apparently needy of the children.

"Blaming anyone is ... like ..." David looked at Christine before he used one of her favorite words, "boring."

She laughed. The other two looked less certain of such a judgment.

"Good night," David said, and he kissed each one, including his grandson.

David looked out at the pale sun of what was an early spring morning, a season in this climate which could easily tip back into winter, and the very fragility made it the more precious. The sap had begun to run in the bare alder and dogwood branches, their tips translucently pink in the light. Dew dripped from all the trees, from the rhododendrons, from the sticks of roses, and the lawn steamed marshily. Down the front path Mary strolled, stopping to greet snow drops, the first of the crocuses, egg yolk yellow, the first pale yellow blooms on the forsythia. "Nature's first green is gold," Patricia had said every spring when they walked together where Mary walked now. David was tempted to join his daughter but thought better of it. This was her second spring as mistress of this place, and, if she was finally going to make it her own, she must do it by herself without either his company or the ghost of her mother.

David realized how little he wanted to uproot Mary.

And it was the garden rather than the house itself, for in the house the furniture was just the furniture, rearranged, reupholstered, replaced as fashion or Patricia's whim took her, but in the garden what was planted grew and became itself, and the nurturing of it was a humbler and more requiring occupation than the similarly perennial taking of drapes to the cleaner, renting the rug shampooer from Safeway or pitching out the year's accumulation of boxes, bags, and egg cartons. "Why egg cartons?" he used to wonder. His wife might have been raised on a farm!

There was nowhere in the house David couldn't encounter hard memories, tensions, sicknesses, sorrows, angers. But in the garden his wife and children came back to him at every season, Patricia embodied in Mary now, his daughters in his grandchildren, having snowball fights, scrambling from terrace to terrace looking for Easter eggs, rolling down the long slope of lawn and heading off to the beach, grass-stained and tangle-haired, jumping in the great piles of leaves on the boulevard before he had a chance to rake them onto a burlap sheet and carry them off to dump into the ravine.

Mary was making her way slowly now off the path along the edge of the iris bed where there was as yet no sign of life. He knew she was going to a large rock, half-hidden in the trees. Both his children had found places of their own. Laura's was down behind a curve of laurel hedge on the other side of the garden where she couldn't be seen from the house, for her moods had always been private. Mary, even in a reclusive mood, hoped to be glimpsed through the trees. David wondered if even now she hoped he was watching her. He turned away. She could not learn to be alone in her own garden without being let alone.

"Have you really given her away?" his sister had asked him. He had thought he had, but offering her the house was a way of calling her home, of filling the terrible empty space with the sounds of young life again. He had abdicated that space fairly gracefully, but it was he and not Ted who had brought her home again this time. "Everyone was holding me hostage," Mary had said. Was he wrong to think that it was only Patricia's power that must gradually wane, that he knew how to abdicate power over the children as she hadn't?

"I am their mother," Patricia would say whenever he suggested that she might be being a bit heavy-handed about her own wishes and judgments and tastes once the children were grown. Yet she would never have made the mistake he increasingly thought he had made. How could it be corrected now without another arbitrary use of his authority? He was thinking like a father of a five-year-old, saying to Mary, "I know you want it, but you can't have it. It's not good for you." And she was responding like a five-year-old, varying temper tantrums with docile behavior, alternately thinking of him as her slave, there to live his life with only her convenience or happiness in mind, and her master, the one person she couldn't finally defy because in the end she never had.

How grateful David was when he could leave the house and make his way to Shaughnessy for dinner with Diana and Constance. He hardly ever any longer thought about the guilt he had carried for years, the ugly gulf there had been, for it was gone. He crossed nothing but the city streets which separated them, always taking a gift of some sort, a book, a good cheese, dinner, tonight a bunch of daffodils from the Chinese grocer near where he caught his bus because it had been a daffodil-colored day out beyond his dark little den. He should have gone out into it much earlier.

Diana greeted him at the door with responding eagerness.

"How long it seems to be now," she said.

The real passage of time, however, was there in Constance's eyes. She did not know who he was. David checked his hurt like a physical pain from which he must not flinch and fell back on his old comic gallantry, bowing, offering up his daffodils as he said, "I'm David, Diana's brother."

She smiled at him, but in her smile was that almost hectic brilliance of will rather than the warmth of recognition. He felt punished by it, as if he had failed in some basic duty of love. And Diana knew he did. He was grateful to her for making no clumsy effort to cover up for Constance, but she did send him almost immediately to the kitchen to make drinks. There he didn't allow himself a moment of self-indulgent grief. He had always known his love for Constance had to be entirely independent of any recognition from her. When she had come to know him, when he had crouched there with her in the shade of the rock, it had been a little miracle, and it was a mistake to have begun to count on that, for it was only his constant presence which had encouraged the small, guttering light that, of course, went out when days passed without him. If she never knew him again, he must refuse to mind, or he would turn all his ease with both his sister and Constance into tension and sadness.

Through drinks and dinner, David was careful not to talk about his family, conversations which always to some extent excluded Constance, and now that they were back on rationed time together, he must make the most of their being three together. He talked about gardens. He wondered if they might one day go to England to see some of the great ones, and gradually Constance relaxed enough to tell him about taking a boat to Kew when she was a child. For David and Diana both, the richness of that deprived childhood always amazed them, and Constance was more present with them in it than she could easily be as herself now, for everything but her childhood broke on the shores of her mind in dissociated fragments which she and often they could not mend into meaning.

Constance did not read to him after dinner. The memory board which she had so resolutely carried with her had been abandoned in the TV room, and, since Diana had not retrieved it for her, David supposed Constance needed a rest from her attempt to live in the present. Instead they listened to music, Bach's variations on a theme, and David had a moment of pure delight in rediscovering the power of that little machine to bring the piano right into the room with them.

When Constance asked if she might go to bed, Diana went with her, and David listened through a whole disc before she returned.

"I'm sorry . . ." Diana began.

"Don't be," David said quickly.

"When she doesn't remember you, I wonder how soon the day will come when she doesn't recognize me."

"D., I'm only a flicker of present light. You've been with her for forty years. She'll always know you."

Diana shook her head almost impatiently and said, "No, she won't, and I have to be prepared for it."

She spoke in the same firm tone she had used when she said, "I have to know how it is for her." She was talking to herself as David had to himself, making drinks at the beginning of the evening. A new understanding confronted David. He and Diana would not lose Constance. She would lose them. For her David was no great loss, and he must see that as a mercy. But how could she live, not knowing Diana?

"Mike's friend Richard has been here again," Diana said. "He has AIDS."

"AIDS?" David repeated.

"Mike's not involved," Diana said quickly. "He's in no danger himself, I mean. But Richard's parents have turned him out, and Mike asked me if I could help. I think I've headed him in helpful directions if he'll take them, but my basic advice to him I find very hard to take myself. We all have to live in the present."

"With the exception of Constance," David said, who hadn't been able to make the shift in concern.

"Constance, too, as much as she's able, and in a way, you know, she does it better than the rest of us."

"Are you sure Mike's in no danger?" David asked then, finally hearing what Diana had said about Richard.

"They're simply friends," Diana said. "Mike's a very good friend."

"I'm so glad they had you to come to," David said.

"I don't feel much like a doctor after all this time," Diana said. "I don't keep up except in a very general way."

"But you could . . ." and David stopped himself, about to blunder into territory that offended her.

"But I didn't," Diana said. "Would you like a nightcap?"

He went to the kitchen and brought back drinks for them both. They sat together without speaking for some time, watching the dying fire.

"I wouldn't say, even to that dying boy," Diana finally said, breaking the silence with a will, "that, yes, I'm gay or queer or homosexual or lesbian. I am Diana Crown, a proud woman nearly turned to stone, but for Constance."

David wanted to protest, but he didn't, for she was talking more to herself than to him. He was there to overhear, nothing more. She did not go on aloud, and in time David wondered if she was even aware that he was still there. It did not matter. He sat in his own chair, exhausted and peaceful.

"You haven't told me about Mary," Diana said finally.

"She's come home," David said.

He got up then.

"Do come before next Wednesday if you can manage it," she said. "You're a great comfort to me, D."

"I love you," he said, a hand on her shoulder as he bent down to kiss her goodnight.

In the morning David looked out to see the first early daffodils in bloom, their thin pale little trumpets no competition for the King Alfreds to come, but it was virtue enough to be the first. He would have liked to go out and work for an hour or two, to find about him all the intimate signs of spring, but he didn't any longer feel free to. He was impatient with himself, to have somehow got himself into this position of being damned if he did and damned if he didn't. It was far too large a garden for Mary to deal with herself, and neither Ted nor the children showed a gardener's interest in it. Perhaps they might if they saw any need to. If he didn't garden, how was he to fill his days?

On the desert, no day was ever long enough, but what had he done but walk into the little town and back, swim, help with meals, be read to, occasionally watch television. If that essentially drab little town could occupy his interest morning after morning, surely Vancouver could provide distractions, but he looked down at the skyline of high rises with distaste.

" 'When the city lies at the monster's feet, there are left the mountains.' " Was it Jeffers?

David hadn't been up Grouse Mountain for years, but the idea of sitting in the chair lift, his legs dangling, naked of skis, among the athletic young had no appeal for him.

He hadn't walked in Stanley Park for years either. He had always thought of it as a place to take children to the zoo or aquarium or for a ride on the little train, but lots of old people without the excuse of children simply walked about or sat on benches at Lost Lagoon feeding the birds, and they were not really what his melodramatic career might have led him to believe, either child molesters or seducers of young boys.

David had to get out of the house, and Stanley Park might do. He even had the forethought to take some stale bread. If the ducks would eat it, he could spare himself having to eat toast which hurt his gums even for lunch toward the end of the week. In a way, he was sorry now that he'd thrown out that old coat and hat, for, if he was going to be one of those sad old men on park benches, he might as well dress the part and not invite muggers. Then he remembered his brown jogging suit. Just the ridiculous thing! With a sweater over it, he would be warm enough and odd enough to cheer himself up. But shoes. He wasn't today setting out to amuse Diana and Constance. He rummaged around in his closet until he found a pair of old blue sneakers. He sighed. Why had even his sneakers been blue? He must have bought them for himself. They would do until he got to a shoe store.

"Something for jogging, will it be, sir?" the blank-faced clerk inquired.

"They should look as if they could jog," David decided.

"Any color preference?"

"Well, brown," David said. "Anyway, something to go with brown."

The clerk glanced at David's jogging pants and glanced away as he very gingerly began to remove one of David's disreputable sneakers.

"They belong in a museum," David said cheerfully, "or

in a theatre costume warehouse."

The clerk reserved any opinion of his own. He went off, leaving David to contemplate his one decently socked foot, for he was wearing a pair of brown socks Christine had given him for Christmas. He sighed. Christine was quite beyond need of him now, for suddenly she had not one boy but several bidding for her attention, and her hours on the phone and nights out had begun to be restricted, a step Ted was much quicker to take than Mary might have been. In fact, he behaved as if Christine were walking out on him, too, every time she went to a movie.

A father is a peculiar creature, David decided, and he is never so aware that he is one as when the children begin to leave him alone. As a husband, Ted suffered something of that quality as well.

The shoes the clerk presented to him were the sort he saw college boys wearing, thick-soled, brown, green-and-white-striped without any shoelaces. David could not imagine them on his feet, but the clerk patiently showed him the velcro opening and shoved his foot into it, wrapping the shoe round with one gesture.

"Good heavens," David said, looking down at the foreign object so simply attached to him.

"Will you try the other?"

"Why not?"

With both shoes on, he got up and bounced gently across the floor to the full-length mirror. What he saw he could hardly credit. He must be at the fun fair, sticking his head over the cardboard cutout of a jogger, for the body and the feet seemed to belong together, but the head was all he recognized, the head of an old man who had been, one might still be able to see, a trifle too pretty in youth. Should that body and those feet do a little running in place to be convincing? But what would the head do, bouncing

on top? Surely Constance would say that these were proper
shoes just by the look of them, and they were in a peculiar
way comfortable, not nearly as heavy as they looked.

"I'll take them," David said, returning to the clerk.
"And I'll wear them. You'd probably better throw those
others away, if you don't mind."

"Eighty-five dollars, plus tax," the clerk said, dropping
David's old shoes into the box.

Eighty five dollars!

"Right," David said.

As he left the store, he heard Patricia say, "You didn't
have to buy them just because you tried them on!" Well,
he had to have shoes, didn't he? She could not be expected
to understand inflation, having been dead for some time
now. He still had trouble with it himself even now when he
considered himself a nearly seasoned shopper.

David was beginning to enjoy himself as he walked
springily toward the park, his bag of stale bread clutched in
one hand—his left hand, he noticed. It was a lovely day.

When he got to Lost Lagoon, he had to compete for his
share of ducks. Nearly half the old-age pensioners of the
West End must be out here getting rid of their stale bread.
If he wanted to do nature a favor, he might better kill a
couple of these obese waddlers and stuff them with the
stale bread for dinner for Constance and Diana.

With some antic coaxing, David did manage to attract
the interest of half a dozen birds, but he'd got rid of less
than half of his bread when an old woman crowded into
his territory and stole his whole flock with bagels.

To hell with this, David thought, and he bounded away
to the sea wall where he had the seagulls to himself, and
who cared if the joggers glared at him as they passed?
There was no law against feeding the seagulls. When he
finally got rid of the bread, he found a trash can in which

to deposit the empty bag, and then he strolled at an elderly pace around the entire length of the sea wall until he came to the restaurant, completely renovated since he had last been there years ago. Men in expensive business suits and women in fur-collared coats and leather gloves strolled across the parking lot. David stared at them, looking into his past life.

Then boldly he joined them, pretending to ignore their critical glances. He had on a pair of eighty-five dollar shoes, which should qualify him to go anywhere. The headwaiter was perfectly polite even though David had no reservation, and the waiter was cheerful and prompt.

"Got a good appetite, I bet you have," he said as he put the large seafood platter in front of David.

"I certainly do," David said and knew his most convincing performance would be eating his part.

At home that evening, enjoying a peanut butter sandwich, a banana and a glass of milk, David reckoned he could not entertain himself so extravagantly every day, but now that he was outfitted, he could afford to be more frugal.

It's not old age, he mused. He had always honored the ordinary, but he had also always wanted to be peculiar at least some of the time. The house above him stirred with peaceful, domestic sounds. Perhaps, after a time, he could relax here again, actually be what he had been trying to be all along, an unobtrusive, uninterfering, occasionally helpful old man, an affectionate father, a supportive father-in-law, benign to his grandchildren.

For some days David entertained himself with jogging suit adventures. He wandered the public gardens learning the names of more flowers and trees, which he brought as offerings to Constance who still did not know him, but, since she was not agitated about it, he schooled himself in his own patience. She asked him if he was a visiting botanist and offered to show him her own garden. She was less willing to share any of the work of it with him. He wandered the grant lands and brought back bags of wild mushrooms to be identified. He and Diana had learned to take spore prints in childhood and rediscovered not only their usefulness in establishing edibility of what he had found but their sheer beauty as designs on paper.

"I must show these to Richard," Diana said. "He's coming now to give me lessons in sketching."

So they learned how to occupy their days.

Mary did not mention the fact that David wasn't gardening. She had begun to take over some of the chores she had before left to him. He saw her eye his jogging suit with some perplexity, but she made no comment about it or his increasing absences from the house. He wasn't even asked to stay at home in the evening with the children though Mary and Ted occasionally went out. As Christine graduated into going out herself, David assumed she had been given new status in looking after her younger brother and sister. Even she didn't drop in on him as casually and often as she had.

David took all these signs as positive indications though he felt much more narrowly at home himself. He did not automatically go for the ladder when he spotted a blocked eaves trough and tried not to feel irritated that Ted hadn't the same alacrity in taking over house maintenance chores that Mary had in the garden. In fact, Ted's behavior made David uncomfortable. After those weeks of candidly depending on David for everything from tending the children to being his father confessor, Ted hardly spoke to him now. David supposed Ted was embarrassed by the intimacy of that time, even regretted it now that he'd been able to take over the reins of family life again. The change had taken place almost immediately after Mary came home. Had she had the lack of good sense to tell Ted she'd come home primarily to save the house?

David hadn't seriously discussed the possibility of selling the house with Ted. Ted was too ambivalent about it already, guiltily grateful about the money it saved him and probably resentful of its hold over Mary. David did not want to make Ted an ally against Mary in such a decision, particularly when it might not come to that. Surely when this period of adjustment passed, David would remain much less involved in their lives but feel less artificially excluded. Time would resolve the awkwardness.

David was surprised one evening to find Ted at his study door. Unlike Mary and the children who had before wandered in and out more or less at will, Ted had respected his father-in-law's privacy and rarely invaded it, waiting to talk when David went up for dinner or was out-of-doors.

"Come in!" David said, surprised at the false enthusiasm in his voice.

"David," Ted said.

David looked at his son-in-law quizzically, for unlike Jack, Ted had always called David "Dad."

"Does that sound okay to you?" Ted asked.

"If it does to you," David said.

"I thought it might make it easier."

"Easier?"

"It doesn't," Ted said in discouragement. "You've been like a father to me."

"You've been like a son," David said gently.

"But not a very good one," Ted said. "You've been very indulgent, and I've let you take care of a lot of things I should have taken care of myself. Both Mary and I have gone on being children in ways we shouldn't. Jack was fairly rough on me, you know. Everyone else talked about how Mary should pull herself together, but Jack said I should stop acting like a sulky kid who could walk away from my family as if they were a bunch of toys I'd got bored with and face up to the fact that I was a husband and father with problems to solve. He's right. And Mary does know now that I don't think of walking out as one of my options. Since it isn't, we've both been making some real progress."

"Good," David said.

"It's been easier for Mary in some ways than it has for me."

David waited.

"I've seen the eaves trough," Ted said. "And I know you're not going to fix it, and I know why. Every day I don't do it myself, I feel guiltier, and then I get mad at you, wondering why the hell an eaves trough is so important anyway."

"I'd be glad to fix it if you'd like me to," David said. "It isn't all that important."

"If you do it, you're fixing your own house. If I do it, I'm doing a boy's chore," Ted said.

"Would you like to move, Ted?"

"No," Ted said. "I'd like you to."

"I see," David said, blinking.

"We could rent this space and add it to what we pay you, and I could add a couple of hundred more to that. I know it's not a realistic offer for this house, but at least you could rent a real apartment for yourself and stop living as if you were a poor relation. I can't buy it from you, Dad, even with the money from our other house, not for what it's worth. Maybe down the way a few years I could, but that's the best I can do now."

"Let me think about it," David said.

"This isn't Mary's idea," Ted said.

"But she's agreeable to it?"

"Yes, if you are. You know, from the beginning everybody thought it was, well, sort of undignified for you to live in the basement of your own house and then turn yourself into a kind of built-in, unpaid servant."

"It hasn't really felt to me like that," David said.

"But it's been like that for us. And we just let you do it."

So the solution to the problem they had perhaps all agreed to was for David to move, something that had never crossed his mind as owner of the house. For he did still, in that sense, think of it as his house, and so it was not easy to think that Ted had any business asking him to leave it—though the others perhaps saw no irony in it?

David sat at dinner with Laura, Jack and the boys, a household in which he had been increasingly encouraged to feel at home over these last few weeks after he'd persuaded Mary to go home. Now he found himself wondering if it had been part of a family plot to ease him out of Mary and Ted's life and into a sterile, respectable place of his own. He found himself less able than usual to be amused at the boys' horseplay or to take an interest in Jack's latest project. He even looked at Laura suspiciously. Was she in league against him? He waited to raise the topic after Ben and Mike had gone off to their rooms to study.

"Have you both decided with Ted and Mary that it would be best for me to move out?"

"Move out?" Laura repeated.

David measured her genuine puzzlement. She didn't blush.

"Ted has asked me to move."

"What?" Jack demanded.

"He says I've become a sort of built-in, unpaid servant,

and you all thought it was undignified for me to live like that."

"We've never discussed it!" Laura protested. "Oh, I guess we did at first. I guess we all worried that you wouldn't be really comfortable."

"Is this another of Mary's pranks?" Jack asked.

Realizing it wasn't a family conspiracy, David shifted his defensiveness from himself to his younger daughter who created enough genuine problems not to be wrongly blamed for this one.

"I'm sure it's not," David said.

"But what right does Ted think he has ..." Jack demanded.

"I don't suppose he thinks of it as a right," David said. "He knows he's in no position to make a realistic financial offer. But, aside from its not being really fair to you, Laura ... it's after all as much your house as Mary's."

"Oh, Daddie, I don't care about that. You know that. It's your house."

"I think Ted doesn't think he can manage to take over the real responsibilities while he's under my nose."

"Surely the real responsibilities include money," Jack said. "He's feckless about it."

"He's generous," David said. "That's not quite the same thing."

"It is if you don't have the money to give," Jack said.

The harsher Jack was the more inclined David was to take Ted's part. Of course, Ted couldn't call David anything but "Dad" because the request he'd made could only be made not as one man to another but as a son to a father. It was not a father's place to drive hard financial bargains with his son. David had made too hard an emotional bargain with both Ted and Mary, not because the associations of the house had forced them to regress into childhood but because he was still there. Why had the obvious been so difficult for him to see?

"At least while you're there," Jack was saying, "you can see that the house doesn't fall down around their ears. Ted's never been any good at those things. Oh, he knows how but he just doesn't see. He didn't do anything to his own house until he decided to sell it."

"He's beginning to," David said. "In any case, there's really no reason for them to live as house-proud as Patricia and I were. Mary's very good in the garden."

"But where would you go?" Laura asked. "You'd hate living in an apartment."

"Well, I don't know," David said. "After the basement, I might like living up in the air and light, maybe somewhere in the West End near the park."

"And be one of those funny old men who sit around in the sun all day with nothing to do?" Laura demanded.

"I've been practicing already," David said. "The only thing I really don't like about it is feeding the ducks."

"David, don't make any quick decisions," Jack said. "Think about it first, and for once think about it from your point of view."

"Do you know the only thing that really troubled me?" David asked. "I thought you were all in on it, and I felt conspired against. I'm getting paranoid in my old age."

When David told Diana of his decision to move, he did not tell her had been asked to leave by his son-in-law. That omission forced him to be aware that conspiracy was not the only aspect of this experience which troubled him. He wasn't sure the residual shame he felt was for himeslf or for Ted. But it was Ted he was protecting from any further criticism, even though his hope that Diana might finally meet this family had grown considerably dimmer. Or was he behaving as he might have with Patricia, trying to protect himself from that old and habitual charge that he had no gumption, that he never stood up for himself? It wasn't bad enough that he'd been a fool in the first place but now he was letting his children ride roughshod over him.

"Do you really want to move?" was the question Diana asked him.

Put to him that simply, the question clarified what had really very little to do with Mary and Ted.

"I didn't know it at the time, but this could never have been anything but an interim arrangement while we all took stock. My little apartment was a good place to grieve, but it isn't really any place to live. It's too dark and too small. I can't have anyone in."

"Do you like to entertain?"

"We always did a lot of it," David said. "I honestly can't say I miss it. I've seen hardly any of our friends for months, and I'm not sure I will now. It's the light really, more than anything."

"I'm going to ask you something I have no business to ask," Diana said. "Would you consider coming to live with us? It would be jumping from the frying pan into the fire, I know that."

"Are you serious?" David asked.

"I shouldn't be, for your sake. I should be saving those empty rooms upstairs for professional help, but I can't bear the idea any more than I can bear the idea of finally having to commit Constance because I can't take care of her. But, if anything happened to me, she'd have no one. It's an impossible thing to ask of you. I know that."

"But, D., I would have suggested it myself if it had ever occurred to me you'd be willing. There's nothing that could make me happier. When we were together on the desert, it seemed to me so natural, so right for us to be together."

"That was a holiday," Diana said. "What we're heading

into now isn't a holiday. You and Constance are very likely to outlive me."

The weight of that statement was heavy on David's shoulders, but it was also familiar. He was under no illusion that he controlled his own destiny, but he was careful. He did know that, if he were left with Constance, he would feel even more excruciatingly inadequate than he had with his children, for whom he couldn't replace their mother. Though he might live the rest of his life with Constance, she would not know who he was. But whether he lived with her or not, he would love her and she would not know him. He was already learning to suffer and accept that.

"Nothing could make more sense to me than living with both of you," David said.

"Think about it," Diana admonished him as Jack had done. "Hoping you don't have the good sense to refuse doesn't mean I won't accept it."

On the third night after Ted had asked David to move, he went upstairs after dinner and found Mary in the kitchen.

"Is this a good time to talk with you and Ted?"

"Oh, I guess it's best to get it over with," Mary sighed. "You're going to sell the house, aren't you? Ted said it's the only sensible thing to do."

"No, I'm not," David said, "but I'm going to move out."

"Oh, Daddie!" Mary cried, and she flung her arms around him.

She was thanking him and clinging to him at the same time.

"Let's go talk with Ted," he said gently, untangling himself from that embrace.

"I've been thinking," David said as the three of them

sat together in the living room. "I could never have afforded to live in this house without help from my own in-laws, and there's no reason why I shouldn't help you if you're sure this is what you both want."

Mary looked at Ted.

"It is," Ted said.

"Then it's settled," David said. "And I'll be moving out in a few days."

"You've already found a place?" Ted asked, surprised.

"Yes," David said. "I'm going to live with my sister."

Mary stared at him.

"Well," Ted said heartily into the silence.

"Is that *your* score to settle with the dead?" Mary asked icily.

"A year ago I might have said, 'In part, yes,' " David answered gently, ignoring his daughter's tone. "I loved your mother, Mary. I also love my sister. She needs me now, and there's no reason for me not to be with her."

"But she's a scandalous person!" Mary protested. "What will your friends think?"

"They were mainly your mother's friends," David said. "I hardly ever see them now, and I don't really much care what they think."

"And you don't care what I think either, do you?" Mary demanded. "You're doing this on purpose."

"I care very much what you think," David said. "I feel partly responsible for what you think. But you're a grown woman, and it's long past time for you and me to stop trying to lead each other's lives."

"You think you own your father, Mary," Ted said. "You don't."

"Why are you both doing this to me?" Mary cried. "I don't even *want* you to leave."

"Isn't it hard enough, damn it!" Ted shouted. "Do you

have to make it impossible?"

"It isn't impossible," David said. "Mary?"

She glared at him through tears.

"I want to show you how to prune the roses before I go."

"Do I have to learn?"

"Yes, my dear, you do," David said.

CHAPTER XIV

The Saturday David was to move in, both Mike and Ben were busy carrying the spare furniture which had accumulated in Jill's vacated rooms to the basement before they drove a rented truck over to pick up David's own things. The cleaning woman did chores around the house, waiting to get into David's rooms as soon as the boys were finished.

"How did I live so long without you two?" Diana asked.

"We've only been much use to anyone recently," Mike said, grinning.

"This is a great set-up for Granddad," Ben said, looking around. "Much better than the basement."

"He'll have to decide about the pictures," Diana said. "There are far too many of them."

"I'd keep them all," Mike said.

"Maybe you'd like to have any David doesn't want," Diana suggested.

Mike shook his head in embarrassment at the extravagance of the offer.

"Well, you'll have them eventually," Diana said, only realizing it as she spoke. "Why not now if they'll only be stored in the basement otherwise?"

"Maybe you could loan one or two to Richard for his new room," Mike suggested tentatively.

"What a good idea!" Diana said.

Diana admired the strength and skill of her two great-nephews as they negotiated the stairs with a heavy, awkward couch. Her aversion to young male bodies had not been sexual; it had developed as an emotional protest when she had had to nurse so many during the war. They had forever shaken her sense of the integrity of the body, that vast complexity of cellular intelligence in its fragile sack of skin. Even now she wanted to admonish, "Be careful!" because she agreed with her brother that males generally are defective in their own defense equally against accident or aggression. Then how baffled they were to discover that they were made of flesh and bone and blood when they lay like the broken toys of their own games.

But these two had been allowed to grow up without the fact of war, instead with the threat of such a war that there would be no place for death-defying heroic fantasies, and they seemed to her gentler, more domestic creatures than her own generation had been, not soft, no, but their strength given to mending, moving, making things. They were great docile beings who conferred authority on their elders as if it were a gift from them rather than a yoke the young were forced to bear.

In her involvement with all the preparations, Diana had for some moments lost track of Constance and went to look for her first in the garden where her memory board would have directed her to go, then into the TV room where Diana found the board and timer. She picked those up and carried them back upstairs to their bedroom where Constance often retreated when the house was a confusion of people. There she was standing before an open suitcase with Diana's bathrobe in her hand.

"What are you doing?" Diana asked cheerfullly.

"I'm trying to pack," Constance said irritably. "I can't find any of my own clothes."

"Well, that's my robe," Diana agreed. "Where are you off to?"

"I'm going home," Constance said.

"You are at home, my darling," Diana said gently.

"This is not time to make jokes. The movers are here. We're finally going home."

"They're only getting ready to move David in. He's coming this afternoon with his own furniture."

"And we're moving out. See for yourself. They're carrying the furniture right down the stairs outside this room."

"It's a beautiful morning," Diana said. "Why don't you come out in the garden? Look, it says right here on your board, 'garden.' "

Constance took the board and stared at it for a long moment.

"I'm tired of this," she said finally. "It gets in my way."

"It helps you remember," Diana said.

Constance took the cellophane and lifted it up. The day's instructions vanished. Then she looked at Diana with a defiant grin. Diana laughed, loving the freedom of that gesture, but it reminded her, too, that Constance also confered authority and could withdraw it at any time.

Constance looked down at the suitcase.

"Where are we going?"

"We're not going anywhere," Diana said. "I'll put that away."

She removed the few clothes, a random mixture of her own and Constance's, and put the suitcase back in the closet while Constance stood watching her.

"Well, tell me where we are if you think you're so smart!" Constance demanded.

"Come into the garden, and I'll show you."

Even in the garden Constance walked about looking at the shrubs and flowers as if they were in a little park. Diana could recognize a garden of Constance's wherever she had designed and cared for it. At the moment Constance couldn't, though it was her own. But she was less agitated here away from the activity in the house.

"I like this," she said finally, smiling at Diana, "but isn't it time to go?"

At that moment, Mike opened the new door and called to them, "We're on our way. Don't forget to fix the front door when you come in."

"Thank you, Mike. I'll be right there."

"You seem to know all these people by name," Constance said.

"Yes, they're my great-nephews."

Constance looked at her oddly. "Do you think you're related to everybody?"

"There certainly are more of my relatives around than we're used to," Diana agreed. "Come on. I'll make us some lunch."

Diana persuaded Constance to rest after the meal, but shortly the noise of David's furniture being moved in disturbed her, and she stood in the doorway of their bedroom peering out at the sound of approaching footsteps and then ducking back behind the door before anyone could see her there.

"Constance, I know you're there," Mike called out in a teasing tone.

She glared at him through the crack in the door.

He called again on his way back downstairs.

"I'm not hiding from you," she said, showing herself to him. "You're nothing but a great, silly boy."

"That's right, so you don't have to play the troll under the bridge because you don't scare me either."

She laughed, and he laughed with her, sounds which came down the stairs to Diana where she stood guard at the open front door, for she was afraid Constance might try to bolt from all this confusion being inflicted on her, some of which, when David settled in, might be permanent. That his presence now might not reassure Constance as it had in the desert, that instead he might prove to be what broke her last ties with this place and made her a stranger in her own home was a risk there was no longer any point in not taking, for the ties were breaking anyway. Diana needed David now. She couldn't any longer manage without him.

When the boys had finished and were saying good-bye to Diana and David in the front hall, Constance came down the stairs to join them.

"I want to go home," she said to Mike. "Could you take me home?"

"Sure," Mike said, and before Diana could object, Mike was escorting Constance down the front walk, leaving David, Diana, and Ben to stare after them.

"Back in a bit," he called after he'd helped Constance into the cab of the rented truck and run round to climb into the driver's seat.

"What is he going to do?" Diana demanded.

"I think he'll drive her around the block a few times and come back. Maybe if we make ourselves scarce," Ben said to his grandfather, "and you're just here by yourself, Aunt Diana, it will seem more familiar to her. There's been a lot of traffic around here today. No wonder it's got to her."

First fright and then indignation flashed and flickered out in Diana, for they weren't simply playing a stupid trick on Constance but trying to invent a way of participating in her doubt to allay it. Maybe it would work, temporarily anyway.

David and Ben disappeared up the stairs to David's new quarters. Diana waited in the living room, watching the street. In a few minutes, the truck pulled up and Mike was helping Constance down from the high cab. How tiny she looked in front of that large machine, at the side of that tall boy, but she was smiling at him and talking to him as they walked up the path.

"This young man was kind enough to bring me home," Constance said as Diana opened the door to them. "Could we give you something? A drink of some sort?"

"No thanks," he said, smiling down at her.

He did not even tip Diana a wink, for it wasn't for him a game he was playing but something he was doing for Constance which he wanted to do well, which he wanted to work.

For the moment, it did. Constance recognized the rooms she walked through, and, when she found the memory board on her bureau in the bedroom, she picked it up with relief. Then she frowned.

"There's nothing on it. I do need it, darling," Constance said earnestly. "Without it I just don't know what to do or where to go next . . . or is it bedtime?"

Diana took the board and wrote on it, "Dinner with

David, my brother."

Constance looked at it and nodded. "Thank you. It's for you, too, you know. Otherwise you have to tell me the same thing over and over again."

It was difficult for Diana, who had always been scrupulously honest with Constance, to acknowledge that forcing honesty on her to the point of flat contradiction didn't any longer serve to reassure her in her most confused moments. Diana simply could not do for Constance what Mike had done and what she now watched David doing. When Constance mistook him for the plumber or the garbage man or the gardener, he quietly took on those roles, not with any archness or flamboyance but with an understated gentleness which was meant to be reassuring to her and was. For his ever-present changing made him appear to Constance a temporary fact of life rather than an established custodian.

"We're getting old," Constance said to Jill as David brought them drinks from the kitchen. "We seem to need so much more help. There always seems to be someone around now, doing something."

Jill smiled at David with an embarrassed apology his eyes refused, for, whenever Constance found it difficult to accept him as one of the company, he did actually become manservant or investment broker or doctor, whatever she suggested to him. Diana was learning not to be embarrassed by it and was the more impatient with Jill because she shared Diana's basic lack of imagination. Together they could never have taken care of Constance as she was cared for now.

"How does he stand it?" Jill asked as Diana walked her

to her car.

"He doesn't seem to mind at all," Diana said. "He did once want to be an actor."

"The butler isn't exactly a prize role," Jill said.

"I'm not sure he'd agree with you," Diana said. "He told me once the minor roles are the hardest because you so often have nothing to do but be."

"She didn't really know who I was today," Jill said. "She was bluffing."

"To please you, if she was," Diana said.

"I'm glad for you that David's here," Jill said, "but it must be odd to have a man in the house."

"He's my brother," Diana said, wondering why she had to remind Jill as she did Constance.

"That would make it more rather than less difficult for me," Jill said. "But I never did get along with my family."

Diana had certainly felt an alien in her own family long before her sister-in-law had managed to alienate her. But it had never seemed to Diana a real family so much as an accidental variety of needs under the same roof. Her mother had never attempted to unite them. She hadn't either the vision or the skill. In her last years the only effort she made was to keep them all apart, out of each other's way. If their mother had wanted or needed their reconciliation, would David have felt compelled to confront his wife's bigotry? Would Diana have felt obliged to forgive her? For families to get along, surely there had to be at least one person who believed it not only possible but important. Well, Jill's mother had, and it produced nothing but farcical holidays until she died, and the siblings fell apart at the funeral. At their mother's funeral, David and Diana were as decorous with each other as they were on their birthdays, and their half-brothers were such strangers to them that they all were no more than embarrassed to intrude on each other's grief. All they had in common was the burden they had been to a woman who had done the best she could under the circumstances. They had never been a family.

Yet Diana said to Jill, "He's my brother," as if it was as natural for her to live with him again as it felt, as if kinship explained it.

"You don't take to Jill, do you?" Diana asked her brother.

"I don't really know her yet," David said. "I suspect she doesn't take to me."

"She lived here with us years ago," Diana said.

"Where I am now?" David asked. "Well, no wonder."

"She's glad you're here. It's not something she could have done, but she does everything she can."

If David had needed a longer explanation, Diana would have given it to him, but he shied away from any conversation which might make him seem intrusive.

Fortunately, he was at ease with the only other familiar of the house, young Richard, who had no prior claims or prejudices for David to deal with. Diana suspected that David had taken advice from Mike in the pictures he chose to eliminate from the collection, for among them were two of Richard's favorites which he caried off for his new room.

"I'd like to give his father a thrashing!" David said, the violence in his tone a surprise to Diana.

"His stepfather," she corrected.

"All the better!" David said. "I could act out all my own adolescent fantasies. And Hugh never even threatened to throw me out."

"You didn't present any hard porblems for him," Diana said.

"What's the hard problem in this?" David demanded.

"The boy's dying! The only trouble he'll be to them in a few months is to their consciences."

"In my experience, the more self-righteous people are, the less troubled they are by conscience," Diana said. "It's a waste of time to be angry with them."

"But he needs help, now," David protested.

"He's getting it," Diana said, "and from people a lot better equipped to do it than his parents. The last thing in the world he needs is people to reconfirm his own worst judgments of himself, that this is a punishment he must accept in all humility. He's better off angry with them than reconciled to them."

"Maybe he is," David admitted. "Does he talk to you while you're sketching?"

"A little, but he has people to talk to about dying. He needs to talk about what he cares about. He's a wonderful teacher."

Diana looked forward to Richard's coming though she had to overcome the first impression inevitable to her medical eye before she could share the hour with him. She gave him lessons in anatomy as he gave her lessons in drawing. His drawing took bolder substance and she began to risk the minimal and suggestive lines at which he was so brilliant. There were days when she knew she took on the only strength he had, but at least that hour was a relief from the black apathy he sank back into, as one opportunistic infection after another had its own way with his defenseless body.

"Some days I'm nothing but a stinking corpse!" Richard cried out. "I'm rotting before I'm even buried."

Then would come a stretch of several weeks when he seemed free of pain, when a frail, happy energy carried him along. He never spoke of being cured, of a miracle that might save him. He was learning to accept as miracle enough any good days he had.

Mike often came to meet him at the end of a sketching session to drive him back to his room if he needed a ride, to take him off to the beach or a movie. Sometimes both the boys stayed to supper. Richard hadn't the ease with Constance that seemed to come so naturally to Mike. Richard could be reduced to staring at her blankly when she derailed a conversation he had been riding with Mike or David, yet Constance touched him more freely and naturally than anyone else could, not discouraged by his initial flinching away because she didn't remember it.

"She doesn't even understand what I have," Richard said to Diana.

"It wouldn't make any difference if she did," Diana said. "It's what she has to give. Let her."

"I've never realized it before, but dying is an alternative to getting old," Richard said.

"Does she frighten you?" Diana asked. "Do I?"

"You did," Richard admitted. "But I'm more comfortable with you now than I am even with Mike. He's all . . . tomorrow, next year. You're always right now."

With Richard, Diana tried to be, and, because she had to keep her apprehensions for him out of the time she spent with him, she was learning how easy it was, particularly when they had such an absorbing pleasure to share. It was not the same for Constance, even when she was reading to David, though it made her feel useful as the gardening did.

Sometimes Diana wondered how it really was for David to move out of the house of a growing family into this mortal climate. She knew him well enough now to realize that his amiability was nearly automatic. Underneath it, there were other darker moods he kept to himself even more now that he lived here. They had had fewer personal talks in the three months of being under the same roof than when they were awkwardly getting to know each other over the year before. Diana needed her brother so much that she was afraid to discover he might regret what he had done.

Jack and the boys came to bottle the wine and now were preparing Diana for the art of using fresh fruit. Diana noticed that David didn't join them but chose instead to keep Constance company out of the way of all the noise and activity. But he did go often on his own to that household, and Laura dropped by occasionally on her own, always bringing something, a batch of cookies, jam, a loaf of bread.

Diana would have felt more generous in making sure that father and daughter had time alone together if she weren't also aware that it gave her excuse to avoid Laura, who didn't get over her eager nervousness with both Diana and Constance. Constance would go on insisting, every time she saw Laura, that Laura was pregnant, and Laura hadn't the knack of turning it into a joke even when David tried to come to her rescue with such advice as, "Don't bite, Snow White!" Constance and Diana had too much fairy tale wickedness about them for Laura to think it funny.

But one day Laura arrived when David had gone off on an errand and Constance was resting. Diana had to put herself to the test of inviting Laura in and entertaining her without aid or distraction.

"Daddie's very happy here," Laura ventured.

Diana braced herself to deal with the inevitable "but. . . ." It didn't follow. Instead Laura went on to say that he had a real life of his own here, which made him feel useful.

"It was the right move for Mary and Ted, too," Laura continued. "They needed to be on their own. But . . ."

Here it was then.

"Did you know Daddie hasn't seen Mary since he left there?"

"No, I didn't," Diana said, not admitting that she had suspected as much since David rarely mentioned his younger daughter and never referred to visits with her as he did to Laura and her family.

"He won't talk with me about it. And that's not like Daddie. Did you know that Ted asked him to leave?"

"No," Diana said. "He simply told me he'd decided to move out."

"Mary won't talk about it either. She just goes on as if nothing had happened, as if nothing were wrong."

"I don't know your sister."

"I know you don't," Laura said, flushing. "She's always been very close to Daddie. Do you think you might talk with him?"

"What would you want me to say?" Diana asked.

"I don't really know," Laura said sadly, "but I don't think it's right, not for either of them. They're both acting as if the other one didn't exist. I know he misses the children. He always wants to hear about them."

"What's to prevent them from coming to see him?"

"I don't know. They may have been told not to," Laura admitted.

Diana studied Laura. Their mutual distaste for this conversation gave Diana a new, hopeful respect for the young woman, usually so pathetically anxious to please.

"You're afraid of making me angry, aren't you?" Diana asked.

"I suppose I am," Laura said.

Diana's relief that what troubled David was still his younger daughter rather than his move to this house made her feel nearly recklessly generous.

"Why don't I have a talk with Mary?" Diana suggested.

Laura could not hide the alarm on her face.

"I may be the only one of you who isn't afraid of Mary," Diana said. "We might even like each other."

"Oh, Aunt Diana, Mary can be terrible!"

Diana paused to catch her breath after making her long slow way up the steep path through the garden. She was nearly drunk with roses. Surely there must be an easier way in, probably from the back alley. But what a lovely place it was, she had time to observe as she looked back down on the way she had come and then up over the trees to the mountains, the air on this summer day nearly as clear as the air of the desert, everything in sharp, clean focus. Diana rang the bell.

Mary opened the door, her pretty face puzzled but tentatively welcoming. She was not as tall as Laura, fuller bodied, more declaratively attractive. Diana smiled.

"Do I know you?" Mary asked.

"We've never met," Diana said. "I'm Diana Crown, your aunt."

"Oh!" Mary exclaimed, surprise catching her off guard. "Well, come in."

"Thank you," Diana said and moved with as quick deliberation as she could, her cane claiming the door sill.

Mary led her down the hall to the living room, full of light and flowers.

"You have quite a hand with roses," Diana said.

Mary did not smile or make any polite reply, nor did

she offer Diana a chair. Mary stood her ground and waited
for Diana's first real move. Diana sat down on the couch,
her back to the view. Mary took a chair in line with the
couch, half-turned to the view so that she could look
directly at Diana without staring into the light behind her.
They studied each other in a growing silence until Mary
finally broke.

"What is it you want?" she asked, sulky in that first
defeat.

"Just this," Diana said.

"To be in this house?" Mary demanded.

"The house isn't of any concern to me," Diana said.
"You are. You haven't seen your father in three months,
and I think I'm the excuse for it. I haven't kidnapped him,
and I want you to know that you and your husband and
children are perfectly welcome to come and see him."

"He hasn't come to see me," Mary said.

"Have you invited him?"

"Why should he have to be invited into his own
house?"

"Because he doesn't live here any longer," Diana said,
and she smiled.

"You don't look anything like him," Mary said.

"No," Diana agreed, thinking that Mary did look like
her father.

"But you sound like him."

"Do I?" Diana asked.

"Did he send you?"

"Heavens no!" Diana answered cheerfully. "He hasn't
even mentioned the fact that he hasn't seen you in three
months. He's being as pigheaded as you are."

"I didn't think I wanted to meet you," Mary said.

"Well, now you have through no fault of your own."

"Over Mother's dead body."

"I don't think this is about your mother," Diana said, "or me."

"Isn't it?" Mary asked.

"Life goes on over people's dead bodies, Mary, soon over the likes of your father and me as well."

"He might as well be dead!" Mary burst out.

"Are you still such a child?" Diana asked, almost gently.

"I'm his child. How can he forget that?" Mary demanded, "just forget it?"

"You seem to have forgotten he's your father."

"Tit for tat," Mary said, but in that sulkines was a glimmer of self-consciousness.

Diana wanted to shout at her, "Don't be such a silly little fool!," but any impatience now would ruin whatever little good she had done. She was here to remove excuses not to give Mary any more. Then Diana saw the easy tears welling up in those eyes so like her father's.

"I won't stay for that," Diana said.

She got up and saw herself out. As she made her way back down through the garden, she understood better the haughty game David had been playing with this daughter, the reason he could not talk about it. They were in a power struggle they both had to lose, and they knew it. Diana really had been nothing more than a confusing excuse. Well, not any longer.

"I went to call on Mary this morning," Diana said to David at the lunch table.

She saw in his look the first signal of trespass he had sent her.

"I thought it was time," Diana said.

"I hope she was civil," David said coolly.

"Civility isn't Mary's strong suit surely," Diana said,

smiling. "She let me in. She was a bit sulky. She says I sound like you."

"You do," Constance said, surprised by information which obviously confirmed a suspicion of her own.

"I'm Diana's brother," David said.

"You're anybody I want you to be," Constance said.

"Sometimes that's a tall order," David said, smiling at her.

"I know," Constance said. "But you do sound like her. That's how I tell."

Was it not the radio after all but some shared timbre in their voices? Constance certainly did know David again, momentarily anyway.

"I didn't want to be the excuse," Diana continued, "for what's going on between you and Mary."

"Excuse?" David repeated.

"I told her I didn't think either her mother or I had anything to do with it."

David refused to encourage Diana to say more. She had to go on uninvited.

"Mary says you've forgotten you're her father."

"Forgotten!" David exclaimed, hurling his napkin to the table.

He left the room obviously unwilling to let his sister see his own defeating tears.

Of all the misfunctions of memory, grudge-holding was perhaps the worst, for it fixed in stone episodes which should be carried along in the flow of time, diluted, finally forgotten. Diana's grudge had died much more slowly than its victim, but she had finally put it to rest in Patricia's child, Mary, whose temper, not so murderous as Diana's, might save her from similar mistakes. Perhaps after all, it helped to cry.

"He'll have to give in first," Diana said.

"Like me?" Constance asked.

Diana laughed. There was no one in the world like Constance, and she wasn't, as Jill once bitterly complained, ridiculously misnamed; she was constant in will to herself even now against the blanks, the confusions, the terrors.

"I love your honesty," Constance said, "even when I have to go on believing you."

"Keep me in mind," Diana said.

"Yes, and what's his name," Constance said, nodding to David's half-eaten lunch.

"David, my brother."

A few of the publications of
THE NAIAD PRESS, INC.
P.O. Box 10543 • Tallahassee, Florida 32302
Phone (904) 539-9322
Mail orders welcome. Please include 15% postage.

MEMORY BOARD by Jane Rule. 336 pp. Memorable novel about an aging lesbian couple.   ISBN 0-941483-02-9 $8.95

THE ALWAYS ANONYMOUS BEAST by Lauren Wright Douglas. 224 pp. A Caitlin Reece mystery. First in a series.
ISBN 0-941483-04-5   8.95

SEARCHING FOR SPRING by Patricia A. Murphy. 224 pp. Novel about the recovery of love.   ISBN 0-941483-00-2   8.95

DUSTY'S QUEEN OF HEARTS DINER by Lee Lynch. 240 pp. Romantic blue-collar novel.   ISBN 0-941483-01-0   8.95

PARENTS MATTER by Ann Muller. 240 pp. Parents' relationships with lesbian daughters and gay sons.
ISBN 0-930044-91-6   9.95

THE PEARLS by Shelley Smith. 176 pp. Passion and fun in the Caribbean sun.   ISBN 0-930044-93-2   7.95

MAGDALENA by Sarah Aldridge. 352 pp. Epic Lesbian novel set on three continents.   ISBN 0-930044-99-1   8.95

THE BLACK AND WHITE OF IT by Ann Allen Shockley. 144 pp. Short stories.   ISBN 0-930044-96-7 $7.95

SAY JESUS AND COME TO ME by Ann Allen Shockley. 288 pp. Contemporary romance.   ISBN 0-930044-98-3   8.95

LOVING HER by Ann Allen Shockley. 192 pp. Romantic love story.   ISBN 0-930044-97-5   7.95

MURDER AT THE NIGHTWOOD BAR by Katherine V. Forrest. 240 pp. A Kate Delafield mystery. Second in a series.
ISBN 0-930044-92-4   8.95

ZOE'S BOOK by Gail Pass. 224 pp. Passionate, obsessive love story.   ISBN 0-930044-95-9   7.95

WINGED DANCER by Camarin Grae. 228 pp. Erotic Lesbian adventure story.   ISBN 0-930044-88-6   8.95

PAZ by Camarin Grae. 336 pp. Romantic Lesbian adventurer with the power to change the world.   ISBN 0-930044-89-4   8.95

SOUL SNATCHER by Camarin Grae. 224 pp. A puzzle, an adventure, a mystery—Lesbian romance.
ISBN 0-930044-90-8   8.95

THE LOVE OF GOOD WOMEN by Isabel Miller. 224 pp. Long-awaited new novel by the author of the beloved *Patience and Sarah.*   ISBN 0-930044-81-9   8.95

THE HOUSE AT PELHAM FALLS by Brenda Weathers. 240 pp. Suspenseful Lesbian ghost story.   ISBN 0-930044-79-7   7.95

THE BURNTON WIDOWS by Vicki P. McConnell. 272 pp. A
Nyla Wade mystery, second in the series. ISBN 0-930044-52-5   7.95

OLD DYKE TALES by Lee Lynch. 224 pp. Extraordinary
stories of our diverse Lesbian lives.   ISBN 0-930044-51-7   7.95

DAUGHTERS OF A CORAL DAWN by Katherine V. Forrest.
240 pp. Novel set in a Lesbian new world. ISBN 0-930044-50-9   7.95

THE PRICE OF SALT by Claire Morgan. 288 pp. A milestone
novel, a beloved classic.   ISBN 0-930044-49-5   8.95

AGAINST THE SEASON by Jane Rule. 224 pp. Luminous,
complex novel of interrelationships.   ISBN 0-930044-48-7   7.95

LOVERS IN THE PRESENT AFTERNOON by Kathleen
Fleming. 288 pp. A novel about recovery and growth.
                                        ISBN 0-930044-46-0   8.95

TOOTHPICK HOUSE by Lee Lynch. 264 pp. Love between
two Lesbians of different classes.   ISBN 0-930044-45-2   7.95

MADAME AURORA by Sarah Aldridge. 256 pp. Historical
novel featuring a charismatic "seer."   ISBN 0-930044-44-4   7.95

CURIOUS WINE by Katherine V. Forrest. 176 pp. Passionate
Lesbian love story, a best-seller.   ISBN 0-930044-43-6   7.95

BLACK LESBIAN IN WHITE AMERICA by Anita Cornwell.
141 pp. Stories, essays, autobiography.   ISBN 0-930044-41-X   7.50

CONTRACT WITH THE WORLD by Jane Rule. 340 pp.
Powerful, panoramic novel of gay life.   ISBN 0-930044-28-2   7.95

YANTRAS OF WOMANLOVE by Tee A. Corinne. 64 pp.
Photos by noted Lesbian photographer.   ISBN 0-930044-30-4   6.95

MRS. PORTER'S LETTER by Vicki P. McConnell. 224 pp.
The first Nyla Wade mystery.   ISBN 0-930044-29-0   7.95

TO THE CLEVELAND STATION by Carol Anne Douglas.
192 pp. Interracial Lesbian love story.   ISBN 0-930044-27-4   6.95

THE NESTING PLACE by Sarah Aldridge. 224 pp. A
three-woman triangle—love conquers all! ISBN 0-930044-26-6   7.95

THIS IS NOT FOR YOU by Jane Rule. 284 pp. A letter to a
beloved is also an intricate novel.   ISBN 0-930044-25-8   7.95

FAULTLINE by Sheila Ortiz Taylor. 140 pp. Warm, funny,
literate story of a startling family.   ISBN 0-930044-24-X   6.95

THE LESBIAN IN LITERATURE by Barbara Grier. 3d ed.
Foreword by Maida Tilchen. 240 pp. Comprehensive bibliography. Literary ratings; rare photos.   ISBN 0-930044-23-1   7.95

ANNA'S COUNTRY by Elizabeth Lang. 208 pp. A woman
finds her Lesbian identity.   ISBN 0-930044-19-3   6.95

PRISM by Valerie Taylor. 158 pp. A love affair between two
women in their sixties.   ISBN 0-930044-18-5   6.95

BLACK LESBIANS: AN ANNOTATED BIBLIOGRAPHY
compiled by J.R. Roberts. Foreword by Barbara Smith. 112
pp. Award winning bibliography.   ISBN 0-930044-21-5   5.95

THE MARQUISE AND THE NOVICE by Victoria Ramstetter.
108 pp. A Lesbian Gothic novel.   ISBN 0-930044-16-9   4.95

OUTLANDER by Jane Rule. 207 pp. Short stories and essays
by one of our finest writers.   ISBN 0-930044-17-7   6.95

SAPPHISTRY: THE BOOK OF LESBIAN SEXUALITY by
Pat Califia. 2d edition, revised. 195 pp.   ISBN 0-930044-47-9   7.95

ALL TRUE LOVERS by Sarah Aldridge. 292 pp. Romantic
novel set in the 1930s and 1940s.   ISBN 0-930044-10-X   7.95

A WOMAN APPEARED TO ME by Renee Vivien. 65 pp. A
classic; translated by Jeannette H. Foster. ISBN 0-930044-06-1   5.00

CYTHEREA'S BREATH by Sarah Aldridge. 240 pp. Romantic
novel about women's entrance into medicine.   0-930044-02-9   6.95

TOTTIE by Sarah Aldridge. 181 pp. Lesbian romance in the
turmoil of the sixties.   ISBN 0-930044-01-0   6.95

THE LATECOMER by Sarah Aldridge. 107 pp. A delicate love
story.   ISBN 0-930044-00-2   5.00

ODD GIRL OUT by Ann Bannon   ISBN 0-930044-83-5   5.95
I AM A WOMAN by Ann Bannon.   ISBN 0-930044-84-3   5.95
WOMEN IN THE SHADOWS by Ann Bannon.
                                     ISBN 0-930044-85-1   5.95
JOURNEY TO A WOMAN by Ann Bannon.
                                     ISBN 0-930044-86-X   5.95
BEEBO BRINKER by Ann Bannon   ISBN 0-930044-87-8   5.95

Legendary novels written in the fifties and sixties,
set in the gay mecca of Greenwich Village.

VOLUTE BOOKS

JOURNEY TO FULFILLMENT   Early classics by Valerie   3.95
A WORLD WITHOUT MEN   Taylor: The Erika Frohmann   3.95
RETURN TO LESBOS   series.   3.95

These are just a few of the many Naiad Press titles—we are the oldest
and largest lesbian/feminist publishing company in the world. Please
request a complete catalog. We offer personal service; we encourage and
welcome direct mail orders from individuals who have limited access to
bookstores carrying our publications.